Anthrax: The Game

Anthrax: The Game

A Novel

Dwan G. Hightower

ISBN: 0-9720495-3-3

Dream Catcher Publishing, Inc.
P.O. Box 14058
Mexico Beach, Florida 32410

FAX: 888-771-2800
Email: DCP@DreamCatcherPublishing.net
Website: www.DreamCatcherPublishing.net

This book is printed on acid-free paper.

This book was written in 1997 and I would like to thank the following people for their help and support. There are so many to thank. To Richard Noegel for the first edit. To Theresa Moss and Linda LaChanse for reading and commenting on it. To Pat Gould for his enthusiasm. To Dr. Joel Greenspan for his "go for it". To Dr. George Schmid for his encouragement and technical assistance. To Linda LaChanse for her gracious constructive criticism and especially to Robert Overstreet for the final edits and the friendship that I treasure. To Dr. Michele Pearson and Dr. Mary Chamberland for an exciting learning adventure in the CDC's Emergency Operations Center (EOC) following the national Anthrax scare in late 2001. And especially to my muse of 1996, who provided the inspiration for this book . . . Ben Grove.

This book is dedicated to my two daughters Lei Rhyne and Dionne Thompson, who made my life complete, and to Allen, who made all of this possible.

Anthrax: The Game

Prologue

His blood was pumping quickly and his heart was pounding as Dr. Norm Bishop pulled the sheet over the body, covering the face of Joshua Evans, a fifteen-year-old high school student. Joshua had just suffered an excruciating death by a vicious and as-yet-undetermined virus or bacterium. He had been admitted to the local hospital two days earlier with a preliminary diagnosis of anthrax. He had the signs of anthrax: fever, malaise, a cough, and a sudden onset of pneumonia, and then the coma that had ended his life. Dr. Bishop knew he had admitted three more patients himself, like Joshua. He patted the arm of the dead boy, one of his favorite people in their small town. Dr. Bishop was more determined than ever to find out how this had happened in his town, in his hospital.

He looked up at his assistant, Dr. Clifford Yalkes, and said, "Call security, and the Virology Department. Get a quarantine unit set up. I don't care if they have to rearrange the whole hospital, get those three suspected cases away from the staff and other patients. Stat! See to it personally. Whatever we're dealing with, the two of us have already been exposed so get going NOW!!"

Yalkes knew from the tone of his boss's voice that whatever this was, it was deadly.

His face paled. "I'm on my way."

"Thanks, Clifford." Dr. Bishop managed a smile. "And keep this one under your hat. We don't want a panic. See me after you're set up."

Bishop ran back to his office and, closing the door, grabbed the phone. He punched in the numbers for the Centers for Disease Control and Prevention. He spoke quickly, "This is Dr. Bishop in Bayside, Maine. I need to speak to Dr. Patterson, please. This is an emergency."

"One moment, please." The few moments seemed like an eternity.

"Tom Patterson," the rushed voice came over the phone.

"Tom? This is Norm in Maine. How are you?"

"I'm fine, Norm, but I get the feeling you're not. What's up?"

"I have something strange going on. I'm not sure, but I think its anthrax. The test results should be back any minute. I have eight cases and one death already."

"Jeez, Norm, you do have something. Have you done the preliminaries?"

"Yes, they are almost finished with those. The cultures are pending."

"Good. I'll be there before dark. I'll call Robert Norton, the State Epidemiologist, and also Larry Weiss, the Health Commissioner. I'm sure they will be there before me. Hang in there, Norm. We'll take care of this."

"Thanks, Tom. See you later."

Two hours later Dr. Larry Weiss and Dr. Robert Norton were at the hospital. Dr. Bishop walked Weiss and Norton out of the morgue and down to the lounge. Pouring his third cup of black coffee, he turned to Norton. "I need to do some paperwork on this to get ready for the press. I'll be in my office if you need me."

He felt the quickening of his breath and the sweat on the back of his neck. Popping two more Advil, he returned to his spacious office and sat down, wiping his sweaty palms on his handkerchief. He opened the desk drawer and took out the asthma inhaler. Taking a deep draw, the third time within two days, he picked up the picture of his family. He had a wonderful wife, Carol, and two sons, Eric and Fred, ages eleven and nine.

The sharp pain in his chest was excruciating, making his breath shorter and harder to bring into his lungs.

The picture fell from his hand, shattering the glass as it hit the floor. Dr. Norm Bishop would be the second death from the outbreak today.

A silent, solitary traveler sat down in a window seat on the plane and brushed back his thick black hair. He leaned over and pushed the silvery metal briefcase under the seat. Even if the briefcase was checked at the next airport, security would find the vial empty.

Pulling his jacket open he checked his coat pocket again. Where was the diskette? Damn! Looking in both pockets he wiped his brow and replaced his handkerchief. Using the illegal entry lock kit, it had been so simple to break into the office and remove the inhaler from Dr. Bishop's top desk drawer and replace it with the contaminated one. He had spent a few moments admiring the family in the picture on the desk. He checked his bag and his jacket pockets again. Where was it? His throat tightened momentarily. Where was the diskette? Maybe he had dropped it back at the library or at the hotel. Oh, well, no matter. If a maid found it she would just toss it. He relaxed, and a strange secretive half-smile passed over his smug visage.

Chapter 1

Atlanta, Georgia

Denise sat at the bar and toyed with the swizzle stick in her drink. She had just left her office at Incline, a special unit of the FBI, and she had the feeling something was in the air. Too many bigwigs running around and too many closed doors. She didn't want to think about it, so she sat enjoying her drink and gracefully avoided eye contact with the man in the three-piece suit at the end of the bar, and the jock with the massive biceps and greasy hair. She didn't want any company. She just wanted to drink and listen to her favorite "oldies" at Hemingway's, her favorite place. She was reminded of her teens and dancing to the Righteous Brothers, and the Beach Boys. . . . Time flies.

Since the incident in DC three years ago, with the accident, the problems, the unanswered questions, she hadn't been able to get past those feelings so she could approach another man. She had been lucky during the intervening years because the men she had dated had been content with theater, concerts, and dinners without the pressure of a more involved relationship.

"Can I buy you a drink?" The jock broke into her thoughts.

"No, thank you. I am waiting on my date. He will be here shortly," she replied.

"Okay, but just whistle if he doesn't show up."

What a joke! She got so many propositions, so many offers, and they didn't even cross her mind. She glanced at her watch and realized she needed to head home. She didn't want to stay in this place too long. The ringing of her cell phone startled her. "Hello, Denise Gibson here."

"Where are you?" Barrett's rushed voice came over the phone.

"I'm at Hemingway's, why?" She recognized the tension in his voice.

"We've got a big problem in Maine. Head home and I will meet you there in a few minutes."

Denise dropped a ten-dollar bill on the bar, leaving a generous tip, but she didn't have time to think about that now. Something was happening again.

She let herself into her condo and slipped into a sense of relaxation despite the concern Barrett had created with his call. She was home in her restful haven. Her home, the one she had taken special time and effort in decorating to reflect her personality.

In the foyer was the antique mahogany end table that held her vase of fresh flowers that arrived the first of each month from an old love who knew how much she loved flowers. He was one of the few men who listened when she said she didn't like roses, except yellow ones, and then only once a year. She moved down the hallway past the large dining room with the long table that seated twelve because she loved dinner parties, large ones or small, intimate ones, because she loved to cook for her friends. The large table was covered by the Irish-linen cloth her grandmother had given her on her twenty-first birthday. The polished cherry wood buffet that held the silver tea service and silver chafing dishes that had once belonged to her mother back when she frequently hosted Sunday afternoon teas.

The kitchen was decorated in the New Orleans style of black and white. All the appliances were white and the counter tops were black with splashes of black in the all-white wallpaper and the large black and white square tiles on the floor. She loved her kitchen with the huge white-boxed island in the middle of the floor where her friends sat and sipped wine while she cooked.

Her library was not the typical library with wooden paneling but a Florida room-type library with one wall of floor-to-ceiling windows looking out over her garden and the other three walls with floor to ceiling bookshelves containing all of her favorite books. She kept her favorite books in this room, with the rest of her books upstairs in her second library, which was a cream-colored room with touches of sea-mist green and mauve. Neither of her libraries fitted the description of the "normal" library.

She sat down in her chair, the big overstuffed chintz with the rolled arms that offered her so much comfort and warmth. She needed to have the chair re-upholstered, but she couldn't bring herself to it. Every worn area reminded her of happier times and experiences in her life. She had sat in this chair on many a rainy day and watched a trickle of rain race down the windowpane to embrace another trickle and race together to the bottom of the pane.

She had sat in this chair in her dorm room when she wrote her first composition in English Composition 101 titled, "How to Make Love to a Book." Her professor had loved it. She had gotten an A+. No, it wasn't time to change the cover yet, not just yet.

Denise climbed the back stairs to the hallway passing her small library and her two guest bedrooms. As she walked into her bedroom she thought of the possibilities of what could have happened to get him so worked up. Her blue room. Where had the "blue mood" come from? Blue had never been one of her favorite colors, but for some reason she had gone crazy with blue in decorating her bedroom.

The walls were of a dark blue with white trim. The wicker chair and table and make-up table where a pale baby blue and the comforter and drapes were a mixture of soft blue-and-white check. It was restful and calming, but it certainly didn't reflect her personality or her bedroom personality at all. It surprised her that she had left the room this color. She would have preferred an accent wall of

3

hunter green with beige and green decor, but she had left it blue. Maybe because in this one room, her bedroom, she could let herself be vulnerable, her true self to be exposed.

She stood in front of the full-length mirror to undress. Sometimes this was torture because she could definitely spot the extra pounds she had put on, or the new wrinkle or dimple that had appeared. Maybe that was the reason her self-inflicted tortures of workouts were good for her: to help her stay in shape.

She slipped off the silk shirtwaist dress and the pink bra and panties to put on her jockey panties, and the striped dress shirt she had taken out of Barrett's office one day. She donned it without a bra. He was probably still thinking he had left it at the cleaners or somewhere else. He probably wouldn't recognize it after all this time.

She slipped on the shirt and picked up reading glasses and the new "veggie" recipe book and headed back downstairs to the kitchen. Tonight she would whip up a wok of stir-fried vegetables. She wasn't hungry. The two drinks at Hemingway's had deadened her appetite.

Flipping on the soft light in the kitchen over the window instead of the full ceiling one relaxed her a bit. She enjoyed cooking in the dusk of evening with the use of no more light than necessary. She pulled the wok out of the closet and set it on the stove, turned on the burner, and poured the oil in so it would get hot before she added the rice.

She placed the steamer on the other burner and added the dumplings, and the egg rolls she had made last night. The sizzling rice with the soy sauce had a delightful, fragrant, salty aroma. She knew it would taste delicious.

Denise placed the veggies and dumplings in a small bowl and put it on the tray with the rice and wine. She carried the tray to her library and set it down at the small table that she used for her breakfast and dinner next to the large window. She could sit here and watch the other world in her back garden. The birds were chirping, the frogs around the lily pond were croaking, and the bees were buzzing. It was heaven. The only thing that would make it better would be to have Barrett here to enjoy it with her.

Denise was jarred out of her thoughts by the ringing of the doorbell. She opened the door to her associate, Barrett Hayden.

"That didn't take long. What's up?"

"Big problem up north. Martin received a call earlier today. We have an outbreak and a big problem in Maine. He wants us to be there first thing in the morning. I hadn't left the office for the day when in he came, grunting and roaring and making all his demands."

"What is it?" she asked now in a whisper voice, as she knew Barrett never got this upset unless it was serious. "What's going on?"

"There is a suspicious outbreak in Maine. Several cases have already been admitted to the hospital and there have been a couple of deaths."

"That is serious. What do they think it is?" She sat down to help breath slower and waited.

"It could be anthrax. It's serious, whatever it is, and it has everyone running," he said as he moved past her and headed for the bar. Barrett dropped his briefcase by the sofa and poured himself a shot of Scotch.

"Anthrax? Are you crazy? We haven't seen that in years. What are the symptoms? Have they got the tests back yet?" she asked, still in a daze.

"Not yet," Barrett answered as he drank the first shot quickly and poured a refill. Dressed in a dark blue suit and baby blue tie, Barrett Hayden looked the average business man-except that he was cuter than most. He had the physique of one who worked out often and tanned complexion from hours of playing tennis. He had dark brown hair that was still a bit long for this day and time and those deep, penetrating green eyes that always had a hint of mischief in them. No one would guess that this man had spent ten years at Harvard Medical Center working on a

5

serious study of germ warfare and had then been recruited by a special intelligence unit. He had worked as a liaison between the medical establishment and the military forces. The two were coming from a different point of view. The strain of the job had gotten to him and he had left.

As Barrett once said, he had gotten tired of the mind games, mind wars, the stress, the strain, and the realization that people there never thought of the consequences of their actions and of what they were working on at the time.

Watching Barrett as he poured another drink for her, Denise thought of all the things he been to her: friend, big brother, confidant, but never a lover. It had crossed her mind once or twice when they were in the field and things were slow and they had shared one too many drinks, but he had never made a move and neither had she. They had remained close friends.

"What do you think it is?" she asked in a whispered voice as she could sense his concern.

"We have an outbreak of what looks like anthrax in Maine and Martin wants us on it right away. That is all I can say. I had Teale make our flight plans and reservations. She's taking care of replacing the voice messages on our services and email accounts, notifying people that we'll be out of the office for a few weeks. I took the liberty of picking up your laptop and your files on this area and bringing them with me. I left all of it in the car. I can bring them in if you want to look at them tonight. Incline has had several calls to investigate this one," he said, as he handed her the drink. Incline was a small, elite, investigative unit of the FBI. It dealt primarily with bioterrorism and germ warfare. It was composed of several bright scientists and researchers who also served as federal agents.

"No, I can wait to look at that, but what is the theory now? What do they think is going on?" she asked.

Barrett looked at her concerned expression and noticed how the soft hazel eyes showed her every emotion. She could hide nothing from him or anyone, and she certainly never could be accused of having a poker face. He knew this lady; he cared for this woman, and he had not realized how much until he had watched her go through several serious misfortunes in the past year. He glanced at her shapely legs beneath the thigh-length shirt. He didn't have to ask; he knew whose shirt it was, but how had she gotten it? Never mind; he really didn't want to know.

"They think its anthrax. There are several cases, but we won't know for sure until we get there. Nice outfit," he smiled trying to help her relax. He sipped the second shot of Scotch more slowly as they sat on love seats across from each other.

"Thanks, I was just getting comfortable. Have you eaten? Do you want something? I made some stir-fry," she said as she glanced over at the half-eaten tray on the table.

"Yes, that would be nice. I haven't eaten since lunch today, and I have been running like crazy on the other issue. Yes, let's eat, and I'll fill you in on this while we eat. Can I help?" He rose with her.

"No, stay seated. I'll bring you a tray. We can eat out here. I'll finish my dinner with you as you fill me in. Although I have to admit I don't have much of an appetite right now," she said as she walked back into the kitchen to prepare a plate for Barrett and to pour some water to replace the wine for both of them. At this point they both needed to relax, but not with the help of Scotch. She really needed a clear head right now.

"Thanks, this looks great," he said as she handed him the tray. I didn't realize how hungry I am. There are a couple of things you need to know right now, and the rest we can get into tomorrow on the flight up to Maine."

"Yeah, just give me the basics and let me sleep on it," she said as she sipped the wine.

"Well, Martin thinks we'll be out in the field for a while, so make all the necessary arrangements for the house as soon as you can. Teale will take care of your office needs. Also you need to know that Martin has gone ahead and placed a call to NCTR, and I am sure we'll be meeting some of their representatives there when we arrive."

"NCTR already? Couldn't he have waited?" she exclaimed, as she set down the wineglass and gazed out the window with the fixed look of concern. NCTR. Paul was still with that agency. Would he be the one they sent to investigate this? Would she have to deal with him sooner than she thought?

Martin Alfonso, her chief, was a brilliant researcher on the subject of germ warfare. He was in his mid fifties, with silver hair and a round belly from his love of good food and good wine. His Italian heritage added to his vigor and his passion for life. But the one thing she always felt concerned about was Martin's tendency to move too fast on certain issues. He was always one to jump the gun. Shouldn't they have discussed it before he made that call, or was this just her reluctance and concern of possibly having to see Paul again?

"Denise, are you okay?" Barrett broke into her thoughts.

"What? Oh yes, I'm fine. I was just wondering whether Martin hasn't jumped the gun on this one. What do you think?"

"I don't think you need to worry about it. What's done is done, and we'll get through this, no matter who we have to deal with." He paused, and then said, "Is it still that painful?"

She smiled. Dear Barrett, always taking care of her. "No, it's not that. I just don't want the publicity and the notoriety we get whenever NCTR is involved. Also I can do without their heavy-handed military style of handling things." Her years of dealing with NCTR had not always been perfect.

"I understand, but we can't keep this out of the press completely. They always get wind of it. We'll keep a low profile ourselves and let the big boys handle the media."

He reached into his briefcase and pulled out a yellow folder.

"Here's the schedule for the first few days - meeting the patients, medical staff, lab people, and family members of the deceased. I thought I'd leave this with you tonight, and we can go over the rest tomorrow. Our flight's at seven o'clock. I'll meet you at the gate." His face brightened and his tone of voice changed. "Now let's try to enjoy this delicious food, and then I'll be out of your hair for a few hours." He smiled.

He watched her sip the water as her eyes gazed out the window. She never bothered to touch her food. He knew her thoughts were wandering back to outbreak in Connecticut three years ago and the streets of D.C. years ago where she had had an assignment that had almost destroyed her. Sometimes he felt as though that assignment had lasted a lifetime for both him and Denise.

Chapter 2

Atlanta, Georgia

Henry Osgood was more rattled and disjointed than usual at dealing with the simpler things today, but his brilliant, keen mind was working harder than ever on the serious problems that faced him and his staff. His mind was on the latest rumor he had heard about another outbreak up North, but he would wait until he had heard from Martin before he reacted. He also had wasted a half-hour looking for a file on NCTR, which he had misplaced in his office.

He was tired, very tired, turning the key in the lock of the heavy, ornate oak door of his house. He could hear Brigade, his beautiful golden retriever, shuffling his paws as he came across the hardwood floor to greet him. He'd lean his head against Henry's knee for his accustomed pat on the head which was his complacent way of saying "Hello and welcome home, I know it has been a hard day and that you are tired, so I will let you go on to your chair and rest."

Too bad Ingrid didn't welcome him even with a simple hello, but that had stopped years ago. Ingrid, the Garbo-looking lady who had stolen his heart the moment he laid eyes on her, knowing all the time she was not anything she seemed. She really was the closest thing to the real Garbo, in more ways than looks, especially when she had started to retreat into her own cocoon and stay there.

Henry dropped the mail on the table in the foyer and walked down the hall into his study. He opened the drapes to let some sunshine into his sanctuary. This was his; this was his cocoon. He retreated as often as possible into this hideaway to spend time with himself, his memories, and his fantasies. He flipped the switch on the stereo and pressed the button on the CD player, and it immediately started the Beethoven piece he always relaxed to. He untied his tie and tossed it carelessly onto the sofa and sat down in his big green overstuffed chair. He picked up the stack of mail and his favorite-notices of garage sales-and removed his loafers.

He tossed the shoes to the side of his roll-top desk and walked into the kitchen to get a drink. How bad had today been? Did he need a beer? Wine? Or a martini? Today hadn't been too bad. He thought of the study and research he was caught up in so a beer would do. He opened the fridge and removed a Miller Lite and walked back into the study, glancing, as he did so, over his shoulder at Brigade, who had gone back to his safe corner in the kitchen. He would protect the house and its occupants, but only from his haven.

Henry sat down in the well-worn chair that greeted him every night. He felt relaxed, safe and protected.

Sitting in his chair with his rumpled hair and rumpled shirt, he glanced through his mail and then looked up at the roses Ingrid had cut from her garden and placed in his room. A nice gesture to say "I know you want more. I know you wish it could be the way it used to be, but it can't. And this is my peace offering to say I am doing the best I can."

He flipped through the mail; the usual: phone bill, letters from the insurance company, advertising circulars. What was this? A post card from Greece. He turned it over. It was from David, his old friend. David had surprised him by phoning last week after a period of months with no communication and had said he was going away to Greece for a month's vacation. He needed the time and the space to regroup and find himself. Henry had never thought David was lost. Although they had not seen each other in years, they still remained in contact, with infrequently made phone calls and with cards now and then. Henry thought David had always seemed the most confident and sure of his friends. David's large size helped that: he was an imposing figure at 6'3" and 230 pounds, with large hands and that dark heavily matted hair, the brown eyes surrounded by deep lines that got even deeper with the rustling sound of his laughter. Henry ran his hand through his rumpled, flyaway gray-tinged brown hair that always seemed mussed. He always had a frazzled look about him. He had the typical look of the absent-minded professor.

David had smoked too many cigarettes in his life, and it showed in his face and his raspy voice. But his imposing figure was emphasized because of his confidence in his ability as a man and as a doctor. Henry could never imagine David being unsure about anything.

Henry sipped the beer and read David's post card. *'Great time, sun, fun, beach, food, booze, books all that I need. You should join me. We could do some fishing, whatever fishing they do here.*
Take care.
David.

He was having a good time. Relaxing and enjoying the beach and the culture. While Henry sat at home in his easy chair trying to decide what he was going to whip up for dinner. He really wasn't very hungry, but he might as well put something together and eat. Besides, he had promised Ingrid he would prepare something for her before he woke her up to work her graveyard shift at the hospital.

How did we get to this point? he thought as he walked into the kitchen and removed the mixing bowl from the cabinet and the eggs from the rack in the refrigerator. He thoughtlessly, almost automatically, cracked the eggs into the bowl. He had decided to do a western omelet with toast and fresh sliced fruit. When did she decide she preferred to go to work just after he arrived home? When did they decide they worked better away from each other than together?

There had once been a time when her dancing green eyes could make his heart pound and his breath quicken, but not now. Now he wondered what she was thinking or what would make her happy or really how unhappy she was.

His routine each day of coming home to Brigade's welcome and relaxing to his music and having a drink had been going on for years. He wasn't unhappy with it. It was just a routine he had fallen into and it never changed.

The toast popped out of the toaster, a golden brown. For a second it reminded him of Ingrid's skin after her first few days in the sun. Her skin would be a golden brown before it eventually went into a deep nut brown from hours of playing tennis and swimming. He spread butter on the toast and reached for the apples and strawberries. He washed the strawberries and watched the water glisten off the green stems as the water had glistened on her skin the day he noticed her swimming at the corporate pool. He arranged the fruit in a crystal bowl and dropped a piece of fresh mint from Ingrid's window-box garden on top. He arranged the tray with the two omelets, the toast, the fruit bowls, and the fresh orange juice for her and the fresh martini he had just mixed for himself. He felt he needed a strong one now because she was entering his thoughts more and more, and he had to control them. She was showing signs of that deep depression again when it was hard for her to get out of bed. When she had no life left in her. No amount of talking and teasing could get her interested in anything. It was not easy on anyone when Ingrid got depressed. She was known to hurt not only herself but other people also. He was hoping for a better side of her today.

He climbed the stairs to the bedroom he shared with Ingrid and pushed the half- open door all the way open. Placing the tray on the nightstand he sat down on the bed. He looked at the woman who had spent the past twelve years with him and remembered the beauty he had fallen in love with, this beauty whose quick sense of wit and amazing intellect had intrigued him. He reached over and smoothed the gray-streaked brown hair off her cheek and gently shook her.

"Ingrid, wake up. Wake up, dear, it is time. I've cooked something for you."

Ingrid rolled over and gazed at Henry. Her sleepy eyes opened slowly to reveal those incredible green pools that he used to lose himself in.

"Hi," she whispered.

"Good evening," he replied. "Rest well?"

"Yes, it was nice. How was your day?"

"The usual," he said, as he began arranging the tray.

Ingrid propped herself up against the huge oak headboard, the headboard they had purchased in New England years ago on one of their many antique junket vacations.

He set his plate and drinks on the nightstand on his side of the bed and put her tray on her lap. Some time ago, the ritual had started of their eating in the bedroom as soon as she awakened, because she was always famished then.

She leaned against the headboard, and the cotton tee shirt pulled against her breasts as she raised her arms over her head to stretch and yawn. She still had a firm, full, shape, just not as tight or as young as Denise. He gulped his drink quickly, which took his breath away and he coughed.

"Are you okay?" she asked as she leaned over to pat him on the back.

"Yes, just went down the wrong way. Sorry," he said.

"A little early for a martini, isn't it? Bad day?"

"No, not really. Just the same old thing: busy day."

He watched her slice into the omelet and lift the chosen section to her lips. She had those round, full lips that once upon a time could give him so much pleasure. They had spent hours exploring each other's bodies with their lips, and her touches and kisses used to drive him to distraction. How long had it been since the last touch, the last kiss, the last lovemaking?

"Thanks for the roses in my den. They really are nice," he said.

"I just wanted to brighten your room," she replied. "Sometimes when I walk in there I feel as though I have walked into a tomb. You are trying to seal yourself away from me, from the world, and I don't know how to stop you. So I try to remind you that there are beautiful things still in the world, and one of them is roses from my garden."

"I'm sorry if I've seemed distant lately," he said reaching for her arm. But she pulled away quickly, and both were reminded of the wall. There was that invisible wall that had been created some time ago. The wall that had gone up so many years ago and neither really know why. But no one questioned it or knew how to take it down.

So they both sat in a sad, reclusive, uninvolved life and ate their dinner. They chatted about the day's events, carried on small talk about Brigade's aging process, the new wild flowers in the garden, and the trivial things that would get them through the meal.

After the meal, Ingrid rose to go to the bathroom and take her shower, do her makeup and style her hair. Henry would go downstairs and read the paper and then watch the television for a short time. Then Ingrid would leave for the hospital where she worked as an ICU nurse, and he would have his sanctuary to himself. Protected by Brigade.

15

After Ingrid had left, Osgood settled into his favorite chair to read the paper, but he was as usual lost in thought. He was one of the few people who could lose himself in nothingness and he was roused from his daydreams by the ringing of the phone. He walked over to the desk and lifted the receiver. "Hello?" he said.

"Henry?"

He recognized the voice, "Yes Martin, this is Henry."

"I need you and now! Make plans to leave town for a few weeks. We have a big problem in Maine, and I'm sending you, Barrett, and Denise up there to take care of the situation. I've asked Teale to take care of the arrangements. You need to be on the first flight out tomorrow."

"Martin, Martin, slow down. What's going on, where, when, and how?"

"We have a small possible outbreak in Maine. We have a few confirmed deaths and some other cases. We need to get a handle on it before it spreads any further."

"What is the outbreak exactly?"

"This is preliminary, but it looks like anthrax, yet not exactly like the common anthrax. Because it looks like it was planted. No intervention with animals, no characteristics we usually find. It's also hush-hush right now because of the way the outbreak may have been generated. I'll get some coverage for your lab."

"Yes, I'll be there," Henry replied, as he felt the swirl at the pit of his stomach. He did not like the phrase 'not characteristic.' His mind raced ahead to the thought of sabotage and why and who? But he shook his head as he tried to clear it.

One nervous Martin was enough. He didn't need others running about getting ahead of themselves and scaring the public. He needed to think calmly and clearly and make clear, concise plans.

"Henry? Are you there?"

"I'm here. I'll make arrangements with Clifford to handle the lab. Everything will be okay here at home. I'll come back into the office tonight and pick up my laptop and a few files I will need."

"No need for that," replied Martin. "I took the liberty of doing that, and Clifford will be there shortly with it. If you find I've left something out, send him back and call me and tell me where it is. I'll courier it. No need for both of us to be out and about. Besides, I'll probably be here all night as it is. I just got off the phone with NCTR and the Red Unit so things are popping. They will have their staff there today or in the morning."

"NCTR? Was that a good idea? So soon?"

"Unfortunately, I had to. They would have known within minutes after we got the call anyway. And CDC has already got their team involved because the head physician at the hospital called the State Health Department who called CDC when the first case appeared, as well as the Health Commissioner. So it is going to be a busy place. And we don't have time to waste. We have already suggested they start vaccinating the family members and other possible cases."

"Are you sure it is not naturally contracted and inflicted?" Henry asked.

"I am not sure of anything right now, that's why I'm sending you. But all the signs point to a big problem. We shall . . ." Martin broke off. "Henry? Got to go, some of the staff has arrived for last-minute briefing. Clifford will be at your place soon. Call me if you need anything else, and stay in touch. As soon as the secure line is set up I'll let you know the code. And thanks, Henry."

"Sure. Bye, Martin. I'll be in touch." Henry replaced the receiver as Brigade rose to his feet, sensing someone at the door.

"Relax, boy. It's just Clifford with my next work assignment," Henry said as he walked to the door and opened it to Clifford, the youngest member of the research team. Clifford was a handsome boy, with light brown hair and clear green eyes that reflected a great sense of humor and an incredible IQ. He did not mind being the messenger boy as he worked his way up through the ranks. Being the messenger had been his idea. He wanted to learn from the bottom up so he would know all the ins and outs.

"Hello, Clifford, come in." Henry opened the door wider for Clifford to enter with his arms full of folders and Henry's laptop.

"Thanks, Dr. Osgood. Dr. Alfonso wanted me to get this to you right away. I think things are really popping. He gave me your laptop and these files, but I picked up a couple of extra ones you may need. I think I got it all. We didn't go into the locked file because you have the key, but if you need anything from there, Dr. Alfonso said to tell me the file you need and give me the key, and I will bring it back to you."

Henry glanced at the files Clifford had brought and recognized the purple folder labeled "Pugwash Review." That was the one he wanted, and the others would do fine. He didn't want anything removed from his secure file unless absolutely necessary.

"Thanks, Clifford. Have a seat while I look through these." Henry pointed toward the sofa. He followed Clifford in. They unloaded the stack on the desk and Clifford sat down on the sofa, where he reached over and patted Brigade on the head.

"He is a beauty, sir," he said, and he continued to pet Brigade as Brigade nuzzled his nose into Clifford's leg, loving the attention.

"Yes, he is nice. My best friend truly. He keeps me company all the time," Henry answered absently as he thumbed through the folders.

"Clifford, do you remember hearing about the Pugwash Incident in the early 1980's in Russia? I think the location was one of the regions now known as Ekaterinburg. When it occurred the Soviets released articles stating that it was an anthrax outbreak among livestock, and that the people had become infected after eating contaminated meat products."

"Wow, what happened?" Clifford asked as he leaned forward now, ignoring Brigade's loving pawing on his knee.

"Well, as you can imagine it created a hell of a political hoopla. We thought it was a laboratory accident that had gone awry and the accidental release had drifted south of the lab. They found the majority of cases in this small area. We never got the true facts and figures, but we think there were about 77 cases of inhalation anthrax. It was one of the largest inhalation anthrax outbreaks ever. Of course we couldn't get in to investigate and it has all been very hush-hush as it would violate the Biological Weapons Convention of 1972, which the Soviet Union, at the time, had signed and ratified."

"Jeez. I remember some of that history, but tell me, Dr. Osgood, is it easily transmitted from person to person? I have heard different theories."

"Not really, though there have been some cases of what was thought to be person-to-person transmission. Not long ago in China there was an outbreak of 10 cases among a hospital staff, but the data could not be found to confirm any details. And remember, industrial infection results from exposure to the organism in its environmental setting or contact with the materials actually being processed. Those employees who work with the materials early have a stronger chance of being exposed and developing the bacteria than those who handle it later after it has gone through the manufacturing process. What bothers me is that this outbreak is no where near a processing plant or animal area so it probably is laboratory introduced."

"Laboratory introduced? You mean someone has been playing with it in the lab and had an accident or . . ." Clifford stood up and gawked at Henry, "deliberately set it?"

"Let's not jump the gun here, Clifford, but that is a very plausible idea. I need to go through this packet again and make a few phone calls," Henry said, continuing to read the papers in the folder.

"This looks good, Clifford. I think we have everything. If I don't, I will call you. Thanks for bringing this over. I hate to have you out running errands tonight."

"It's okay," Clifford said. "I think it will be a long night, and I'm looking forward to it. If you need me in the field, just call and I'll try to get away. Or if you need anything shipped to you, call me. Thanks for the information, Dr. Osgood, even though it's not pleasant to hear. I do want to know about it. Remember - anything I can do."

"Thanks, Clifford, I appreciate that. I'll keep it in mind," Henry replied.

"Dr. Osgood, also remember that if you need anything quick, with the least amount of work or explanation, call me and I will get it to you."

"I know, and I appreciate it. Thanks again," Henry said, as he walked Clifford to the door and closed it behind him. He remembered that the last time he had been out in the field Clifford had been a lifesaver, cutting through the red tape and going over heads to get the needed supplies to the field staff. Clifford had probably been called on the carpet for his dealings, but Martin was not going to let the "golden-haired boy" be reprimanded too strongly, because he was a real asset to the company.

"Well, old boy," Henry said, as he settled back in his chair and stroked Brigade with one hand and combed through the file on "Pugwash Incident" with the other, "let's do some reading."

Chapter 3

Denise saw Barrett and Henry at the security check desk before the terminal entrance. Hartsfield Airport was one of the busiest in the country and today was no exception. Barrett raised his hand and waved when he spotted her.

"We need to check in with security because I suppose you are carrying, aren't you?" he asked.

"Yes, it's easier than trying to retrieve it from the luggage later." Denise had never gotten comfortable with her .38, but when she went out in the field on assignment, it was required.

After the security check, the papers, and ID badges, they walked through the terminal to the waiting lounge.

"Guess what?" Barrett said when Denise reached his side.

"I am afraid to ask." She smiled.

"Oh, no, it is something good. We have first-class seats. I think maybe Teale slipped one over on Martin this time."

"Or maybe Martin requested them because he knows we are flying into the heart of danger," she replied.

"It won't be that bad and you know it," he said. "We will be in and out of there in no time. It will be a small, naturally-inflicted outbreak. We'll find the host and dispose of it, and get back in no time at all," he said.

"I hope so. But have you read the incident report and the other unusual facts surrounding this case?" She grinned as they boarded the plane and sat down in their first class seats on the second row.

"Yes, but that is preliminary data. Let's see what we find when we get there, okay?"

Denise took the window seat because she had never really learned to love to fly, and she felt more secure next to the window. Barrett never objected and always sat in quiet composure next to her during the taxiing, take off, and landing. On some of their trips, he would reach over and press her hand if he noticed the white-rimmed knuckles gripping the armrest. She always laid her head back against the seat, closed her eyes, and tried not to think about the theory of flying, the cockpit, or anything that dealt with aviation.

As she felt the plane start to taxi, she laid her head back and closed her eyes. Barrett took that moment to admire the two-piece beige suit she had chosen with the brown silk blouse. The jacket fitted perfectly across her raised chest, and the skirt rose just a bit above her knee. He noticed the uncomfortable expression around the eyes and the look of intensity on her face.

He reached over and cupped her hand in his and said, "Relax, 'Nise," his nickname when he wanted to calm her or tease her.

"We'll be off the ground in just a second, and I'll get you a glass of champagne or wine or whatever, and you can sit back and enjoy the ride. I think this is a good time of year to be in Maine if we have to go." He smiled as he squeezed her hand.

She squeezed his hand back but did not comment. She had never been able to talk until the plane had leveled off and her panic was over. She was glad Barrett was with her. She would have to remember to thank him once things had settled down.

As she felt the plane level off, she opened her eyes and looked at Barrett. His beautiful green eyes were examining her face with a look of concern? What would she call that? Ah, yes- concern. A good friends concern because of her uneasiness with flying.

"Thanks," she said as she release
know I never tell you how much I appre
with this one phobia of mine. I do appreciate
"You're welcome. Besides, what
suppose to do except save the fair maiden? .
your only phobia? I wonder sometimes. May
delve into that one night over a lingering dinner .
too much wine." He smiled and his devilish eyes s
She had never noticed before how irresistible he cou
She felt sure many women had found that to be true.
was the one thing they never shared, even as close frie
and associates- they never discussed their love lives.
knew about the relationship in Connecticut because no
only had he met the man, but also he had helped her pick
up the pieces afterwards.

"Well, Sir Lancelot, now that I have recovered.
Look at this, did you see this file on the map?" She pulled
the computer-generated map out of her briefcase. "This
area has never had an influx of anthrax, and it is not
populated with animals or stock of any kind."

"I guess you have been up all night, generating
these maps and charts, instead of sleeping, although I must
say you look very nice and rested." There was that gleam
again and that hint. Maybe she was reading too much into
it.

"Well, thank you, kind sir, for the compliment. At
least you didn't say I look like a hag. I do appreciate that.
And yes, I did get a good night's sleep after I ran off a few
charts."

Reaching for her laptop under the seat, she brushed
her leg against his and he flinched. He then reached over
and helped her remove the laptop. She put the tray table
down and laid out her laptop, flipped the screen up, and
booted up the system. Thank goodness for these small,
light accessible computers of today. Being a computer
analyst in the medical field and having spent the past few
years with Incline she could appreciate good technology.

"Look at this," she said, as the map exploded onto the computer's color screen.

"This is the area that the first confirmed death was found in, but the other seven cases were not in this area. It's in an open urban area, with, according to the questionnaires, no one going hiking, or biking in the last few weeks, and with no wooded area. It needs to be looked into a lot more. Unless this is a new strain of anthrax that has mutated. And can reproduce in other animals or plant life. I think we definitely need to look at what the lab in the Health Department found . . ."

"Excuse me. Denise."

She looked up into the face of Henry Osgood. She had been so intrigued with the screen she had not even noticed him walking up and watching her.

"Henry? How nice! How are you? Where are you seated?" she blurted out as one quick question.

"In the back. Nice seats. First class. I am afraid Teale didn't get around to doing that for me." He smiled.

Denise realized he was sitting in coach and she and Barrett were up front in the first class seats. "It was just an oversight, I am sure," she said.

"Oh, it's okay, believe me I have flown under worse conditions," he replied.

"Here, Henry, take my seat," Barrett offered as he rose. "I think she wants to pick your brain anyway about this outbreak. She has come up with some explosive material in the past few minutes. Maybe you can concur or dissuade her from taking it too far. What is your seat number? I'll sit there for a while. I need to do some reading and some security checks on a few people where we are headed, anyway."

"Thanks, Barrett. My seat is 16 B. This is very nice of you. I think Denise could probably come up with explosive ideas anywhere," he said as they began to move. Denise glanced up at Barrett as he headed toward Henry's seat. He smiled at her and winked.

"This is the reason I don't think it has mutated. The conditions are just not right, but I won't rule that out right now," he said as he broke into her thoughts. "There is no serious threat from livestock in this area, no processing plants and no bio-weaponry labs anywhere nearby."

"What? Oh, okay I see what you mean," she responded. "But what do we start looking for if this is not a natural occurrence? Labs? Anything specific you are looking for?"

"Yes, the possibilities of places like Plum Island, Ft. Detrick with the Army, operations that handle this bacteria, I don't know," he said. "I don't want to jump to conclusions. Martin has already done that by calling in NCTR, but I need to see more data, the patients, their history and what the Maine lab came up with. I think if you could focus on a program that would let us read data such as location, spores found and the practical data such as seasonal, personal identifiers, age, characteristics, sex, and so forth that would help a lot. I don't want to go with the old studies and I think we may have to start a new one now at this very moment. What do you think?"

Denise smiled at his concise, quick question on what he needed. She knew she could deliver and replied, "I was thinking the same thing. So let me clear this screen, and here we are. A clear screen, ready for your use. Give me the variables you want to look at and what databases you want to compare them with and we will see what we come up with. Look at this, the area where the young Evans man was found had no contamination. It was as though he contracted the bacteria somewhere else and died in the wooded area which they have quarantined. It doesn't mean that it is the contaminated area where he first came in contact with the illness."

"You are on top of this outbreak, aren't you?" he replied. "Always one step ahead of the game. Great! I want you to know that I am looking forward to working with you on this project. You ... and Barrett." he added with a smile.

"Thanks, I think we'll make a great team, the three of us."

The rest of the flight was spent with Henry's telling Denise the needed data and Denise's setting up a database and a questionnaire that could be printed as soon as they arrived at the labs. A few minutes before landing, Barrett returned to his seat, saying, "Sorry, Henry, but I need to take my seat back, because my carry-all is overhead."

"No problem," said Henry. "I know what you mean. I need to get back to my seat and remove my bags also. I hope my input helps Denise. Thanks for getting started on this so promptly. It will save us hours once we get out into the field. See you later at the car and the lab," he said, as he rose to return to his seat.

"Okay?" asked Barrett looking at her.

"Yes, fine, thanks. And thanks again for coming to my rescue. Not many people know about my phobia, and I don't care to share it with Henry or anyone, not yet anyway," she said, as she replaced the laptop in the case and pushed it under her seat, putting up the tray table to prepare for the landing. She clutched her left armrest with her left hand, but for some reason this time she grabbed Barrett's biceps with her right hand and held on. She leaned back and closed her eyes and wished this landing, among other things, would soon be over.

As the three departed the gate, they saw the health specialist from the Maine Department of Health holding up a sign that read: Party from Incline.

"Hi, I'm Denise Gibson. This is Dr. Barrett Hayden and Dr. Henry Osgood. We're from Incline," she said, smiling at the serious-looking young lady from the Health Department.

"Hello, I am Sierra Connor, your liaison for the rest of the epi-aid. I have a car, and I'll take you to the hotel. We have you at the Mayfield Inn, which is downtown close to the Health Department, not too far from the Mercury Labs. They are the ones handling the lab work. I am glad you caught an early flight. The news media haven't picked up on this too much yet. They have reported the two deaths, but not the other cases, and they have no idea anyone is coming in from NCTR. So we won't be bothered yet by the media," she exclaimed, all in one breath.

"Hello, Sierra," replied Henry, "Are you by any chance related to Dr. David Connor?"

"Yes, yes, I am. He's my brother. Do you know him?" she asked, taking a studied look at the three people in front of her.

"Yes, we were in medical school together. He was a brilliant student and a good friend," Henry replied.

"Thank you. He is my favorite brother. Maybe we can share some stories during your visit. I would love to hear about him during his days at Old Med. I bet he was fun."

"He was. And I'd be glad to discuss those days with you later," Henry said. Denise felt a twinge up her back hairline. What was this? Jealousy? Sierra was just a kid, and they had just met. Henry was only trying to be polite. But as she thought this she caught Barrett's glance and knew he knew what she was thinking also. Too much information too soon.

"Follow me and we'll pick up the baggage and be on our way," Sierra said leading the group toward the baggage claim area. Denise couldn't help noticing that under that cotton print dress was a young, tight body and on top of that was a delicious face with twinkling dark-brown eyes, two big dimples surrounded by a perfectly cut page-boy of dark brown hair. She had very little makeup on, if any, maybe a touch of lipstick, and she moved with grace and confidence across the waiting area. She was glad to meet these distinguished guests, but they did not intimidate her. This impressed yet disturbed Denise.

The ride to the Mayfield Inn, through the city of Augusta was made with polite conversation as Henry sat up front with Sierra, and Denise and Barrett sat in the back of the sedan. Sierra pointed out various landmarks and public buildings as they passed.

The hotel was a gabled New England building with high ceilings in the foyer. Many antiques were scattered about, and yet it wasn't furnished in the dark colors and heavy tapestries of the Colonial period. It was very bright and cheerful in its spring colors. Denise noticed that off to the right of the registration desk was a small dining room. She would probably be eating many breakfasts there, and having late night coffees. Sierra informed them that the main dining room was one flight downstairs and had a delightful menu of seafood and that the bar was next door to the restaurant and stayed open all night, with a piano bar attached.

Denise rode the elevator in silence as she listened to Sierra acquaint them with the day's agenda. After a brief rest and a cup of coffee downstairs, they would head on up to the Health Department. Since their arrival was so early, there was no one else in the office yet.

Denise unlocked the door to her room and entered a brightly-colored suite of honey beige with green drapes and light blonde furniture. She had a working desk and sofa and chairs; it would be a comfortable setting for the time she was here. She walked into the large bedroom with a king-size bed and a large bathroom and dressing area. The bedroom colors were a soft baby-blue, like at home. She felt very comfortable in this place. As she laid her bag on the bed, she heard a knock from the adjoining room door. She unlocked the door and opened it – there stood Barrett.

"Hello, roomie," he said. "I thought I would check out your place. Nice, nice indeed. Especially since we have to be here for an extended time."

Denise smiled. She couldn't decide whether she was pleased or disappointed that Barrett was next door.

"Yes, it is nice, and yours?" she asked.

"Nice. See for yourself." He motioned to his room.

"Not now, maybe later. I want to unpack and set up few things before we head to the department."

"Sure, maybe later, later on one evening," he smiled.

There was that devilish grin again.

"Thanks. See you downstairs in about an hour," she said as she closed and locked the door.

Chapter 4

Bayside, Maine

Denise, Barrett and Henry aarrived at the Health Department, which, as Sierra had told them was a short distance from the hotel. They were shown to a makeshift conference room with the morning light shining brightly through the windows. Denise started on her second cup of coffee, offered by Sierra.

"Thanks, I seem to really be drinking this stuff these days," she said setting the cup on the desk as she surveyed the offices she had been given for her staff of three. It was a large conference room, but the tables that were usually arranged in a square for meetings had been divided into tiny corner offices. Each office had a small but comfortable desk, a chair, and a visitor's chair with a personal computer already there, phone, file folders, notepads and pens.

"Sorry about the accommodations, but it was the best we could do on such short notice. You know what our budget is like these days," Sierra said, straightening the accessories on the desks.

"That's okay, Sierra. We know what it's like. Besides, most of us brought our laptops and will be using those. We'll be out in the field a lot and other times doing work out of the hotel. So don't fret. But how about a tour of the ladies' rooms, the corridors and the labs as soon as I finish setting up?" Denise placed her briefcase on the table and began to unload her supplies. The box included pencils, pens, tablets, questionnaires, a few medical journals, a medical dictionary, and the latest reprints on anthrax. After she had placed the stacks on each desk, she turned to Sierra. "Now, about that tour."

The corridors of the health department were painted the traditional dull light green from floor to ceiling. Even the door and door facings were the same color. The walls were in definite need of repainting. There were signs of years of misuse and abuse. The beige and white scuffed flooring had been recently mopped and waxed but the high-gloss luster could not hide the many years of wear and tear. The overhead florescent lighting was harsh but necessary for the small offices and the number of people the building accommodated. The offices, small as they were, had been cut into again to accommodate more employees. Quickly thrown-up partitions of gray plastic stood in the middle of the rooms to make smaller cubicles.

The ladies' room was a typical facility with four stalls, and four sinks, and the soap dispensers. At least there was a shower room off to the side, with lockers. Denise took note of that in case she should have need of it later on during her visit here. Denise brushed her hair, applied fresh lipstick, and glanced in the mirror. She was ready for the day. No matter what it would bring.

Barrett had joined Sierra outside the ladies' room. He had changed into khaki pants and a polo shirt and was wearing tennis shoes. Denise wished she had thought of that, but there would be time for that later, when she would spend days in her jeans and tee shirts.

"Looking a bit relaxed, aren't we?" she teased Barrett winking at him.

"I never know where I'll be or when I'll be back on these outbreaks so I am going to be comfortable. I suggest you do the same," he said noticing she was still in her beige suit and heels. Not that he objected; he just wanted her to be as comfortable as possible for the rest of the trip.

"I plan to get comfortable before too much longer." she replied, "I want to tour the labs and talk to the technician and get some feedback as to exactly what we are looking at. I think we'll be out in the field in the general area by this afternoon. We also need to check in with the local police department and find out what they have so far. How far away is the site, Sierra?" she questioned.

31

"About twenty miles. We can drive out there any time today, whenever you are ready. Also we have placed several government cars at your disposal so that as you become familiar with the area and no longer need a guide you can take yourselves around and check out other areas." She smiled as she quickly gave Barrett the once over with his boyish charming green eyes and the tan set off by the khaki pants and the yellow polo.

"Dr. Osgood is already in the lab, so follow me, please." Sierra led the team down the hall to the secure area of the labs.

As they walked along the dark, drab hallways, Denise noticed the sprinkler system set in for emergency showering in case of a spill from a deadly vial inside the labs. It was an antiquated system compared with what other high-tech labs now had in place, including CDC.

"Are all the cultures here at the health department or at Mercury Labs?" Denise asked as they entered through the secure door, opened by Sierra's card-key. She would have to make a note to find out whether they could obtain one or whether they would always need a cleared member of the health department before entering this part of the building.

"Our labs are so small and unsophisticated that we have only a few of the specimens. It was the first case and the first death in this outbreak. The others are at Mercury Labs, and we have already taken a sample from that specimen and sent it to Atlanta. Our labs are a bit outdated, but we still get some good work done here and diagnoses made." She glanced up as they entered the second locked door and the buzzer sounded. This small closet-size room held the protection garments. Sierra pointed to the small open locker and Denise started putting on the yellow rubber space-like suit, hood, mask, gloves, goggles and rubber booties. She entered the small lab and smiled at the doctor who was showing Henry a culture under the microscope. Denise noticed that Henry had not changed. Showing through his gowned outfit was his rumpled gray suit, loosed tie and his hair that was always awry.

"Hello, Henry," Barrett said as they entered the room, donned in the lab protection gear. "Already up and at 'em?"

"'Fraid so, and so far this is very interesting. You might want to take a look yourself. By the way, Dr. Terry Vogt, this is Dr. Hayden and Denise Gibson from Incline. This is Dr. Vogt. I am sure you've read some of his papers on anthrax and other virulent diseases."

"Yes, how are you, Dr. Vogt? This is an honor. Thank you for your hospitality and help in this matter. I know you hate to see all of us converging on you right now."

"I'm fine, and please call me Terry. No, it's a pleasure to have you here. We need all the help we can get. The team from the CDC has arrived and is out at the field site already, gathering samples and interviewing some more candidates. Miss Gibson, I understand you have devised a questionnaire for us that we can get out to the field staff fairly soon."

"Yes, hello, and please call me Denise," she said looking at the man of about fifty with graying temples and thick glasses. He was about six feet tall, with a husky build and a pleasant smile and appearance. She had not read any of his writings, but knew his name from the earlier publications in the medical journals and from his latest book warning of lethal outbreaks to come.

"The questionnaire is being printed right now by your staff, and we should have copies when we leave for the field this afternoon." She glanced over at Barrett as he took a look at the culture under the microscope.

"SHHHHH," he said as he let out a breath of air. "That's the real thing, isn't it, Henry?"

"Yes," replied Henry, "it's exactly what we were afraid of. It's the same strain. Look at those gram-positive rods. It has the same make up with blue tinted ends as the other. It is the Iowa strain, just like the ones created in black market labs over the years. Look at the pX01 and the pX02. It certainly has the three components of edema toxin, lethal toxin and capsular material with protective antigen. That is the same poly-D-glutamic acid we have seen before. Another place, another time. I ran several of the assays three times just be sure. The results are the same. All are positive. I can follow up with some other tests, but those results will take a while."

"Look at this, Denise," Barrett said moving away from the microscope.

"God!!! How can something so beautiful . . . be so damn deadly?" Denise sighed as she turned to Barrett. "Now what?" She asked noting the concern on Henry's face and the strained expression in his clear hazel eyes.

"Now we start that investigation I told you about on the plane. Now we start from square one, with your questionnaire, my security search and Terry's and Henry's expertise in this area, and we might come up with an answer-and soon. The lab folks have already started swapping the cases' homes and offices trying to isolate the bacterium. Let's hope they will come up with some cultures that we will understand today. We are sending the cultures back to Atlanta and they are sending out their Hazard-Van for work on site."

"Don't forget that Dr. Wagner has been sent from NCTR along with his associates," Terry said. Denise hoped her reaction to the mention of Paul's name was not obvious to the others in the room.

"I take it you three already know Dr. Wagner?" Terry's voice came across the room as he removed other cultures from the refrigerator and carried them to the next microscope they would be looking through.

"Yes, we worked with him some time ago on an outbreak in South Africa and then again on some research and clean-up in D.C," Barrett replied, as Denise smiled gratefully in his direction. She wasn't sure she could talk at this moment, after the mention of Wagner's name. So now it was confirmed that he would be here heading up the team. She held onto the counter top of the large sink and hoped no one noticed, but she felt Barrett's eyes on her back. She turned, and he gave her the "everything will be okay" wink that he gave her at times like these. She could not act like a child now. She had a job to do, and she had to get this personal baggage off her and deal with the health issue at hand. She was a professional and had never in her years at work let any private matter enter into her work arena. But then again, she had never met anyone like Paul Wagner before. No one had ever taken her life, her heart, her mind, and her soul in one movement and obliterated her. She had always thought herself a strong, independent woman until she met this man, who had overwhelmed her so totally.

"Well, Sierra, thanks for the tour. It was nice meeting you, Terry. Henry, I think Barrett and I will head on back to the hotel so I can change, and then we'll go out to the site. I'll pick up the questionnaires from your staff and distribute them to the team so they can start gathering information. Is there anything else we can do here for you?" She asked in a fairly calm, normal voice, surprising herself.

At that moment, a voice came over the intercom telling them a computer printout was ready to be picked up. The list would contain the names of cases and of patients who had died so far.

Leaving Dr. Vogt in his lab and removing their protective gear in the closet-like room, they went back into the hall.

"Here's the list of cases and deaths so far at the hospital. Do you want to look at this, Barrett?" Sierra asked as she took it from the young attendant.

Taking the printout, Barrett read, "The case looked like pneumonia, but the lungs were clear despite the patient's history of asthma. All the serological testing has been negative for influenza virus. Everything is coming up negative: urine cultures, blood cultures, sputum cultures'. They have wasted their time testing for malaria and other parasites, with nothing coming up. Now, maybe they will start running the right tests for anthrax and we can get on with it. Here, Henry, look at these numbers."

"Thanks," Henry said, taking the list.

"Look at this, Henry. It's seven cases with three deaths and all different sexes, ages, races. Nothing in common, not jobs, locations or anything."

Henry looked at the list and his face turned white. "Dear God," he said.

"Henry, what is it?" Barrett questioned.

"If that is Dr. Norman Bishop from Boston, I know him. He used to be a professor of mine, during undergraduate school."

"You're kidding! I'll do some checking to make sure, and when I find out I will let you know. Do you want to go with us or stay here? We need to catch up with NCTR and find out if they have anything."

"No, I'll stay here with Terry and look at a few more cultures and run a few tests. I think we need to be a bit more aggressive in some testing areas. We need to get something down and on paper soon. I'll see you back at the hotel later maybe for drinks or dinner," he said, watching
Dr. Vogt through the glass door looking into the microscope at the latest slide.

"Ready?" Barrett interrupted her thoughts of Paul and also of Henry's surprised reaction to the case list.

"Yes, thank you." She meant thank you for the supporting arm on her waist more than the offer of a ride to the hotel and the field site. She didn't dare look up at him. She knew she would see the concern he had for her and her pain right now and she didn't want to acknowledge that pain or any of her feelings.

Denise looked back into the lab and received Sierra's smile and noticed her excitement at being left behind to work with Drs. Osgood and Vogt. It was a young doctor's dream to be on this team.

"You okay, 'Nise?" Barrett questioned her.

"Yes, I'm fine. Let's stop by the office and pick up the copies and head on out to the hotel so I can change, and then to the site."

"If you want to talk..."

"No, I am fine," she interrupted him. "We both knew there was a chance he might be here, heading up the team. He *is* here and I have to deal with it. I'll be fine. I just don't want to get into it now. I'm okay, I promise." Once again she didn't look at Barrett but kept walking toward the front office to pick up her copies, thankful for the distraction to get away from his questioning looks and direct questions.

Barrett walked into the front office to pick up the keys to the rental car, which was the standard dark-blue sedan. The secretary told him he had a phone call. As he took the phone, Denise motioned to him that she would be waiting outside.

The morning sun was glistening on the freshly-washed sidewalks as Denise stepped out of the health department building. She smelled the sweet fragrance of jasmine and noticed off to the side of the walkway the brilliant blooms of purple and white petunias. Underneath the large maple was a well-kept wildflower garden filled with beautiful blue, red, yellow and lavender blooms. For a moment she was homesick for her home and garden. But it lasted only a brief second she had to get on with the job at hand.

"We have to make a stop on the way to the site," Barrett said, walking up behind her.

"Why, what is it?"

"It seems that Bob, one of my guys, has picked up an interesting tid-bit. He's at one of the local hotels."

"Great, a sleazy place, I bet."

"Always. Some of my favorite places," he teased. "No, I think it might be important."

Barrett parked the car in the closest parking space to the rental office of the hotel, which really was sleazy.

"Stay here and lock the door," he said. "I won't be but a minute."

Denise watched Barrett go through the glass door and talk to a tall, well-dressed man. The man handed Barrett a package and shook his hand.

Barrett got back into the car and opened the package.

"Shit, look at this!" he exclaimed.

"What?" Denise said looking at the computer diskette.

"Look at the listing of names on the label," he said.

Denise took the diskette and read the label. The handwriting on the label said Dr. Norman Bishop, Bayside, Maine; Dr. Richard Bean, Madison, New Hampshire; Dr. Stanley Grant, Nags Head, North Carolina; and Amherst College.

"Is that Henry's Dr. Bishop?" Denise asked.

"I don't know. I'll check. We couldn't be so lucky! Put this in your magic laptop and tell me what you see," he said pulling his phone out of his bag and dialing the number of the Maine Health Department.

"May I speak to Dr. Henry Osgood? He is a visiting scientist; he should be in the labs with Dr. Terry Vogt right now."

After a few moments' wait that seemed so long Barrett said, "Henry, this is Barrett. Now listen carefully. A while ago you said you knew our Dr. Bishop. Do you know a Dr. Richard Bean or Dr. Stanley Grant? Also, did you ever attend Amherst College in Massachusetts?"

"You do? From where and when? What about Amherst?" Barrett listened to Henry's explanations, shaking his head as each answer surprised him.   He fastened his puzzled and excited gaze on Denise.

"Okay, thanks, Henry, I'll get back to you."

"What?" asked Denise as she loaded the diskette into her laptop.

"All of these doctors were professors at Henry's old college, Boston University. He knew all of them. He didn't attend Amherst, but he did teach some microbiology classes there during summer sessions. Jesus!"

"How did you get this diskette? Where did it come from?" Denise was already reading the data that started to flow across the screen.

"A librarian found it in the floppy drive of one of the public access computers in their communications room at the library. She tried to find the guy, but he had given her a bogus address and phone number. She was watching the news on TV and recognized the name of Dr. Bishop as a recent death in town and then noticed that the name on the diskette was Dr. Bishop. She also recognized him because he would come into the library to check out books. Sheer luck! She called the Health Department, and they called us. Thank God, Bob got there first. What do you have on the screen?"

"I have a list of professors, classes, students, dates, and times. Let me open this next file." She clicked on the next file and said, "This looks like the chemical makeup of a large portion of an agent. I can't figure it out yet, but I bet Terry or Henry could tell us the makeup. But whatever it is, it's a large amount of chemicals or bacteria."

"Anything else?" Barrett asked.

"Yes, one more file. It's a diagram of a campus, a lot of buildings; it could be a building complex or a college. Dear God! It could be Amherst?"

"Maybe. I'll make some calls and send some of our folks down there. I'm not sure what we're looking for but we need to let them know to be on the lookout. Anything else? Dates, time, places?"

39

"Yes, a note at the bottom of the calculations that has the date of July twenty-third. That's seven weeks away. What do you think the date is for?" She was clicking on other files and trying to find some data that were readable and that she could understand.

"I don't know, but I don't like the sound of it," Barrett said, as he speeded up on their way to the outbreak site near Bayside, Maine.

Reaching into his briefcase in the back seat with one hand and controlling the steering wheel with the other, he handed Denise another computer printout with the information of NCTR. "Thought you might like to do some light reading and sharing with me, if you don't mind," he teased.

"As long as you keep both hands on the wheel while you're driving, please. Do you want me to read all of this to you?"

"No, just the high points, I think we both know what is there." Denise settled back in her seat to read the paper: NCTR BRIEF HISTORY.

"'Studying the biological effects, especially any adverse health effects, of potentially toxic chemical substances in our environment is the major job of the FDA's National Center for Toxicological Research (NCTR). Created by a presidential order in 1972, this Center also emphasizes the development of improved methodologies and tests for evaluating the safety of chemical toxicants.

All government agencies have responded to the Presidential Decision Directive by combining forces to develop plans and procedures to combat bioterrorism. In collaboration with The Department of Justice, The Department of Health and Human Services, and the Department of Defense, NCTR researchers are working on three areas of research: Identification of virulent biomarkers using mass spectrometry, rapid detection of microorganisms using polymerase chain reaction (PCR)

40

technology, and exploring sage and efficacious neuroprotective strategies to

protect exposed populations. NCTR is well suited and well situated to contribute to the efforts to combat terrorism. The Center is geographically located in the center of the country, physically

adjacent to the U.S. Army's Pine Bluff Arsenal, and has enjoyed a long history of formal agreements with the Army. In addition, NCTR has an unusual breadth of toxicological expertise, thus providing a strong base of knowledge and experience that can be applied to this area. Though NCTR received no resources to support this work, initial efforts continued; including collaboration with the Department of Defense concerning mass spectrometry assessment and identification of bacterial proteins (biomarkers), and in conjunction with the Food Safety Initiative on PCR characterization of bacteria. NCTR researchers have developed a novel approach to rapidly identify biomarkers of toxicity using a mass spectrometry-based method for detection of microorganisms.'"

"This place has really been moving on with their program," She said to Barrett.

"I know. Read some more of it to me. I just got a chance to glance it, but at least we know these folks know what they are doing, no wonder Paul went to work there. Impressive."

"Okay, shall I continue out loud?"

"Yes, let me hear it all."

"I am just picking up in the middle so bear with me. This spectrometry-based procedure is designed to identify and detect biomarkers for the presence of specific genes that identify biological agents or those that could be introduced into otherwise harmless organisms. The value of this technique is that important traits of microorganisms manifest themselves across species and offer species independent markers. Identification of these biomarkers can be associated with the identity or properties of the types of biological warfare agents that would be used in a terrorist threat. After identification of the biomarker-proteins using mass spectrometry, it should be feasible to develop field diagnostic kits to identify these biomarkers."

"God, let's hope so, let's hope these guys have some of their new kids out here at the site, I'm not sure what our group is bringing. We can use all the help we can get," Barrett interjected.

"'In a terrorist situation, the timely identification of the problem agent will be critical,'" she read.

"No kidding," he said.

"Are you going to comment on every detail? Should I read or do you want to read it later?" she asked.

"Sorry, I just get lost in all that is involved with what we are dealing with. Please continue."

"'Molecular biology studies associated with the government-wide Food Safety Initiative are also applicable to the bioterrorism initiative. Scientists at NCTR have used PCR technology to identify and classify twelve food-borne pathogens and have developed molecular procedures to individually detect known determinants of antibiotic resistance. Through safety assessment drug trials and outreach activities via the Interagency Committee of Neurotoxicology and CTR/FDA-organized International Neuroprotective Conferences, NCTR researchers will continue to build a strong research base on which to contract/develop predictive systems for neuroprotective drugs. Many of the agents used to conduct terroristic activities are nerve agents for which few techniques are available to protect humans. The application of new non-invasive imaging techniques can be used to determine if exposure has occurred and can be used to assess the utility of neuroprotective strategies. The development of prophylactic approaches to protect against bio/chem terrorism depends on determining the potential toxicity of neuroprotective approaches. NCTR plans to acquire the non-invasive imaging capabilities to explore neuroprotective concepts likely to be effective in humans by first testing in laboratory rodents and primates.' The rest is about the location and such, want to hear it?"

"Why not, it will keep us busy until we get to the site and meet the real boys."

"'NCTR is located on 496 acres in Jefferson, Arkansas. Physical facilities include 35 buildings owned by FDA valued at $225 million, one million square feet of floor space, and approximately $20 million in capital equipment. The NCTR laboratory complex, accredited by the American Association for Accreditation of Laboratory Animal Care (AAALAC), houses both general purpose and high containment laboratories, specific pathogen free (SPF) barrier laboratory animal breeding and holding rooms, conventional laboratory animal holding rooms, primate research facilities, diet preparation facilities, pathology laboratories, and hazardous waste disposal capabilities.' How is that?"

"At least we know who we are dealing with. Thanks for reading. I just wanted to get a handle on this group."

Chapter 5

Bayside, Maine

The ride to the field site through the countryside was exactly what Denise needed. She had stopped at the hotel and changed into her jeans and polo shirt and work boots. As she was changing, Barrett had taken the opportunity to pack a small cooler with sodas, sandwiches, and chips in case they needed a snack. Neither of them knew what the facilities would be like at the site or whether there would even be place close by that sold food. She was always amazed at how thorough Barrett was in these matters. The thought of food and drink had not even entered her mind. She turned the map over and said, "The next exit to the right should take us through Bayside, where the cases and deaths were isolated and then on out to the site they have set up."

Barrett eased the car into a right turn and whistled slowly. "This is out in the boonies. And look at this, nothing but trees, scrubs, and a hiking area. No open grazing land. I think Henry is beginning to make sense. This is not the normal location for anthrax. I hope we're not dealing with a new strain that we can't monitor or treat. I hate to think of the possibilities of that." He frowned as he gazed across the land and studied each area they passed.

"If it is new, then what? Would you think man-made and man-set? If that's true, what's the next step?"

"Well, my dear, that is the reason I'm here. The security on this has got to be kept at a maximum, and the data has to be lily white and perfectly documented. Remind me as soon as we get to the site to put in a call to Martin and get the secured line. He needs to get more information on our three doctors. He needs to locate Dr. Bean and Dr. Grant and just check in with them. I don't know, what you say to someone whose name you have found on a bloody death computer disk."

"Do you remember the name of the new kid at the agency who follows Henry around like a dog?" he quietly asked.

"Yes, ah, Clifford. Yes, Clifford. He's a bright kid. I think everyone is pleased with his performance and lets him stay where he is. I am sure he is being heavily groomed. Why?"

"Yes, Clifford. I want to talk to Henry about him. We may need to make use of Clifford's handiwork soon. I think I'll need a few more things than what we brought in, and more information, and I think Clifford will be our man. Have your heard the names of the teams coming from the Center yet or from NCTR?" he asked.

"No, I am sure from CDC it will be a couple of epidemiologists and the state field man, and one of their experts. The Feds usually send in a small team and then add to it, as they feel necessary. Well, at least we know Paul will be here. Don't panic; I am fine with that," she said. "This is a job, and I'm sure I'll be too busy to think or worry about Dr. Wagner. I am being honest with you, and I don't want you worrying about me either. As for as the rest of his team I've no idea. I have been out of touch with him and his agency for some time so I have no idea who is on board now. Why?"

"I want to get a feel for who we will be dealing with, their background, their contacts, their ideas, maybe even their political affiliation . . ." he turned and flashed that mischievous grin.

"You can't be serious? One of the field team might be behind this outbreak? Aren't your reaching a bit? I would think if it is man-made and man-set then it would be someone totally removed from these three agencies."

"That, my dear," he smiled in his sweet, but condescending way, "is the reason you are in computer security and I am in people security. Now think about it, if someone wanted to breach your security system, would you think a novice would attempt it, or someone familiar with computers? Or better yet, why not someone from the company? Someone who had an axe to grind, or just wanted to show the big boys it could be done. There are a million reasons someone would want to sabotage a system."

"Sabotage? You're getting pretty dramatic, aren't you?" She glanced over at him and saw that the expression on his face with its deeply furrowed brow made her realize he was very serious and that he'd given it a lot of thought.

"Maybe, maybe not. But it is food for thought and that's just between the two of us. I am sure it has already gone through Henry's, Terry's and Martin's minds. I would be willing to bet Martin is already compiling a list of interesting characters in his office as we speak. And we are not just talking about international terrorists of various religious facets, but domestic ones also. We have a lot of people in this country who feel they have an axe to grind with our government," Barrett said, slowing to a crawl as they entered the city limits of Bayside.

Bayside was a small town of maybe 2,300 people, about twenty miles from Augusta and ten miles from the coast. The economy relied mostly on farming and the tourist trade-tourists who had wandered off the beaten path to enjoy the flavor of small-town New England. There were one main street and several side streets. The shops were freshly painted in white, with a few that had pastel trim on the doors or windows. Most of the shops were antiques stores or nautically related. Denise spotted an interesting-looking diner on the main street next to a dress shop. She would have to remember both of those. The streets were fairly quiet. The tourist season was not yet in full swing. The sign showed that the post office was down a side street. She didn't see a notice for UPS or FedEx but she could use the facilities at the health department.

She liked the looks of this place and looked forward to getting to know it and its residents better. She would prefer this to Augusta, the busy state capital.

"Nice setting, peaceful, quiet, almost romantic?" Barrett read her thoughts. She glanced at him and at once saw that mischievous glint in his eyes. He was a study in nature for her.

"Yes, I like it. Peaceful looking, isn't it? I wonder if anyone here has any idea what is going on out in their peaceful fields?" She said.

"Well, let's not spoil it for them yet. Did you bring your swimsuit? I know the ocean water is probably fairly cold, but our hotel has a pool, and we might even find a local lake during our investigation," he laughed.

"Yes, as a matter of fact I did. I always try to get some laps in. I not only swim for exercise, but to clear my head. And the more we delve into this case the clearer my head needs to be. Did you see that diner back there? The name is KC's. Advertised 'great seafood.' Maybe we can check it out one night. Get to know the people and at least make our presence known. What do you think?"

"Sounds good to me. I could use some great seafood. The last I had was a few months ago in Boston, and I'm ready for some steamers, lobster, and all the other good stuff," he smiled.

The drive through Bayside took only a few minutes. Following the map, Barrett drove to the end of the state highway. Turning onto a county road and then taking a left, they entered a pasture, where the site was set off with two large tents, and several four-wheeled drives. The Maine Public Health Department's pickup truck and a van with "NCTR" on the side were parked at the site. Off to the left, apart from all the vehicles, were two men in white coverall safety suits. The men wore their Level-personal protection equipment, knee-high florescent-green boots and the yellow-covered headgear with face shields equipped with respirators. No matter how many times Denise saw it, it reminded her of a scene from some 1957 sci-fi movies.

"Looks like they are fairly well set up. And all the players are here. Ready, kid?" Barrett asked as he switched the car off and reached into the back seat for his briefcase. She knew his question was not concern for the outbreak, but concern for her at spotting the van. He had noticed it at the same time she had-, as soon as they had pulled into the field and parked.

"I'm fine. Let's get on with this. I'll try to establish a working point for the laptop and secure lines."

"Sierra has put a folding table and chairs in the trunk. She's sending a canopy later today," Barrett went on. "I think for the time being we need to set up our own little operation. We can share data later if you want, but for now *our* data, *our* findings, stay with *us* at all times. I'll brief Henry on this but I think he will agree. The less anyone knows about our work and findings the better off we are. So let's do it! Let's save the world!" he joked, as he stepped out into the warm mid-afternoon sun.

Denise flipped open the trunk to the sedan and looked at all the accessories Sierra had sent. She had been thorough in her packing. The folding table was on the bottom of the stack and there were three sturdy but uncomfortable gray, folding chairs. There was also a flashlight; a medical kit; a box of more tablets, pens, and pencils; an address book for health department; colored markers; computer paper for the small printer; maps of the local area; and a local telephone book. And on top of the box was a large fifteen-inch bowie knife. Interesting choice?

"Do you think our Sierra has a sense of humor or a sense of drama?" Barrett asked as he started removing the equipment and laughed at Denise's response to the knife.

"It is a bit much, isn't it?" she agreed.

"Maybe not. Maybe it is in place of scissors. The wild outback cutting bushes, limbs, strings, you know. Roughing it, so to speak," he answered.

"Grab the box. I'll get the heavy things and we will set up our little office. As soon as we are up I need to call Martin. Where is the cellular phone?" He glanced at her still-disturbed look.

"It's in my briefcase. The kit with the phones and the codes and all the information. I'll set it up for you as soon as I can. I will get Martin on the phone for you also," she said.

"Thanks. After the call, you and I can do some exploring of territory and people. I am really eager to get into this arena and find out who the players are and what the agenda is." She could tell by his flushed face he was getting geared up for this moment. He always loved a bit of excitement and adventure, and it was showing now on his face.

Setting up the small outdoor office took no time. Then they got on with setting up the tables and chairs, covering the table with the needed computers, calculators, journals and papers. The men from the health department showed up with the canopy to put over the makeshift office. The canopy of white and green stripes was a bit out of place, looking more like a wedding reception tent than a secured office area for the study of a deadly disease outbreak.

After the outdoor office was set up, Denise got Martin on the secure line and handed it over to Barrett, who walked away from tent to engage in security issues and concerns. He wanted Martin to start a search on the people whose names were on the diskette and to get more information for him.

Denise did not feel left out. In a way, she didn't want to hear all of those conversations, and she knew Barrett well enough to know that he would tell her anything he felt she needed to know or that was pertinent to the case.

She busied herself with setting up the laptop and pulling up the questionnaire on the screen and double-checking her entries. She knew the questionnaire had been distributed to the department staff and was being taken door-to-door in Bayside. She hoped the department would not start distributing questionnaires in Augusta for at least a few more days. No cases had been reported from that city, just from Bayside. She wanted to keep the investigation as quiet as possible and questioning people in Augusta would only alert the media. Right now, they needed all the quiet working time they could get.

Barrett walked back into their "office."

"Well, I was right," he said firmly. "Martin has already started composing a list of people who might have an interest in starting this outbreak. He gave me a few of the names on the phone but will FedEx me the others tonight. He has also started researching the names on that disk. This looks really homey," he said, stepping back and observing how organized the small working area had become in just a few minutes. "Aren't you just the little homemaker?" he teased.

She smiled. "If we are going to be here for a while we might as well make the best of it."

Barrett went on. "We have another problem, though. The contaminated site is not here. It has been traced to a group of contaminated asthma-medication inhalers. Apparently Dr. Bishop had asthma, and that's how he contracted the agent. Even though a case was found in this area, this is not the site of disease."

"What are you talking about?" she asked.

"The first death occurred in this area, a young man named Evans, who was brought in from this site, but the police have found that Dr. Bishop's inhaler was contaminated with anthrax. There was a large amount of bacteria found in his system. The lab was checking other possible sources of infection and there were no bites on skin, bleeding into the skin, although his skin did have a slightly dusty coloration. The pathologist found lots of bleeding and inflammation between the lungs, which included the trachea, the esophagus, the main bronchial cavity and the vessels, and some of the lymph nodes."

"Meaning what?" Denise asked sitting down in the chair, hardly believing what she was hearing.

"Meaning that after a brief look about, the cops, with the help of the hospital staff, found large traces of the bacteria in Dr. Bishop's mouth. Also they noted later that all the other victims admitted to the hospital were asthma suffers. They have traced one of the cases to a bottle of "saline solution" that Dr. Bishop bought to clean his inhaler. They have found the drug store it was purchased at, and have pulled all the other containers off the shelf. We can close up shop here in a little while and head for the hospital and talk to the staff and the family members. We may also be dealing with an airborne virus, which leaves little room for thought."

"You mean someone has broken into Dr. Bishop's house or office and injected anthrax into his medication?"

"Yes, and the others contracted it from contaminated supplies they'd bought at a local drug store."

"Dear God, do you know what you are saying?"

"Yes, this nut is crazier than I thought."

"What is his reason for this?"

"That I don't know yet, but I intend to find out," Barrett replied, walking off to make another phone call.

Chapter 6

Bayside, Maine

"Good afternoon, folks. My name is David O'Brien, and this is my associate, Sasha Kemp." Denise and Barrett hadn't noticed the couple who had walked up to the tent. David O'Brien was a man in his mid-forties with a deep tan, short-cropped sandy-blonde hair and a handsome face with deep blue eyes. He was about six feet tall with a very muscular build, shown off by his tight blue jeans and cotton plaid shirt. He reached over to shake hands with Barrett.

"Hello, I am Barrett Hayden, and this is my associate, Denise Gibson. We are with Incline. We just got here. Looks like things are getting started and moving quickly."

"Yes, we've been out since early this morning," replied the striking blonde of maybe five feet ten inches, standing in mid-calf boots, faded jeans, and a pink polo shirt that suggested a very nice shape underneath. She had the greenest eyes, a flawless complexion, and unnaturally blonde hair pulled back with a pink pony-tail holder. Denise's first thought was this lady had not spent much time in the field.

"We flew in early this morning. Who are you with?" Denise asked trying to sound interested. But for the first time in her life, she felt unattractive standing next to this beauty. She had already noticed Barrett doing his once-over from head to toe of the lady who extended her hand to Denise in greeting. Denise could not wait to hear his description of Sasha when they got back to the hotel later. She knew he would be sharing it with her.

"We are with NCTR," said the blonde. "We got in late yesterday so we have had a few hours to get set up and ready to go. This is an out of the way place, isn't it? But beautiful country. I'm looking forward to checking out one of the seaside towns later this week. That is if my slave-driving boss doesn't keep me too busy. He has a . . ."

"That would be me . . . the slave-driving boss," replied the deep husky voice behind Denise. She recognized it at once. She felt the chill rush down her back, a slight tingle in her ears and the hair rise on the back of her neck. She turned to face the man who still had that effect on her.

"Paul." She hoped it came out as a statement and not a question or exclamation. She hoped no one had noticed the rise in her voice or the slight blush she felt creeping up from her neck to her face.

"Hello, Denise, Barrett. I see you've made it here safe and sound. It is a lovely location, and regardless of what my young friend has to say, I think I *will* let her check out the beach. And I *may* check it out myself," he said as he reached to shake first Barrett's hand and then hers. His eyes quickly moved to Sasha, and he smiled. So, thought Denise, she is probably more than a friend after all. He always did have great taste in women.

"I didn't realize you three knew each other," said Sasha, noticing the effect Paul's presence had on both Denise and Barrett. Paul had never mentioned Denise to Sasha before.

"Yes, we worked together on an outbreak several years ago. And you're right, it *is* peaceful and quiet here," replied Barrett moving closer to Denise in case she needed some moral support.

"We were impressed with the small town we just drove through, with the selection of shops and diners. It looks like a pleasant area. Thank goodness we are not here during the winter, coping with the cold, bitter New England snow."

"Ahh yes, but Maine in winter can be beautiful and a lot of fun for us skiers. They have some fantastic lodges and great slopes. It also makes for some beautiful wintry scenes," Paul said, staring deep into Denise's eyes as though trying to read her thoughts. He had probably picked up on her body language now as she was still trying to get control of herself.

"This is interesting," said Sasha reaching over and picking up the Bowie knife. Denise had left it on the table and had not had a chance to put it back in the trunk of the car. "We are going back to Daniel Boone days, aren't we?" David asked, as he reached for the knife. "This is different. I haven't seen one like this in years. I used to have one similar to this when I was growing up in Montana. They will cut through anything and clear off small brushes, limbs, and other things that get in your way. Even though it should be used only for cleaning and skinning." He turned the well-made knife over in his hands. Denise could feel Paul's eyes on her, but she stood her ground and stared at the knife.

"Well, as interesting as this is, we need to get back to our tent. Coming, Paul?" Sasha asked.

"Not yet. Why don't you and David go set up the testing table for me. I will be there in a minute. I'd like to discuss a few things with Barrett. We have mutual interests of sorts, and I need to get some of his ideas," said Paul.

"Sounds like a good idea," said Denise walking out of the tent. "I want to walk this area anyway and check out the terrain and meet the guys from the Health Department. Excuse me please." As she walked away, she could feel all four pairs of eyes on her back. But she didn't falter. She was not ready for this, not yet. She knew it would come when she had to meet him again face to face but she was shocked at how unprepared she really had been just now.

She walked briskly to the pickup truck that belonged to the health department and engaged the men in conversation. She knew she was making idle chatter, with introducing herself and asking questions about the location and other pointless stuff, but at least she was away from *him* and it would give her some time to collect her thoughts and regain her composure.

After a brief discussion with the men, she walked over to the makeshift CDC tent and introduced herself. She would try to get some information on their personnel and get an idea of who was with them so she could discuss things with Barrett when she joined him later. Even if she couldn't do too much thinking now, she could at least try to gather useful information. Besides, she needed a distraction. Any type of distraction.

"Anyway, this is our second trip out this week," came Dane's voice as he was answering Denise's question about the requests they answer on calls for epi-aids and how often and where and when. She could tell Dane was a seasoned lab technician who traveled all over, investigating various outbreaks. He was in his mid-forties with graying-brown hair and a wrinkled face that showed lots of weather exposure. She felt soothed by his Southern drawl. It was real, not fake and not syrupy, just nice and comfortable. She would have to make a mental note to remember this man because with his knowledge and background and intuition he would be a valuable asset later on.

"We just stay packed most of the time," Dane continued. "I grab my bag and run whenever the call comes. But I'm not complaining. This traveling has taken me to some very interesting places from South Africa to Hawaii, and that's a stretch. I've seen deserts, rain forests, the Alps, volcanoes, and wild natives. I've met more people than I can ever remember, but I have also seen some terrible things, including death and various stages of fatal diseases. But I have to be honest, Miss Gibson, this one looks different. I hear the whispers, and I see the questioning stares between the crew, so I know there is more to this than meets the eye."

"Please call me Denise, Dane. And I have to agree. We felt the same way after we read the preliminary data, but we'll wait and see what we come up with tomorrow. I left Dr. Osgood in the lab with the state's Dr. Vogt working away on some new specimens. So we'll just have to wait and see. When you were in South Africa, did you meet Dr. Stephens and his group?" she asked as she tried to move the conversation away from the real interest, so as not to share her and Barrett's concern about this outbreak. She also just needed to hear someone else talk so she could answer with noncommittal responses until she was back on her feet emotionally.

"I had rather be here in the outdoors than back in Atlanta at the home base. Those folks are catching it right now. They turned the main auditorium into makeshift offices for fifty to sixty people. The telephone people had to set up at least sixty phones with the hot line and the IT folks had to install fifty personal computers overnight. And they did it. Somehow it all came together, but then again a great organizer and thinker, Dr. Geoff Foskey, is running CDC and he knows how to handle things. He's an old hand at setting up in the midst of a crisis." Dane continued, "Dr. Foskey has the auditorium set up in a crisis mode divided by teams that will handle the calls from the public. And the calls have started. Before we left they were handling hundreds of calls a day. The bullpen, which handles the majority of calls before they're farmed off to a specific team, is being manned by EIS officers and other professionals. If there ever was a public health issue, this anthrax scare is one." Denise stood listening to Dane's explanations of what it was like at his office in Atlanta. She knew her office was under the gun, but they did not have to respond to the public the way CDC had to reassure the public that all was well.

"Our folks in the bio-terrorist unit are working 10-14 hour shifts in-house and the ones out here will be up all night and day trying to catch a few naps along the way. We can't afford not to as we have to have some answers and have them soon. And let's face it, we at CDC are the ones the public is looking to for leadership."

"How do you think they are doing back in Atlanta?" Denise asked as she sipped a Coke, fascinated by Dane's excitement in telling the guts of CDC.

"Hell, we got it under control, even with our limited budget and this being the first real scare we have had in years. We are trained for this. I bet some of our EIS officers are thriving off this. And those folks who work at CDC to serve the public good feel that they are contributing and making a difference right now. Do you know any of our people?" Dane asked as he pulled a Coke from the cooler.

"Oh, yes, one of my old buddies is Dr. Doug Stephens, in virology. Do you know him?"

Dane smiles. "Yeah, I know Doug. This is the type of action he lives for. He is in the middle of it in Atlanta and handling it like a champ. And trust me, those folks are under pressure not just from the public, but from Washington. I think they are expecting some senators, cabinet members and maybe even the President to visit in the next couple of days. It is going to make some change in CDC. Hopefully, for the better. Maybe more money, more jobs, construction of facilities and buying equipment to handle outbreaks like this. It is too bad that it takes a national emergency to wake the public up to the potential hazards out there in the real world. But at least we have our dedicated folks ready to go out and investigate and take care of the situation." He laughed again.

"Forgive me. Sometimes I get carried away with our agency. I think it is because I love the work so much and the excitement of working on some of these outbreaks. How long since you last saw or talked to your good friend Dr. Stephens in Atlanta?"

"Unfortunately, it has been a while. What with both of our schedules, it is hard to maintain contact sometimes," she said.

"Well, let me enlighten you about a few stories that he may not have shared with you," Dane said, sitting down next to her in the plastic lawn chair. Denise spent several minutes living the adventures with her old associate Doug Stephens in South Africa, and then suddenly Dane was called away. He was needed inside the CDC van to look at the maps of the area. She thanked him for his information and reminded him they would have to get together soon for a drink to share more war stories. He seemed very pleased with that idea.

Chapter 7

Bayside, Maine

Denise walked through the clearing just beyond their workstations and came to the top of a small incline overlooking a small pond in a lush green setting. Huge green stalks of cattails with a few water lilies surrounded the pond. On the shore was a small two-seater fishing boat with two oars and rusty bait can in the bottom. The field around the pond was covered with green grass and wild flowers of purple, yellow, blue and red. It looked like the pastoral setting from a peaceful painting by Monet. No one would ever think of the chaos that was taking place just several hundred yards behind her.

"It is lovely, isn't it?" Paul said, as he quietly walked up behind her. She took a deep breath and gathered herself to deal with this here and now.

"Yes, it is. So peaceful," she said, without turning around, and continuing to stare at the Monet-like landscape. She wanted to be in full control of herself before she faced him again.

"It's hard to believe any place could be this quiet and serene and yet be threatened by anything as deadly as what we're looking at, isn't it?" he said as she turned to look at him.

She caught a glimpse of Barrett standing back at the health department truck and knew that he was keeping on eye on her, but would not approach unless she gave a needful signal. Then she took in the full figure of the man who had taken so very much from her years ago. That gorgeous copper-red, below-the-ear hair, the soft brown eyes encased in gold-rimmed shaded-lens glasses-glasses that hid the expression in his eyes and those soft, full lips surrounded by a well-kept short beard and forming that grin. The broad shoulders and well-developed chest and arms were enhanced by the soft, worn, plaid, cotton shirt. He wore faded jeans and the boots. His trademark, the boots. He had a pair of boots for every occasion.

"It's nice to have this close by," she motioned toward the open field, "to look at to remind ourselves there is a beautiful, tranquil world around us no matter what we are dealing with at this time and place. That there is beauty and peace in every corner of this world." She could hear herself rambling on making no sense at all, she was just staring at him, letting her mouth continue without the help of her mind.

"Is there peace and love and harmony anywhere in the world? I wonder sometimes." He smiled down at her and then once again turned to look at the landscape. He was more relaxed than she was; yet she felt he was a bit uncomfortable. He gave a deep sigh and continued to stare at the pond without speaking. She could actually *feel* his body just a few inches from hers. She could catch a brief whiff of his Stetson cologne and feel the heat generated not only by the sun, but also by his body. His body temperature always ran a few fractions of a degree higher than most people did. She glanced up at him and saw his eyes taking in the scene, and she could tell his thoughts were miles away, but she couldn't tell whether he was reliving a good experience or a bad one. The two of them stood there for several minutes that seemed like hours to her.

"How are you?" He turned and asked.

"I'm fine. I've been very busy at the office. I haven't been traveling as much as before, but that's okay. It gives me time to take care of my garden and attend the symphony with my friends and catch up on my reading. I've started a book club with several friends, and we are enjoying that . . . " She stopped, realizing again that she was just running on. "I am fine, really. And you?" she smiled and asked. She could feel herself relax and get comfortable with him again. It felt the same. As though she had no reasons to put up defenses to protect herself. This was the man she had loved, the man she had given everything to at one moment in time, the man she thought she would be with for the rest of her life. But she caught herself. She thought, be careful. She did have to protect herself and not relax too much.

"I'm fine," he said. "I've been very busy this last year. But I miss you. I miss us. Nothing. No amount of work, travel or people can take the place of you. I miss you. You ended it so quickly, so fast. You never gave me a chance to explain. We need to talk. Not here, not now, but soon. You never returned my calls, and let's face it; I am not the type of man to chase you forever. I won't show up and demand your attention, although I still kick myself sometimes for not flying to Atlanta and dragging you off somewhere to make you listen to me. But nevertheless," he slowed down and turned to her again, not touching her, but looking into her eyes, "I miss you, I need you, and I do want to talk to you . . . soon."

"You're right, I can't get into this now. Not at this site, not with the way things stand at the office. We have a lot of work to do, and I can't be distracted. I will make a deal with you. Let's be civil, let's be friends, and let's work together, because you know we are going to be thrown together a lot. If you will do that for me now, I promise we'll talk in a few days. We'll find a nice, quiet place and talk, and I will listen. I don't think you can explain away what happened, but I do owe you the courtesy of listening."

He smiled, turning back to look at the work site and the people and Barrett standing guard.

"Thank you. I do appreciate that, and I do have answers for you and for myself. I see your trusty friend Barrett is still on the lookout for you. Haven't you two started dating yet? I guess that's none of my business, but surely you know the guy is crazy about you. Or did you know that? Anyway, thanks for the offer of a discussion time later. And yes, we can work together and things will be fine. I have to admit it won't be easy. It is not easy standing here next to you now."

He reached and placed his hands on each of her shoulders and turned her to face him. "I can hardly be this close without remembering, but I won't touch you again. But believe me, it's not because I don't want to. No matter what you think or believe, it was real. It was real for me, and it was real for you. Never doubt that."

He released her and walked back to the site. Denise turned back to face the valley and the pond. She could feel the tears welling up in her eyes, and she wasn't ready to face anyone or anything. She shook her head briefly and wiped her eyes. He could still get to her and she would have to keep her guard up. After several deep breaths, she turned and headed back to the tent. She passed by the NCTR van since it was parked in a position that she could not avoid passing, and she glanced at Sasha, looking up at her. David was on the phone, and Paul had disappeared. She kept walking straight to her tent, watching her step as she walked through the heavily overgrown brush. She finally looked up to see Barrett walking toward her with a soda in his hand.

"Okay?" he asked. Sometimes he could be such a good friend with his one-word questions or comments. "I thought you could use this. I couldn't help but notice you had a visitor on your walk. I didn't want to intrude. I figured you could handle the situation and if not you would call. I gave you the last few minutes to get yourself together. You look fine, except a tiny tear streak and a lighter shade of pale. Thank goodness for sunglasses, huh?"

"What would I do without you?" she smiled as she accepted the soda and took a deep gulp. "Thanks for the thoughts. I am okay, but I must admit I was surprised at my reaction to him and how he still gets under my skin. I knew he could, but not this much. I just need time. He and I have a truce to work together on this and not get involved. I did promise him one dinner with conversation. I think I owe him that much, but it will be later, much later in the week. And that's all I want to say for now except, thanks again. Now what do we have here?" she asked as she picked up the latest print out of Barrett's data. "This looks interesting, really interesting. Remember the anthrax outbreak in Russia in 1979?"

"Yes, it was on a much larger scale, but this disease frightens me, really frightens me. I am more than a little concerned. It is nothing like anything I have ever seen before. We have a lot of work to do to find this culprit, and I mean both of them. I want the organism and the person. And I mean that seriously," Barrett said as she looked up and saw the very disturbed look on his face. "The other thing is that Henry called, and he feels the same way I do, so the three of us will get together later for dinner and go over some of this info."

At that moment, Denise looked up to see the small, black rented car go by with Sasha and Paul, leaving the site. Sasha waved; Paul kept his eyes on the road. Denise turned back to Barrett and said, "Yes, let's do dinner. By now Osgood and Vogt should have some idea of what's happening."

Getting into the car Denise rested her head on the back of the car seat and remembered . .

**Three years earlier,
Atlanta, Georgia**

Denise had been waiting patiently in the conference room for ten minutes before the door opened and Martin, General Gordon Saunders, Barrett, Susan, and the tall nice-looking red-haired man walked in.

"I am so sorry to keep you waiting, Denise," said Martin, "but things are very busy. Paul's flight was late, and he has just walked in, and it took me forever to get Gordon off the phone. Need I say more? By the way, this is Colonel Paul Wagner as well as Dr. Wagner, one and the same. How do you like to be introduced, Paul? Paul, this is Denise Gibson."

"Colonel Wagner or Dr. Wagner, either one is fine with me," he answered. "Hello, Denise. It's a pleasure to meet you. I have heard good reviews on your work, and I look forward to working with you on this project." He extended his hand. As Denise took it, she liked the grip, but more important she liked the eyes and the generous mouth. She had heard of this rebel, cavalier doctor who had taken the medical community and the military by storm. He had taken on the task of making the two entities work together and somehow agree on the same platform to address the issue of bio-warfare; a daunting task for anyone especially one so young. But unless appearances were deceiving, he was the man for the job.

"Thank you, Colonel Wagner. I look forward to working with you also. We will offer any help that we can to NCTR." She was not going to tell him all she had read about him earlier. He had been an early graduate of Harvard Medical School and then on to the University of Washington graduate school in Microbiology. He was one of the youngest men ever to be promoted to full Colonel. His reputation in the field, in the office, and in the society columns preceded him. He was probably already very much aware of himself and his accomplishments.

She couldn't help noticing the broad shoulders and the athletic build hidden beneath the soft gray suit, with the traditional white shirt set off by a Jerry Garcia tie of multi-colored balloons. The tie itself was an in-your-face statement of its own. Topping off the unique wardrobe was a high-gloss pair of black cowboy boots. Not dress boots, but western boots. Being in the Special Unit of NCTR, he

64

could get away with this dress. Apparently he only was in military garb when on the base or the occasion called for it.

She had heard a lot about this man from different reports in the office, gossip at the coffee shop, at Incline, and from the few things she had read in the local newspaper. He was considered by the medical community to be a young biology genius specializing in germ warfare. He was also a brilliant military officer and she couldn't decide whether the boots were part of the military garb or just his own preference.

His presentation on what they had found in the outback of North Carolina was well- developed and presented with color slides and containing many statistics and much data, precise and to the point without overkill. He was good at analyzing and presenting his case. Martin followed Paul's presentation with a few short remarks about the urgency of this anthrax outbreak and the large amount of work ahead of each of them.

As Denise was walking out of the conference room, she heard, "Excuse me, Denise, have you got a minute?"

She turned and looked at Paul. "Sure. By the way, that was a very good presentation. It answered a lot of my questions and gave me some idea of what you are looking for so I can do the research to develop something you can use."

"Thanks, I appreciate that, but I was wondering if we might have lunch today and discuss it further?" he asked.

"I wish I could, but I have plans today, and I can't cancel. Maybe another time," she said.

"Dinner tonight?" he asked.

She wanted to jump at the chance but she couldn't appear too eager so she stopped and smiled and said, "Sorry, plans again, but what about lunch tomorrow? I have no plans, and I'd like to discuss this North Carolina project with you. I have a lot of questions."

"I guess you can't change your dinner plans, either?" he questioned.

She shook her head and smiled.

He smiled and said, "Okay, then. Lunch tomorrow will be fine. Do you have any suggestions for a place to eat?"

"Yes, there is a nice little Italian restaurant, just a few blocks away. A bit crowded at times, but worth the wait. We can meet in the front lobby of this complex at 12:00 tomorrow and walk to the café."

"I was thinking of a more secluded, quieter, romantic place, myself." He grinned boyishly.

"That would be nice, but both of us are going to be very busy tomorrow and all this week. So let's just stick to the Italian café and we can relax and enjoy the food."

"Okay, but maybe tomorrow I can talk you into having dinner with me one night this week," he said, sounding disappointed.

"Perhaps, Dr. Wagner. I am really not playing hard-to-get, I'm just very busy, and as I am sure you are also." She didn't want to push him too far, because she did want to spend some time with him and get to know him, but she didn't want to seem so eager either.

"I understand how busy both of us are, but we both still have to eat and we might as well eat together. If you know what I mean?" he teased.

"I know what you mean, so I will meet you for the walk to the Italian café."

Denise walked back to her office with a light step. She closed the door on her sanctuary, the large office on the fourteenth floor. It was painted soft beige, with a deep burgundy sofa and chairs and a splash of burgundy in the pale green drapes. Her desk was a century-old oaken writing desk she had found at an antique store years ago. Her staff could not believe she wanted to move her own desk into her office instead of using one of the nice, lean, heavy, mahogany desks supplied by the agency. But once they saw her desk, they understood why she had brought it.

She started to work immediately on the notes she had taken during the meeting, designing the type of questionnaire and analytical program they would need during this project. Every once in a while she would stop and think about Paul. She wished, in a way that he would drop by her office and visit with her. She kept glancing up at the door hoping he would knock and walk in, but he didn't. In fact she didn't see him again until they met in the lobby the following day.

Chapter 8

Three Years Earlier

The bright sunshine streamed through the sheer curtains at Denise's bedroom window. She woke tired and restless. She had spent an uneasy night thinking about her meeting with Paul. Now, she was trying to decide what to wear. She had not worried about dressing for the office in a long time. She couldn't wear the green silk; that was a bit much for the office. The light brown shirtdress was too conservative. Finally, in a last minute decision, she chose the beige silk blouse with the soft gray suit. It revealed her figure without being flashy. She finished her attire with gold earrings and a small gold herringbone necklace.

Later, after a hectic morning with phone calls, she met Paul in the lobby, "Hello, how are you?" he asked as she walked toward him. She could see his eyes go up and down her body taking in the blouse, the skirt, and the jacket, apparently meeting his approval. He was wearing a dark blue pin stripe suit, with white shirt and the traditional yellow 'power tie,' and his black boots. The contrast between the red hair pulled back with a dark blue rubber band and the dark blue suit was incredible. His shaded lens let through just enough of those brown eyes that Denise knew he was very pleased with himself and with their being together.

"I'm fine. And you?" she asked. "Has your day been very busy or do you have a handle on all of it now so that you can relax?"

He laughed, "I wish it were that easy. No, I have just started to settle into this. I'll be leaving tomorrow to be on the site for a few days and talk to some folks, and then a brief trip to D.C. I should be back here by next Thursday, so maybe you can leave Friday night open for me?" He took her arm and guided her through the door and they headed down the street toward the restaurant.

"Maybe," she smiled, "Let's get through lunch and then we'll talk about next week. What if you have terrible table manners, or I don't like your conversation? Then I would never want to see you again, or you may not want to see me."

He squeezed her elbow. "I doubt that, because I think we both know we have a lot in common, and we will enjoy each other's company a great deal. Especially the more we get to know each other. I think this is going to be a great relationship."

She motioned toward the restaurant, and he opened the door for her. She felt the cool air conditioned breeze hit her face, a nice relief from the warm weather and the warm sensation that she had just experienced from the blandishments of this Montana man.

"Hello, Denise," Roger, the restaurant owner, greeted her as they walked in. "How nice to see you again," Roger said.

"Hello, Roger. A quiet table for two please," she said, and Roger immediately led them to the back of the café to a secluded table next to a window.

"How about this one?" he said and he pulled out her chair for her.

"This is fine, Roger. Roger Adams, this is Paul Wagner. Paul, Roger." She wanted to introduce to two of them and also take some time to clear her thoughts, because her heart was racing now.

"Roger, you have a great place here," Paul said shaking Roger's hand.

"Thank you. It's a pleasure, sir. I'm glad Denise is having lunch with a friend. Although I love her company and her business, sometimes she eats here too often and mostly alone with her work. I keep telling her to leave the work at the office and go out and enjoy herself."

"Thank you, Roger, for your concern," she said curtly so as to cut him off before he told all her family history and interests. Things that no one needed to know, especially the man across from her. She'd rather he didn't know about her lifestyle, and her days, and her nights. Roger made her sound like a little old spinster schoolteacher.

"I think that's true for all of us single workaholic folks, unfortunately, but I'm glad she has such a good friend as you to be looking out for her," Paul replied.

"Well, I do try, but sometimes she can be very hard-headed," replied Roger.

"What are the specials today?" Denise cut into Roger's speech.

"The special is the manicotti with an Italian salad. Everything else is on the menu. But I do have a new case of Burgundy wines that are excellent."

"Thanks, I'll have the manicotti," said Denise.

"So will I," said Paul, "with a small house salad. And bring us a bottle of that Burgundy."

"No, no wine. It is lunchtime and I need a clear head when I go back to the office. I have a meeting with Martin and a lot of work to do," she replied.

"That is the reason you should have dinner with me tonight, or should have last night. And, Roger, don't rush. We're not in any hurry," he teased her. She looked up to see the smile on Roger's face. He was enjoying every minute of this.

"Okay, a compromise, a glass of your Burgundy for me and, Roger, don't take his statement to heart, so let's have a reasonable time frame for lunch because I do have to get back to the office," said Denise.

"Lunch in a reasonable time frame, that I can do," replied Roger, walking away with a smile.

"A bottle of wine? Really, Dr. Wagner!" She glared at him.

"Paul, remember, Paul. Well, I thought we could at least start the day off right and also work in a good send-off for me since I will be away for sometime. Also, I didn't want to hurt Roger's feelings since he was so excited about you having someone to eat lunch with today." His soft brown eyes crinkled at the corners.

"I couldn't have dinner with you because I had other plans," she said, "and don't worry about Roger. He sells enough of that wine. Furthermore, I don't have lunch or dinner alone everyday." She could hear the rise in her excited voice and it angered her to let him see her so upset.

"I am glad you do not eat alone all the time," he said. "I know you work hard at your office, sometimes late, so I am glad you have someone in your life to take you out and help you relax. What is this young man's name so that I can thank him?" he asked.

"There is no one special in my life. I have several friends I see. Sometimes I have more than enough things to do." She had no idea why she was explaining her life to him. She knew she wouldn't be able to get away from it so she might as well go ahead and tell him. And anyway, he did seem interested.

"How about you? Anyone special in your life?" She smiled, wanting to let him know she could get to him as well as he could get to her.

That boyish grin again, "Now, in my line of work it is very hard to start, much less continue, a relationship. You know what it's like. We are constantly traveling, moving around. And time in the service is no piece of cake either. I was doing tours of duty in various places and having to leave at a moment's notice. I had a hard enough time adjusting to it myself; I couldn't expect anyone else to accept that type of life. Even now that I am settled with one place as home, I am still on call twenty-four, seven."

"From what I have heard and read about you, you have had a very colorful life. One of the youngest full colonels in the service, not to mention a microbiologist. You have been very busy. I bet you have some interesting stories of outbreaks, scares, and intrigue. You could write a book," she smiled.

"I can't comment on any of that. You know that, but I have to admit it has been interesting. Besides what I have read about you and your life is just as colorful."

"So you have been checking up on me?"

"I had to. Once you were assigned to my team from your agency. Then once I saw your picture, I wanted to know more. Like for instance, how did such a gorgeous creature as you get involved in this game of germ warfare? You certainly don't fit the bill for a computer analyst with a background in deadly bugs," he said, smiling.

"Well, it was just fate. I was in the computer courses in college and then got intrigued with what was happening in the labs where a few of my friends were majoring in dirty little bug work for Uncle Sam. It just took off from there. I didn't want to do the work in the lab, but I knew the docs needed backup with computer sources and information to follow through on the projects that were going on around the country. So I majored in computer science, minored in microbiology, and spent a few years with a small federal agency, and that's about it."

"Your salads," Roger interrupted, setting the plates in front of them. She could feel Paul sizing her up and trying to imagine what she was like in her college days.

"Thanks, this looks fine," was Paul's reply to Roger. He went on. "So what is your interpretation of what happened in the North Carolina mountains? Unless you don't want to discuss business at lunch?" He smiled again.

"No, I'm glad you asked. I thought your presentation yesterday was very good. But I need more data. I felt like you were holding back on what you were delivering to us. I couldn't decide whether it was for security reasons or whether you didn't have a handle on it. I just kept getting the impression that you are not telling all."

"How insightful of you. You do have a second instinct. I felt that about you when we were introduced. That is not

72

flattery that is an honest observation, which is very important in our line of work. Am I wrong?"

"No, you are right," she smiled. "I have been accused of having too much insight into people. Almost witch-like." She laughed.

"No, I wouldn't say witch-like; I would say life-saving. Am I correct?" He lowered his voice as she lowered her eyes to the white linen napkin in her lap. She knew at that moment if she closed her eyes she could once again see the red blood seeping through the white bandage, so she raised her head and looked him directly in the eyes.

"Yes, it is a life-saving trait, although one time it proved to be a bit late, and it cost a life, but I think that comes with the territory," she said reaching for the wine and hoping he did not notice her shaking hand.

He took her hand and squeezed it. "I know. Been there, done that. I read the file. I'm sorry you had to go through that, and as callous as it sounds, yes, it comes with the territory. I think you have done well handling it. If you ever want to talk about it, I am here. I won't push; I just want you to know that I have big ears. I am a good listener, and I don't think you could ever shock me with anything you might share." He stared into her eyes, and for the first time she realized he was being very truthful. No bullshit. He had been to that dark corridor, had walked through and come out. Not unscathed, but he had come out of it.

"Thank you. I figured you had already read the dossier and we might talk about it some time, but not now. Besides, here comes our lunch. Roger, it looks delicious! I think once again you have outdone yourself!" She smiled up at Roger, thanking him for his timely interruption.

"Thanks. I thought if Paul was going to be around and coming to my place I had better impress him today."

"You have impressed me," Paul smiled. "And I can assure you I will be coming back. I can't wait to try one of your dinner entrees with Denise." He released her hand and reached for his fork.

"Let me know the night, and I will prepare something special for you two," Roger said. "I do love to cook and it makes me even happier when my favorite customers enjoy it and let me know. Enjoy, and if you need anything else, let your waitress, Julie, know. Or me. I may be in the back for a few minutes. We have the Rotary Club today in the private dining room. So please excuse me, and, once again, Paul, it was very nice meeting a friend of Denise's." He reached over and shook Paul's hand.

"Thank you, Roger. The pleasure is all mine. It is great to find a good restaurant, meet the owner, and then be assured of special attention because of my friendship with a special lady."

"Do join us again," replied Roger as he hurried off to the loud and growing noise in the back room.

"He's a pleasant man. A good friend to his friends. I think he really cares about you. You are very lucky," Paul said, as he placed the first forkful of manicotti into his mouth. "This is delicious. The man does know how to cook. This is excellent."

"Delicious as usual," Denise said. "Yes, I am lucky to be Roger's friend. We have known each other for years, and he loves to play the part of a concerned uncle." She was glad for the silence demanded by eating so she could gather her composure and breathe easier in the presence of this man who could prove to be as much as his dossier stated.

After the delicious meal and pleasantries about the day, the office, the staff, and a cup of steaming coffee, Paul settled back into his chair and said, "Back to the subject at hand. Yes, in answer to your question several minutes ago, I did hold back, and it was for security purposes and other reasons. I figured if no one in the crowd could pick up on it then nothing was lost, but if someone did, I would explain more details to them. Is that what you want, more details?" he asked, lowering his voice as though to warn her she was wandering into deep, dark waters now.

74

"I want the details, but not here. How about after my 1:30 meeting? Can you drop by my office and discuss this further? I do need some answers."

"I wish I could, but as I told you earlier, I have to leave shortly for a briefing before my trip back to the site, and from the site I have to go back to Washington, and I won't be here again until Friday night. Are you up for dinner and discussion then?"

"Yes, that would be fine," she replied realizing she didn't hide the disappointment in her voice as well as she had hoped to. Besides, this would give her a chance to review the material and try to figure out what he didn't say or shied away from in his presentation.

Apparently Paul read her mind as he picked up the check and pulled the bills out of his wallet. He was generous with the tip, but as he had said earlier, it was a delicious meal. He stood up and walked around to pull her chair out for her.

"The answer is an old friend, or an old enemy, depending on how you look at it. Maybe an old associate would be a better choice of words. Someone who was very close to me at one time and now is causing havoc in my life. Does that help?"

"I see I am not the only one with a sixth sense." She smiled, realizing he had picked up on her mental questions about his behavior at the presentation earlier.

"Yes, that helps, and thanks. I think Friday night will be fine. I'll leave my address on your voice mail, and directions and you can pick me up at whatever time is convenient for you." She couldn't believe she was being so thoughtful.

"I have your address. I'll pick you up at 8:00, and why don't you choose your favorite restaurant, or we can come back for Roger's special attention."

She didn't want to show her surprise at the revelation that he had her address, but then he did check everyone out so of course he had her address.

"I think we'll try another place. How about Thai?"

"Excellent. Let's make it a casual, good, relaxing evening. Just what I'll need after this trip, and I'll answer all of your questions on this issue and anything else you want to know."

"Anything?" she teased.

"Anything!" he answered with a stern voice. And she knew that he would give her a complete and honest history. Somewhere during this lunch she had lost control of the situation, and "the relationship," as he had called it yesterday, was moving too fast, and he was driving the bus. She decided to let him drive for a short period as long as she could reach the brakes to slow it down. They both shook hands with Roger, in the midst of his hurried attempts to keep the Rotarians quiet and to please his other customers, assuring him they would be back for dinner some time soon.

The walk back to the office was pleasant, as the day had turned cloudy and was not as hot as earlier. Rain was in the air. Paul kept his hand on her elbow, as he guided her back to the complex. It was as though he wanted to touch her and be close to her and yet not too much. As though he didn't want to scare her. Besides that been some lunch! Within an hour they both had touched on one of the most hurtful, painful, moments of their lives. She had not fully recovered from her memory of the accident. She could tell that Paul was lost in thought as they walked through the crowds hurrying back to their offices.

When they arrived in the cool lobby of the building, she felt a slight chill from the cooling air outside and the brisk cooled air-conditioned air inside.

"We'll talk in your office," he said, more as a statement than a question.

"Thank you that would be fine." She was not about to object to anything this man suggested right now. The moment was too charged, too electric to even think, and she would not destroy it. So much had been said, and not been said. When she glanced up at him and noticed for the first time the tiny scar on his forehead, she knew. She knew that he felt the same vibrations, and neither of them wanted to break the bond. The other people in the elevator took no notice of the silence as they rode up to the fourteenth floor. During the ride, Paul's hand remained on her elbow as though not to steady her, but to steady himself or just to feel a real human being's body next to his. She didn't speak, just led the way down the corridor to her corner office. Her door was closed, and as she turned to open the door he squeezed her elbow, "It isn't easy being us, is it?"

"No, it isn't, but you know that."

"Yes, we both do. I don't want to come in." He took his hand from her elbow and brushed his fingers across her cheek.

"Take care of yourself. I'll see you in three days." He smiled, staring into her eyes.

"I will. You do the same."

He stepped back and smiled not the conceited smile she had come to expect, but a concerned, caring smile.

"Bye."

"Bye." She watched him walk away with part of her heart, mind, and soul.

Denise managed to open the door and close it behind her and then collapsed against the closed door and breathed again. She felt she had been holding her breath throughout the entire walk and elevator ride. She knew now that this man had more control over her than she liked and that she had a lot to learn about him. But not now. Now she just wanted to savor the moment. She wanted to remember his touch, his smell, his voice, and his eyes with that concerned look.

"Denise?" She was jarred out of her thoughts as she walked across the room to the sofa.

"Yes, come in," she called. Teale, her secretary, came in with a big smile on her face.

"My Lord! Who was that? The entire floor and probably the entire building is abuzz with the cowboy. He is gorgeous!" Teale exclaimed. "Tell Auntie Teale all and right now."

"Teale, really. You act as though you have never seen an attractive man before," she laughed.

"Denise, there is attractive and then there is attractive! I don't remember seeing him or being introduced to him. Tell me."

"That's Dr. Paul Wagner. He's here working with us on the North Carolina project. He is single, handsome, intelligent and very nice. Need I say more? Anyway, I can't say more. I have a meeting in ten minutes and I need to get my thoughts together for that," she said, as she reached for the supposed folder for her next meeting. But it was the folder on the North Carolina project. She hoped Teale wouldn't notice the difference in the folders. Denise decided she would do a lot of reading up on this man and this project. "So excuse me. I'll talk to you later."

"If I had had lunch with him I would have to collect my thoughts, too. Maybe drinks later today and you can bring me up to speed?"

"Maybe. Let's see how the day goes. See you later." She motioned Teale out of the office, because she wanted to be alone to think. And also, to be very honest, she didn't know what to share. The hour-and-a-half with this man had been so electrifying! She couldn't remember things said or done. She just knew something or someone had walked into her life and had stirred feelings that she had thought dead for some time. Someone had reminded her of pain and love, and someone had made her feel alive again. She had to think about that. And to top it all off, that someone was Dr. Paul Wagner.

Chapter 9

Three years earlier

The ringing of the phone, days later, was getting to Denise. It seemed every second there was a phone call, an intercom call or a knock at her door. The staffers were handling a great many of the calls and requests for information on the nature of this outbreak. She had spent some time in the lab with Dr. Harold Rushman, her lead lab expert, going over the samples and the data they had already received from the field staff in North Carolina. The cultures from the lung tissue were reading differently from the specimens from another anthrax outbreak.

Looking through the microscope, Denise could see the difference in the outline of the cells.

"See what I mean?" Harold asked, as Denise looked into the lens of the microscope. "There's no comparison. They're completely different from the ones from CDC, but it is the from the same bacterium family. I hate to say this, Denise, and I will repeat this only to you until I do some more tests, but this is man-made anthrax, and if you think about it, it's very simple. Anyone so inclined can steal and create this deadly bacterium. You reinvent it on a stronger scale and then spread it at a not too heavily populated location at the beginning so as not to draw too much attention to the outbreak. People come into hospitals for treatment, and at first it will be misdiagnosed and then finally it's diagnosed as just a few random anthrax cases. Then, if need be, you spread more spores to increase the number of cases and deaths, depending on how much treatment and how good the treatment is that patient gets and Voila! You have germ warfare at its best in a very subtle form. You can then decide what to do about blackmail, demands, or whatever. Because at this time, the toxins in this bacterium do not respond to our antibiotics and unless we can create stronger chemicals for antitoxin sprays, we can't destroy it on the ground or in the air." Denise saw fear on Harold's face.

"What now? What do we do?" she asked, trying not to get caught up in his emotional state. Someone needed to try to remain calm and clear thinking, even if what they were looking at was a new strain of killer on a small glass slide under a microscope.

"I am going to run some more tests and then call Martin and Barrett in and discuss this matter. They will have to make the decision on how to deal with this. I am not talking to CDC about this. The least the Feds know the better, although I don't think it will be much longer before they come up with the same conclusion as mine. And," he added, "Dr. Wagner from NCTR thinks the same thing. This is his field, and I think he has dealt in this area before. I have to admit I'm impressed with the form of this bacterium. To be able to steal this agent and spray it and contaminate an area is unreal! The chemical makeup is completely different from the natural source, so only the creator will know the elements to destroy it. If there is a way to destroy it."

Harold had finished his test and had made his report to a few members of the head staff. Now a meeting was being called to fill the rest of the staff in on what they were dealing with. Denise had spent several hours going over the data, working in the lab beside Harold when she had the time. Both she and Harold were so surprised by this new strain that she kept going back to reconfirm for her head what her eyes were seeing through the lens of her microscope.

Denise was very tired as she settled in the semi-comfortable chair in the conference room to await Martin's 1:00 briefing. There were about ten people in the room; lab workers and some people from PR. They explained how to keep the news out of the paper and to be briefed on how to deny, deny, deny any threat whatsoever. There were a couple of security men she had worked with on earlier "to know only" projects. The only two women in the room were she and Beth Garner, the head of the publicity department with Incline.

Beth was an attractive woman of forty with soft auburn hair, green eyes, and a body in tip-top shape. She was an avid runner and snow skier. She handled the press well and the management at Incline when they had to deal with sticky topics like this new outbreak. Denise did not know Beth well, but she respected her and her position. Beth had to put up with a lot of bullshit not only from her company but also from the public and the press. Denise smiled across the room at Beth, and Beth returned the recognition.

Raising the cup of hot coffee to her lips, Denise found that the flavor was no longer there. The flavor of coffee tends to disappear with the fifth or sixth cup. All she really wanted was a hot bath, a deep, restful sleep, some unhurried time and a relaxing evening alone. It had been a long and hectic week.

She was awakened from her daydream when the door to the conference room opened. Martin, Barrett, Harold, Paul, and an interesting-looking dark-haired man with flashing eyes behind thick, black-framed glasses entered the room. Denise felt a slight chill run across her arms and her neck at the sight of this visitor. Rarely did she respond to anyone this way. Maybe it was his unusual glasses. No one wore those heavy-framed glasses anymore. No. It was more than that; it was the way he carried himself. The way he did a quick glance at the people in the room as though sizing them up in one swift movement and then averted his eyes back to the floor. She noticed that he never made eye contact with anyone, even in his brief appraisal of the people in the room. Maybe she was just too tired and the secrecy and the threat of a real terrorist problem had put the "spook" in her. But she did feel something, and the strongest feeling was that this man could not be trusted.

The entrance of her co-workers and the new man jarred Denise awake and she felt the blood rush to her head. In the hectic week of reading the data and doing the research, her time had been so busy that she had lost track and now realized it was Friday, Paul was back and she looked awful. Did she even have on makeup? She knew she had been dressing down more and more as she spent more time in the labs and less time in meetings. Today she had at least worn a soft pink silk blouse with matching silk slacks. She had run a brush through her hair in the bathroom before making this meeting and had applied a bit of pink lipstick, but she had not taken any care with the rest of her appearance. She glanced across the room at Paul, and he met her gaze. Once again she felt the meeting of the minds as she felt his crinkling brown eyes say, 'You look fine. A little tired, but fine.' Maybe it was her own psyche saying that for her own self-affirmation, but she felt it was his thoughts.

"Good afternoon, everyone." Martin started the meeting. "I'm glad all of you could make it. I know it has been a pressure-filled week and I do appreciate the hours you have been putting in. I know it has been a hectic schedule. Believe me, my wife has no idea what I look like anymore, and my kids may think they don't even have a father." Martin tried to ease the crowd into a relaxed mood before delivering his grim news.

"I'm afraid we have a real problem on our hands. Nothing we can't handle, but something we need to deal with as soon as possible and keep a lid on at the same time. This is proving to be one of our more challenging episodes. But we have a well-trained team of lab technicians, support staff, and security people, and I know we'll come through this in the best manner possible. We are also very fortunate to have Paul Wagner and Dr. Michael Fitzgerald working with us from NCTR. And some members of his support staff.   Also, Dr. Fitzgerald is the head of NCTR's laboratory that will be working closely with Harold.   Now I'll let Dr. Wagner tell you what he has found in his preliminary studies, and then he can introduce Dr. Fitzgerald, who can tell us what they have come up with. I need not remind any of you that this is of a very sensitive nature, and nothing leaves this room. Beth, you and I will meet in my office after this meeting for a briefing on how you will handle the press. The public, CDC, and other agencies are hammering us for more information. Right now I want to keep a lid on this." He smiled across the room at Beth, letting everyone know the complete confidence he had in his PR chief.

"Dr. Wagner." Martin gestured to Paul as and he rose and stood in front of the black board removing a few cards from his coat pocket. Denise noticed that the lines around his eyes and mouth were much deeper now and he had a tired, haggard, lack of sleep look. The small scar on his forehead was a deeper pink from the sun exposure of late, as he been out in the field and the sun had burned the scar tissue.

Paul laid the cards on the table as if the information was too serious to deliver from cards. He would deliver it from his own thoughts.

"Thank you, Martin. Good afternoon, everyone. I have to agree with Martin's words. This is a very intense time for both of our agencies and for the nation and it is imperative that we work in complete secrecy and keep a lid on this. The less the public knows the less chance of a panic and panic's attendant problems. Not to mention alerting the person or persons responsible for this that we are on to them." He glanced up at Denise as though to collect his thoughts and settle himself into a brief discussion of the results from his work in the field. He announced the recommendations his military agency had come up with to handle the problem. The more he spoke the easier his words came, the more relaxed he became, and his calm, cool, voice settled the group down to understand that the situation was serious, but nothing that they could not handle. They had handled outbreaks like this before. But the underlying thought of everyone was that this deadly outbreak was a deliberate and criminal act and could take numerous lives.

"Now, on that note, I'd like to introduce Dr. Michael Fitzgerald, a colleague of mine. He'll give you his lab results and the possible antitoxin to all of this. I do want to stress Martin's comments on the need for secrecy again. We are dealing with a threat to everyone and it is considered a terrorist threat. Right now we don't know if it is a threat from just one nut or from a large organization. The size and the scope lead me to believe it is a well-manned, well-maintained organization." He paused and then turned to Dr. Fitzgerald: "Michael."

As Michael rose to address the group, Paul glanced across the room to catch Denise's eye. And she felt as though he could actually see the slight trace of chill bumps that ran up her arm.

What was it about this man, Michael, she wondered, that put her so ill at ease?

"Good afternoon everyone, and thank you for the opportunity to address your group. Thanks also for the working cooperation between our two agencies. I have been made to feel very welcome by your organization and at this time, with this type of threat, we need all the help we can get on locating, isolating, analyzing the problem and conquering it as quickly as possible."

As Michael launched into his description of his agency's lab tests and results, which concurred with Harold's, Denise glanced across the room at Harold and noted the expression of complete confidence in the man who was speaking. When a colleague impressed Harold, that colleague would have to have a lot to offer and a lot to show, because Harold was considered the expert in his field. He had graduated with top honors from the Northwestern School of Microbiology.

Harold nodded in agreement with the explanations and terms Michael was explaining to the group about how both of them in different locations had isolated the agent and identified it. Between secured-line phone calls, they had been moving at the same rate in analyzing the cultures and the organism. As the presentation went on, Denise watched the reaction on each person's face to his ideas and solutions. In their faces she saw complete confidence and professional awe at a highly intelligent scientist working on a devastating disease.

When Michael started his briefing on the antitoxin he had created, she noted the complete look of shock and surprise that covered Harold's face. At one moment she thought he would interrupt Michael or at least raise his hand, but then his expression changed to one of concern and he turned to her with a look of complete bewilderment. She had seen that face only once before: a few years back when Harold and she had been stumped by a culture that they could make no headway on until by mistake and sheer luck Harold tried a bizarre antitoxin that had worked. She trusted Harold, and now she felt she had found one person to confirm her concerns about Michael, the germ genius. Harold's expression to her for a brief second conveyed the message of "we have to talk later."

"Thank you once again for your help, your consideration, and your attention to this matter. I think we can breathe a lot easier right now. I think we have found the key and that soon we'll make some progress on getting the word out on the use of this antitoxin and also the chemical spray for the area that is saturated with this organism. The results in the lab have been very promising. We'll be using them in the field within the next day or so, as soon as the antitoxin can be reproduced in large enough quantities. If you have any follow-up questions, please see me. I am sure you will be seeing more of me in your offices and in the hallway and especially at the coffee maker. Martin." He ended on a brief note of laughter and gave the floor back to Martin.

"Thank you, Michael. We do appreciate your update, and I must admit I am as amazed and intrigued as everyone else in the room that you may have discovered an antitoxin so quickly, but we're very thankful. Also, for everyone's information, we have given Dr. Fitzgerald and Dr. Wagner the suite of offices on the twelfth floor next to Harold's staff. So you can locate him for more questions and discussions. Now I know all of you have a lot of questions, but we are requesting you to make notes of your questions and hold on to them until later today. We are making a few more inquiries and tests, and we'll be better able to field your questions then. Let's plan to meet back here at 5:00 today. Sorry, no rest for the weary. Beth, I'll see you in my office now." The group let out a collective moan, realizing their plans of an early out Friday afternoon for drinks would have to be shelved.

Denise rose and walked over to Harold. As she did, she noticed Beth out of the corner of her eye, stopping to speak to Paul and placing her hand on his arm. Denise felt a surge of jealousy. She had to get a grip! Paul and she had had one lunch together, although that had held promises of things to come. She had no control of this man and certainly not a relationship with him.

"Harold? What is it?" she whispered to Harold as he moved closer to her. So close she could feel his breath on her left cheek as they both lowered their heads in a whispered conversation.

"Not here, come to my office now. If you get there before me, have a seat. I want to go by the lab to pick up the latest results from some antitoxin tests my staff was running. I can't say anything now, but you and I have to talk and no one else, okay?"

"Sure, see you there." She noted the tension in his voice and in his mannerism. She walked across the room, headed for the door past Paul and Beth and heard Paul say, "Excuse me, Beth, for one moment." He stopped Denise briefly at the door and said, "I will see you at eight o'clock." He walked back to Beth's immediate attention as Denise walked to the elevator to go down to Harold's offices. Harold had taken the stairs because he was in such a rush to pick up his data. Denise walked into the elevator and turned to face out. She couldn't help noticing Beth and Paul walking down the hall in the direction of Martin's office for Beth's meeting. They were walking very close to each other, and every once in a while, Beth would touch the sleeve of Paul's coat. Following behind them were Barrett, Martin and a few other staff members walking down the hall toward their huddle with Martin and Beth.

Chapter 10

Three Years Earlier

Denise sat at a contemporary oak desk, her back to the door. She noticed the desk was laden with research papers, notes, graphs, and charts, all in a mish-mash of stacks. How did he ever find anything in this chaos? But then again, Harold had his own filing system in his head. He could probably locate anything anytime he needed it in this sea of papers.

"Good, you're here!" Harold rushed into the office, locking the door behind him. Walking across the room, he turned the radio to the NPR station, turning up the volume on the Mozart cello sonata, and then pulled his chair over close to Denise.

"Harold, aren't we being a bit paranoid? I don't like this side of you," she teased.

"I don't think so," he replied, laying some papers down on the table and pointing to the latest computer printout of chemical analysis. "Look at that, Denise, and tell me what do you see."

Leaning over the printout, Denise studied the numbers for a few minutes and then looked at Harold. As soon as his eyes met hers, she instantly recognized what he had found.

"It doesn't work! It can't work! The caliber, the mixture of this antibiotic is not strong enough to protect the patient. The antibiotics have been diluted so much that there will be no reaction to the anthrax toxin. It is not strong enough to block the toxins."

"Exactly my point. When I first saw it three days ago, I thought it wasn't going to work and I didn't pursue it. But in one of Michael's calls, he said he was heading in the same direction, so I did a few more tests. I came up with zilch. He came up with a working antitoxin, using the same ingredients. I smell a rat. This is not plausible. This will not work. What do you think?"

Reaching over and looking at the printout Denise wanted to study it again to make sure they were reading the same results and to double-check herself on the numbers. The only sound was the mellow music of the cello coming from the radio. "No, we're right. It will not work. These numbers show the composite is not strong enough. The antitoxin has been reduced by 50% and that will not react at all to kill the spores."

"Good. Now that you concur, what next? We have to keep this under our hat because I have a feeling we're being sold down the river. How about you?"

"Paranoid and schizoid," she teased, until she saw the frightened gleam in Harold's eyes. "I'm sorry. You are correct, and I agree with your summation and with your idea to keep it quiet, but we have to let Martin and Barrett in on this. I think we should confide in those two at least. But we will leave the others out, especially the outside agencies."

"No, I am not paranoid, just careful. I agree we have to let a few others know, but for now, I say let's just tell Barrett and we can include Martin later. I know he was surprised and a bit skeptical of Michael's announcement of an antitoxin. Besides, right now what we need is a security expert's advice on how to proceed, and I trust Barrett. How about you?"

"Okay, I'll call Barrett in now, and we'll talk to him and get his feedback on who and who not to tell. Do you want to meet him here in your office?"

Harold glanced down at his watch, "No, let's take a walk for a cup of coffee, and some fresh air. Buzz him and ask him to join us."

Denise walked over to the desk, skirting through the stacks of scientific journals and boxes of manuscripts and papers on the floor. Maneuvering in this office would tax a well-trained seal. She glanced up at Harold, and she pressed the numbers for Barrett's office intercom.

"Barrett here."

"Hi, it's Denise. How about a cup of coffee?" she asked.

"I would love to except I am swamped right now. I have Bob, one of my security people, sitting here with Paul, and Robert. We have a lot of things to go over. Maybe later?"

"No, listen to me. This is India." India was the code word they used when there was serious trouble, and they used it sparingly. She knew he would get the message. "Just excuse yourself, Barrett. Don't use my name. Meet Harold and me out on the terrace. Bring a coke or coffee. We need to take a brief walk and clear our heads and blow your socks off."

"Sounds good. Be right there. I can finish this later with these guys, right guys?" She could imagine him smiling at the room of people and gracefully excusing himself from their meeting.

"Thanks, and no one, I mean *no one* needs to know this."

"Okay, see you. Thanks." His little touch to make people think it was no big deal to leave a high-level security meeting for another meeting. It usually worked. But one could never be sure with the security leaks and personalities in the business.

Denise hung up the phone, grabbed the printout from Harold's desk and headed for the door. Harold followed behind, staring at the floor as they walked down the corridor. They headed for the stairs instead of the elevator. Old intelligence training coming into play. Never use the elevator, where you could run into people, when you can use the stairs. Also the walk would help clear their heads and give them time to think about how to present this to Barrett. Neither one of them spoke as they

90

descended the stairs. Denise's heels clicking was the only sound in the stairwell.

They exited into the east side lobby of the building instead of into the main lobby, a little winded after a twelve-floor stair walk. Denise turned to Harold. "Got any change for a couple of Cokes?" He looked up at her as though in shock. He had been miles away with his thoughts.

"Yeah, here, I think so." He reached into his pockets and pulled out a handful of change, rubber bands, paper clips, a small two-inch pocket knife, and a small plastic bottle of Visine. He counted out the correct change in to Denise's hand.

"What do you want, Coke, Sprite?" she asked as she walked a few steps to the soda machine.

"Coke, Coke is fine," he answered, still in a daze, staring down at the knife as though it was the first time he had ever seen it.

"I'll take a Cherry Coke; I need all the sugar I can get right now to clear my head, help me think, give me energy." Denise smiled and handed his drink to Harold. For a brief moment she could see her entire day and evening being destroyed by the facts she and Harold had just learned. She still had the five o'clock meeting with the staff. She had no idea how long that would last, and, depending on Barrett's response to their news, she might be tied up in this building for several more hours, late into the night.

"Those things are not good for you," Barrett's said as he rounded the corner from the West End stairwell, carrying a plastic container of bottled water. Denise took a drink out of the can and smiled. "I know, but I was telling Harold I need the sugar boost right now. Let's take a walk. We need to talk."

Barrett looked over at Harold and noticed the look of deep thought and concentration on his face. "Harold, are you with us?"

Harold looked back and came out of his trance, "Yeah, I am here. Denise and I have an interesting printout to show you. Let's walk for a while." They walked through the automatic doors and headed for the terraced area where employees went for lunch and breaks in nice weather. The area was almost empty now since it was after the lunch hour and too early for breaks. A few stragglers were reading a newspaper and smoking.

Denise handed the printout to Barrett and smiled, "If you need any clarification on this, just ask. But I think your background in the field will help you understand the numbers and what you are seeing. Jar your memory for a second. After you dissect this we have a couple of questions."

"Yes, madam," came Barrett's teasing reply until he started reading the sheet, and his expression changed from happy-go-lucky to one of concern.

Denise led them to a vacant table and sat down across from Harold and next to Barrett. Sipping her Cherry Coke while Barrett was reading, she looked around, taking in the delightful terrace garden. She gazed at the small corner fountain with the water cascading down the stones. The water flowing over the stones was the only sound now. Harold was examining another sheet of paper he had brought out with him. Barrett was still reading the printout with a look of deep frustration on his face. Denise just wanted to sit and not think. She felt she had been bombarded all day with news, good and bad. Then she realized Paul was back. Now on top of that there was this major security question on bad information concerning this outbreak itself. She was almost to the point of overload. She took a deep breath, trying to relax and not disturb the other two. They would come around when they had digested the information they were reading.

"Well, well, well. We have a problem here, don't we?" Barrett said. "Harold, how many times did you run the tests on this antitoxin?"

"Three times, Barrett, just to be sure it was accurate. Then I spoke to Denise. I knew in the meeting when Michael gave us his information about his antitoxin that it couldn't be right because I had already run those tests. I almost spoke up in the meeting and then decided it would be best not to. I caught Denise's eye and decided the best avenue would be to go back by the lab, pick these up and start the tests again and then talk to her." Harold's voice was tired, strained.

"Does anyone else know about these tests, these results? Anyone else at all in your lab?" Barrett questioned him.

"My lab tech assistant, Veronica, knows about the tests, but not the results. I had put away the printouts with the results before the meeting. The last time I ran them, she was out to lunch and no one else was in that part of the lab. Here are some preliminary data from another lab that somebody faxed to me earlier. I just picked it up. They show the same findings." He handed the printout across the table to Barrett and reached for the Coke can to take another drink.

"Harold sees a rat. What do you see?" Denise asked Barrett.

"I see a big rat, a big problem, and a dangerous situation. We have got to get on this right now."

"We thought we might tell Martin about these findings. What do you think?" she asked as she sipped her Cherry Coke again.

"No. No one else. Just the three of us need to know right now. Martin would be placed in the awkward situation of having to question Michael's findings. Release these data now and in the process our rat might escape. I have no idea who or what it is, but I don't want it to get away. Forewarned always allows for escape." He leaned across the table and looked Harold straight in the eye. "Harold, you back these numbers? You know they are accurate?"

93

"Yes, they are as accurate as you can get. They are one hundred per cent accurate. Three tests, same agents, no miscalculations. What you see is what you get. They are true." He heard a sigh with his exclamation. "Now what?" He was more a lost little boy than a brilliant microbiologist.

"Let me ask you this," continued Barrett, glancing first at Denise and then Harold. "If we let this go with Martin and Michael's approval, what is the harm done? What if the treatment on the ground for the bacteria is carried out? Will it harm anyone more than it already has? Also I think Martin is planning on using it only on the contaminated sites and not in new areas. So at least they are not planning to use it as a cure-all and spread it across an entire state for preventive purposes, just on the already-contaminated area, correct?"

"That is my understanding. They will spray the contaminated area with this antitoxin and hope to destroy the bacteria. Only it won't. It won't have any affect on the area at all. Since the area has already been condemned, no one will be there except our field people and the lab technicians spraying the antitoxin. They will be safe. They'll wear their 'bio-suits.' If they use this antitoxin in that capacity only, it won't be dangerous to the area. It won't kill a thing, or save anyone, but it won't hurt anyone either. I think if they started spreading it in more areas, then we would have to speak up." Harold's concerned voice broke on the last word.

"I agree. I am just looking to buy time. You understand that, don't you? But I also want assurances that no one and I do mean no one is going to be injured if they spray this at the site. I want to make sure the site team is geared up and that no new areas are sprayed in the next few days. This is a major industry security problem, and we are watching a bio-terrorist at work, and I want to nail the son-of-a-bitch. Okay, Denise?"

"I agree. As long as we have Martin's and Michael's plan on how they are going to use this antitoxin and where and when, then we can protect people. But if we are not in their loop, we are asking for trouble. We don't want any more innocent people contracting this illness."

Harold leaned over to Barrett; "Maybe we should include Paul Wagner in our group?"

"No, I don't think so," Barrett replied. "I have a great deal of respect for Dr. Wagner and his staff, but this misinformation may be coming from his people, his staff. Maybe he is not involved and knows nothing about this. Michael is the head of the NCTR lab. I assume he would check test results or notice if something didn't add up. Right now, I look at him as a 'bad guy.' Maybe someone is feeding Michael bad data and bad tests results, but we haven't worked with this group or known these people long enough yet to include them in anything. Do you see where I'm coming from?"

"Yes," they agreed in unison. "I think it makes sense that this information be limited to the three of us for the time being," Denise volunteered.

"Me, too," said Harold. "Is there anything else I can do or tell you now, Barrett?"

"No, I'll take it from here. I will do another security check on Paul and all of his staff. I will run some clearance on the lab technicians working with Michael, but I think all of those folks belong to us. Do you want to keep these or can I hang onto these papers for a while?" he asked Harold, looking at the printouts.

"You can keep them. I have read them and re-read them. Now I feel I can see them in my sleep."

"Do me a favor, Harold. Go back to your office, make it like a normal day, run other tests. If there are any more of this type of results in the lab or your office, lock them in your safe. Put them away, lock them up for the time being. I don't want to sound melodramatic, but we have got to be careful with this deal."

"Anything I can do?" Denise asked.

95

"Yeah, I am going to e-mail you what seems mindless question games and you answer them the best you can with the information you have at hand in your database. Don't worry about the simple questions or the strange ones; just answer them and send it all back to me. Now I suggest we all go back, as though we have just had a brief, chatty break. I will see you at the five o'clock meeting, and maybe we can find out how much further Martin and Michael want to go with this issue. If you have any concerns or notice anything unusual with anyone, old personnel, new personnel, no matter how silly it may seem, call me. If you miss me in the office, page me."

The three of them rose and walked back into the cool lobby and this time they took the elevator. Denise felt she couldn't make the walk up. Not now. She was as emotionally drained and physically drained from a strenuous workweek.

Barrett reached over and touched her shoulder. "Don't worry, kid, it's just a tiny little rat, and we will catch it quick and soon. Get some rest, and stay in touch. If I don't make the five o'clock meeting, you can fill me in later, but I will try to be there." Barrett left the elevator on his floor and headed to his office. Denise walked off the elevator and entered her office, closed the door, and breathed a sigh of relief. Then she noticed the note on her phone. She walked over, picked it up, and lifted the turned-down top of the paper. She recognized Paul's handwriting, from the many notes she had read in his files: *"WILL PICK YOU UP AT EIGHT O'CLOCK."*

Any other time she would have been thrilled with the message but now she was too worried and too tired to even think of the handsome, brilliant man and what the evening held in promise. She was jarred out of her thoughts by the intercom buzzer on her phone.

"Yes, Teale." She pressed the button on the intercom and replied into the speakerphone, too tired even to lift the receiver.

"Just a quick note: Martin cancelled the five o'clock meeting. He needs more information before he continues. But he has asked everyone to stay in town, stay alert, and he will let us know if we have to come back into the office tomorrow. Keep your pager handy in case he beeps you."

"Thanks, I needed that," Denise replied as she released the button, walked across the room and picked up her pocketbook, and headed for the door. A reprieve. She was going to lock up her office, go home, soak in the tub after all, take a quick nap, and regroup her forces so as to be ready for the evening.

Chapter 11

Three Years Earlier

Denise gave one last glance in the living room mirror as she walked over to answer the door. Paul was standing there with a single yellow rose and that grin of his.

"My, you look nice," he said, handing her the rose.

"Thank you," she replied, placing the rose on the stand next to the door. "We had said a casual, relaxing dinner at a Thai restaurant. Is that still the game plan?"

"Yes, that sounds good to me. Ready?"

"Yes, all ready." She picked up her purse in her right hand and switched the lights off.

The smell of coconut and beef was prevalent as they walked into the restaurant. This was one of Denise's favorite restaurants. The room was dimly lit, with small candles on each table. The decor was made up of many large green plants mixed in with silk-flower arrangements of various shades of blue, pink, and yellow. The bamboo tables and high-back chairs with their intricate woven designs gave an aura of the Far East.

The waiter escorted them to a table in the corner next to the window that overlooked a small park. Paul pulled the chair out for her.

"This is perfect. If the food is half as good as the ambience, it'll be great," he said, sitting across from her and glancing around the room to take in all of the decor and the customers. It was filled with young professionals. No children. People relaxing on a Friday evening, just glad to be out of the office and looking forward to a weekend.

"See anyone you know? Or are you looking for someone?" she asked, as she noticed him glancing around the room.

"Sorry, force of habit. Also I am taken with the decorating. I spent a few months in Thailand, and this is very close to the places there. Thailand is an interesting country and the people are very warm and friendly. They seem to especially enjoy Americans. Have you ever been?"

"No, I have never had the pleasure of visiting there. But a few of my friends have, and they said the same thing. That people are nice and friendly and that it is a beautiful country."

"True. So what are some of the favorite places you have been to and why?" he asked.

"Is this a test, or an intelligence quiz?" she teased.

"Neither, just wanting to get to know you better, and I do have a favor to ask. Would it be possible for you to forget that side of my career? Can you just think of me as a research scientist and that's all?"

"That will not be easy to do, but I will try. Your reputation as an intelligence officer or 'spook' precedes you." She laughed. The waiter appeared at the table with glasses of water and their menus.

"Can we order a bottle of wine?" he asked, jogging her memory of the lunch they had shared only four days ago when she would only agree to one glass of wine.

"Yes, a bottle of wine is fine," she replied.

"Do you have a bottle of Berrenman in the house?" The waiter nodded. Denise did not recognize the name of the wine.

"I saw you and Harold with your heads together after the meeting and then later in the courtyard. Is he trying to make time with my lovely lady?" he smiled.

Denise flinched. So they had been spotted in the courtyard by Paul--and by who else, she wondered. As careful as they were at getting out of the building, she knew the terraced garden was open to anyone with a window office overlooking that area.

"No, believe me, not Harold. Harold is one of my dearest friends and colleagues." She stopped and reached for a quick answer as she remembered Barrett's warning not to include anyone else in the news Harold had given them. "He was just sharing some news. It seems a mutual friend of ours had just given birth to a healthy baby boy." It sounded plausible to her, and it came so easily. She sometimes amazed herself at how easily she could lie when she had to. Years ago she never would have imagined she would ever get to this point in her life. She had always abhorred lying and liars, and here she was telling a lie to a man she was very interested in and wanted to be truthful with. As Barrett had told her months ago when she mentioned her dislike of lying, it "comes with the territory."

"Really. Well, I hope mother and baby are doing fine. I didn't realize you and Harold attended the same college."

"Yes, in undergraduate school. We attended different universities for graduate work. You can imagine what a treat it was to find him at the corporation when I joined the staff."

The waiter returned with the bottle of wine and poured each a glass. "If you trust my taste in wine, may I order for you tonight? Also is there anything that you don't care for?"

"No, I love all Thai food, so please order for us."

After the waiter had left, Denise said, "You could be a knight on a white horse saving the world."

He reached for her hand. "Believe me, the people out there saving the world are not knights on white horses. You do know that by now don't you?"

"Yes, I learned it years ago with the accident." She turned her head away. She could feel the tears rising in her eyes. Each time she broached this subject with him she teared up. She didn't tear up with Barrett or Harold when she had talked about it. Of course she hadn't talked about it in months. It had been so long ago. But it still bothered her.

"Tell me. Tell me about that incident. Can you tell me now?" He squeezed her hand.

"I thought you had read the case file. Young computer analyst falls in love with brilliant biologist. Young couple very happy and successful. Making plans to be married and live happily ever after. One day, young biologist finds important discovery in lab, dealing with germ warfare. Several days later, young biologist is shot and killed outside his home by unknown assailant. Young biologist dies in lover's arms. End of story. Lots of blood, lots of pain, lots of tears. That's it." She was amazed that she had gotten through that dissertation without breaking down. She found that if she treated it the way the police did, as a case, short and to the point with no emotional ties, she could tell it.

"I know. I read about it. I am so sorry. I just wanted you to tell me yourself. I know it was painful. I don't want to ever do anything to hurt you or have anything happen to you because of me."

"No, I am fine. It was years ago, and I am getting better at reliving the incident. The killer has never been caught, and on top of that I never truly found out what Adam had discovered. Martin, Barrett, and all of them confiscated his lab and stored his files away. Of course, I guess I never really wanted to know. But I am okay about talking about it, just not dwelling on it, okay?" she asked.

"That's understandable. I just wanted to hear you say it yourself. I wanted to make sure in my own mind that you had dealt with it, and I think you have."

He looked up as the waiter arrived with the soup. As she tasted it, she knew it was going to be a delightful dinner and evening. It was nice to be able to sit back and be taken care of for a change.

Arriving back at her condo, Denise flipped on the light switch and turned to Paul. "Would you like a nightcap?"

"Yes, just one. I'm afraid I have an early morning tomorrow. I have to fly back to DC and I wanted to get in an early jog before the flight. It seems that another problem has arisen in Connecticut that may be connected to the one in North Carolina so I have to check it out."

"What's going on with this?" she asked. "All of a sudden there are several outbreaks in various locations, and none of them look natural, and we can't put our finger on any of them. It just seems bizarre to me, what about you?"

She crossed to the bar and poured a quick splash of her favorite. He reached for the snifter of Courvoisier she handed him. "I'm afraid that's the problem, Denise. It *is* happening, and DC wants some answers. So does my agency, and yours. We can't even isolate the bug, much less discern the etiology or the host. Although I was impressed with what Michael had to say today about getting a handle on it this fast, and now he might even have an antitoxin. That would be a tremendous help. To stop it before it caused more deaths, and to control it while we are still tracking down the culprit. Don't you agree?"

Denise walked over to the window and gazed out into the night so as to hide her expression of concern as she was remembering Harold's findings and Barrett's warning. "Yes, it was very encouraging, and I hope we settle this quickly, before we are looking at a full-blown epidemic." She kept her voice soft and walked back and sat next to Paul and raised her glass to his. "Cheers."

Paul finished his brandy and set the glass down. "I see you have excellent taste in brandies. It's going to be fun getting to know you." He reached over and cupped her face in his hand and kissed her full on the lips. He pulled back and looked into her eyes. "I have to go. I will either call you or see you one day next week."

He stood, turned and walked across the room, opened the door, turned around, smiled, and was gone.

Denise was stunned. What did she want, she thought as she stood there staring at the closed door. It was a first dinner date, what more did she expect? The food and wine had been excellent. The conversation had been interesting. After the story about Adam he hadn't pressed her for anything else, and the rest of the evening had been spent on sharing mutual likes and dislikes and talking of mutual friends, since it turned out they knew several of the same people. But, after all, they were in the same business and made the same business contacts at conferences and meetings. She walked over to the door and turned the dead-bolt lock and smiled. She would see him again. Soon.

Chapter 12

Three Years Earlier

Late Wednesday morning Denise was in her office after a hectic weekend handling calls and media blitz accusing not only Incline but CDC of responding too slow to the outbreak and too slow to their questions. The entire staff's nerves were on edge. The conference room was packed with reporters from every area. Reporters from small and large papers had converged on the scene and were trying to push past the security guards and rush not only the staff but the building. The number of deaths had now risen to seven and the number of cases had gone up to twenty-four. Denise heard a brief two knocks at her door. Before she could answer, a tired-looking Beth walked in with two styrofoam cups of coffee. She reached across the desk and handed one to Denise and then Beth sat on the sofa, kicked off her low-heel brown pumps, and said, "May I join you?"

"Sure, I need a break. Thanks for the coffee."

"No problem. I was looking for a companion-in-arms to hide out with for a few minutes and to compare notes. But mostly just to breathe. Have you ever seen it like this before?"

"No, it's rather bad. I know you are catching hell between Martin and the press. This can't be easy on you. But you seem to be holding up."

"I'm hanging in there. The press can be hell to play with. At times they can be so irresponsible. They run off with mad headlines scaring the public silly and print things when there is absolutely no basis to them. Just a few minutes ago at the latest news conference, I did a low blow thing to get rid of some of those characters. I dropped the name of a small, rival lab across town that may have come up with an answer and then stood out of way of the stampede. There are going to be some pissed-off reporters and pissed-off people at that lab when that entourage arrives over there demanding a press conference. But that's the name of the game, right?"

"Right. Whatever it takes to get through this ordeal," Denise said, as she sipped the coffee, surveying Beth's dress and mood. She knew there was more to come.

"Before that fiasco, I was in Martin's office going over the press releases when he received a call from Pennsylvania, Dr. Wagner. From the gist of the conversation and Martin's murmured 'son of a bitch' I take it they were dealing with bad news also. So I excused myself and went to the conference room. Which brings up the reason I am here. I heard through the grapevine that you and Dr. Wagner have seen each other a couple of times and I wanted to know where you two stand."

Denise was shocked at the question. She had no idea other members of the staff knew that she and Paul had been out, much less discussing the possibility of a relationship.

"Where we stand? Interesting question, Beth. We are associates and friends. We have had dinner, that's about it," she replied. "Why?"

"I will be honest with you, Denise. I find the man most attractive and attentive, but if you are involved I won't go any further with it. But if it is just a professional friendship I would like to pursue it with him. What do you say?"

Denise used her best-eased voice, hoping not to let on her jealousy of the very thought of the two of them together.

"Please feel free to see Dr. Wagner anytime you wish. There is and will be no competition, I assure you." She looked over at Beth hoping she would buy the explanation. Thank goodness Beth was looking at Denise's dying plant that was in bad need of water and attention. If there had been a concerned look on Denise's face, she would have missed it.

Beth looked up at Denise. "Good. You understand I had to ask. I don't play office politics or office romances, but you have to admit this guy is one of a kind, and I do want to get to know him better."

"He is attractive and has a dossier that reads like a military, medical, and political encyclopedia. Have you seen it? Has he asked you out?" Denise asked, hoping her voice was calm enough to sound like an interested friend and not the crazed woman she was about to become.

"No, not yet. And he does have an interesting file. I looked at his file after that first meeting when he was introduced to us with his buddy, Michael. He was fairly friendly after that meeting. Later, after Martin's discussion with me, Paul appeared in my office to discuss a few security features of dealing with the press." As Beth continued her recollection of the meeting, Denise realized that Beth's office overlooked the terrace and that that must have been where he was when he had seen her, Barrett, and Harold discussing the results of Harold's tests. If he did see them, then he knew they were also looking at and exchanging the printouts and that Barrett had walked off with the papers Harold had brought to him. She would have to remember to mention this to Barrett and the three of them would have to be more careful about their meetings and discussions.

"Besides, that guy, Michael, gives me the creeps." Beth's voice brought Denise out of her thoughts, "Have you ever seen glasses like that? I think the last pair like that was worn by my chemistry teacher in high school." She laughed. Beth rose from her relaxed position, walked to the door, and turned: "Thanks for the talk and the go-ahead. I just wanted to double check before I made a move. If there was something going on between you and Paul, I didn't want to start any trouble."

"No, there's nothing going on. Feel free to call him or whatever to get his attention. There is no problem with me. Take care. And get some rest. You look tired."

"I was here all weekend and it was a long one. I think Paul will be returning in a few days. That's the reason I wanted to talk to you. Well, back to the real world. I'll talk to you later." She smiled as she closed the door behind her. Denise felt a knot in the pit of her stomach. She did not want to appear too inquisitive about Paul. Besides, she had other things to worry about right now. She knew that Paul had seen the meeting out on the terrace. Also, where was Michael these days? She had not seen him in the halls or in the meetings over the weekend. She had to check into that.

She reached over and buzzed for Barrett.

"Yes? Barrett here." He sounded tired and rushed.

"Hi, want to have lunch with your best buddy?"

"How could I refuse an invite like that? Of course. Where and when?"

"How about Roger's in thirty minutes? I'll meet you there. Okay?"

"Sounds fine. Anything going on I need to know about?"

"Not really. I need to fill you in on a few things and I need some input from you. Also, have you seen Michael lately? I've noticed he hasn't been in the briefings, but he may be tied up in his lab doing some work, correct?"

"Funny you should ask. Let's discuss it at lunch. See you in thirty." His voice dropped off.

Denise pressed the release button on her phone console and sat back in the chair with her hand over her eyes. This was too much, too fast. Bombardment of all kinds of data. She was in overload again. She had talked to Harold twice this week, and his findings were the same. He had mentioned to her that he had met with Barrett earlier, and the word was the same. Be quiet, let it work its way through, and don't share with anyone.

As Denise walked across the restaurant she saw Barrett already seated at the corner booth, typing on his laptop. "Hi, there," she said as she sat down across from him.

"Hi, hold on just a minute, let me finish this." He finished typing in some words and hit the save key. Flipped the power key off and closed the lid.

"Just some quick notes before my senile brain forgets. So how are you? You look tired."

"No more so than anyone else. It has been a busy week. I was . . ."

"Good afternoon, you two. What can I get you?" Mike, their favorite waiter, interrupted. They chatted as he took their orders. When he had left them, Denise asked, "So what is the latest with Michael and Harold, and why haven't you been back in touch with me?"

"Wait a minute, slow down. I've been busy. But I have some interesting information. Harold and I met and confirmed that one other lab that ran his tests came up with the same results as his. Therefore we know Dr. Michael is way off base about finding an antitoxin. On top of that, Michael had to leave town for a few days on Sunday to visit a very sick relative. Martin OK'd that because Michael had given the formula to his staff to start replicating the antitoxin, and they've almost finished with that. Soon it will be out in the field, being sprayed on the contaminated area. I decided to do some checking on my own, and I booked a flight two hours later than Dr. Michael's flight to his sick relative in Pittsburgh and checked that out. It was his favorite uncle, mother's brother, who is in the hospital with lung cancer. Short time left and all that. I spent a couple of hours there. Flew on over to DC and had a tête-à-tête with our friend, Paul. He asked about you by the way." Denise felt the blood rise in her face and hoped Barrett didn't notice the blush.

"It seems he has found some interesting data in DC labs that he'll share with me later this week when he gets back. And that is a very sweet blush. Anything you want to tell me?" As Denise started to respond, Mike showed up with their drinks.

"Thanks, Mike," she said, feeling saved for a few moments.

"So Michael is visiting a real sick relative and all that looks on the up and up. Harold's test results are the same, so we're back to square one. What next?" She asked, hoping to divert the conversation from herself and Paul and back to the outbreak.

"We wait. Maybe Paul has found something in the labs that we can use. At least there haven't been any more outbreaks. So far it has been confined to North Carolina and I hope it stays that way. If you don't want to answer my question about you and Paul, you don't have to," he grinned. "Have you decided on when you are going up for the Microbiology Conference in DC? You know, it's a bad time for all of us to be out attending this thing, but I know Harold is real excited about going, and I think he wants to get away from the lab for a while. I know Paul plans to attend. He mentioned it to me. And what will you wear to the black-tie event? I can hardly wait to get back into my monkey suit."

"I had almost forgotten about it. I'm glad you reminded me. I'll go out in the next few weeks and pick something up. Now be honest, you know you look marvelous in your tux. Women swoon when you walk into a room," she teased. But it wasn't all teasing. She had noticed him at other formal events, and he *was* a very handsome man in his tux.

"And I don't mind answering your question. There is nothing to tell. We had dinner. We talked. It was nice. We laughed. We said good night, and that was about it," she concluded.

"That's it?"

"Yes, except I did want to let you know he mentioned seeing the three of us meeting out on the terrace. I made some lame excuse about sharing news on an old college friend, but if he saw us talking he also saw the exchange of papers, and I think if the three of us meet again, we'll have to be more careful."

"You're right. I think we'll meet less often and in a more secure area and when it is a 'need only' situation. Everyone's nerves are on edge, and everyone is looking over their shoulder. We need to be aware of that. One last thought before Mike gets here with our lunch. I don't mind you dating Paul, but I do have to warn you to be very careful in that arena, both emotionally and professionally. He comes with a lot of excess baggage. You need to tread lightly in that area, and if you are not sure about where you are headed, then don't even start off in that direction. Do I make myself clear?" His stern voice came across the table.

"Yes, I get your meaning. I can handle this, and if I feel it's getting out of hand I will step back. Besides, spending some time with him I may find out some more useful information for us."

"Let me make this clear," he whispered. "I do not want you seeing him just to get to play spy. I don't want you in that situation because you are not equipped to play that game."

"Lunch, folks!" Mike set down their salads and smiled.

"Thanks, Mike, it looks great." Denise smiled up at him and leaned across the table to Barrett and whispered, "Need I remind you I spent three years with the company in the field? I think I did okay in the cat-and-mouse game, and I can handle this."

"This is not cat-and-mouse, Denise. This is serious. This is the threat of a bio-terrorist, and I hate to say, we are no closer to an idea of what is going on today than we were three days ago. So you be careful and leave the big stuff to the tough guys."

She placed a forkful of lettuce into her mouth, chewed it slowly, and then said, "Barrett, you don't even know if Paul is involved in this. It sounds to me like he is out busting his ass to come up with some answers himself. And I will be careful and watch what I am doing, okay?"

"Okay. But not just the danger of the physical. Watch the emotional, okay?" He looked at her with those green eyes that, at times like this, cut straight through her to her soul.

"I will, friend. I promise."

The rest of lunch was spent in discussing Harold's findings, and the latest news from the front office and pressroom. Denise did not want to tell Barrett about her earlier conversation with Beth, so she avoided that issue completely.

Walking back into her office with Barrett's warning ringing in her ears and her feeling of appreciation for his concern, she noticed her red message light flashing. She hated to check because she knew even though she had been gone only an hour or so she would probably have several messages. She was right. The first two were from the computer room about a certain program she had requested on micros. They had found it and were e-mailing it to her. The next one was from Teale, her secretary, saying that she was leaving early for a doctor's appointment. The next one was that voice. He was asking her to meet him Friday night at Roger's for dinner at eight. He left his number in DC. No, she decided; I have another idea. Instead she dialed the number at his office in her agency that had been assigned to him, knowing she would get his voice mail and not have to talk to him directly. As the message left off with "Leave a message." she replied.

"Hello, thanks for the call and the invitation, but why not have dinner with me at my place Friday night at eight? I'll cook Italian, and you can bring some wine. If there is a problem with this plan let me know. If not, I'll see you Friday at eight at my place. Have a good week."

111

Short, to the point, but pleasant. She was pleased with herself. She walked out of the office and headed to the computer room. She decided she'd rather pick the software program up than deal with downloading it from her computer. Besides, she needed the exercise.

Chapter 13

Three Years Earlier

As Denise ladled the rich tomato sauce over the meat and Ricotta cheese mixture of the lasagna, the doorbell rang. She placed the covered dish in the oven and walked to the door. Wiping her hands on her tacky, bright yellow apron, she opened the door to a completely relaxed, tanned Paul with his gorgeous copper-red hair pulled back into a ponytail held with a rubber band. He was dressed in a soft, worn-out white dress shirt, with tattered cuffs, faded blue jeans and well-worn brown boots. Placing a bottle of rich Burgundy in her hand, he leaned down and kissed her on the cheek. "That's a very domesticated look," he teased, squeezing her shoulder with his hand.

"It's the best I could do. I am such a messy cook," she laughed. She was a bit uneasy with the comfort level of the moment. It felt as though no time had passed since the last time they had been together. In the past seven days she had not seen him or heard from him except for his brief message about dinner tonight.

"Oh, I highly approve! I think it's cute!" He released her and looked down into her eyes as though to find her soul and steal it.

She turned and took a deep breath. "What can I get you? Scotch, beer, wine for starters?"

"A beer would be great. I'll open that wine later and let it breathe before dinner. Can I help?"

"Sure, you might as well earn your keep." She walked over to the sideboard and took a stack of plates with napkins and silverware on top and handed them to him.

"Something smells delicious. May I ask, or is it a surprise?" he chuckled.

"It's regular old lasagna" she replied, as she turned back to the task of mixing the green salad with the tomatoes, cucumbers, and radishes.

He stepped over to the other side of the china cabinet and took down two of the Waterford goblets and two clarets. He placed them on the table in the correct position. The man had been around a fine table.

"What else?"

"That's it for now. The salad is finished. Let me get your beer and my wine and we can sit and talk, while the lasagna finishes cooking." She opened the refrigerator, removed his beer, popped the top off with the church key and poured it into an iced mug. She refreshed the glass of white wine that she had been sipping before he arrived. She handed him his beer and guided him to the sofa.

"So, how was DC and your whirlwind tour of the North Carolina site, and everything else that has been going on?" she asked.

"DC is DC. The main office asking all the questions from everything that is going on around the country. You know that. Hurry up and wait. I did find out a few interesting things, saw a few old friends, ran into Barrett. Did he mention it to you?" going on before she could answer. "The North Carolina site was in turmoil. They have several new cases, one being a seven-year-old child. The Health Department is trying to sit on the fact that it's a planted outbreak of anthrax. A few of the press members are getting fairly close to the truth. So all in all it has been a hectic week. And yours?"

"The same as yours. Hectic. Fielding questions from the field staff, the office, and the press. Developing a new program for the analysis of what we are finding in the labs. And yes, Barrett did mention to me that he had seen you, and you shared some information with him, but had a promise of more to come. So he is very interested in getting together next week if not sooner."

"It will be next week. I hope to be tied up this weekend," he grinned. "Did he also mention the Micro Conference coming up in six weeks in DC? He told me that all of the grand party from Incline would be there. That includes Harold, Barrett, Martin, you and me. Is that true? Are you going?" He turned to her and searched her face for the answer he was hoping for.

"Yes, I'm going. In fact, I plan to go shopping this week to find a dress. If I can find some time in the next few days I'll sneak out of the office long enough to make it to Saks."

"Shop for a dress! I bet you have several in your closet, and besides, you could put on sackcloth and still outshine anyone there," he replied.

"Are you sure you're not Irish, with all that blarney?" she laughed. "I haven't looked in my closet lately, but I think a shopping trip is what I need right now to clear my head," she said, as she felt him reach for her shoulder with his free hand and pull her to himself. She didn't resist, and his lips closed on hers with a demanding need and she responded to that need. He slipped his arm around her, pulling her against him as she balanced her wine glass, trying not to spill it and yet losing herself in his mouth, his chest, his arms.

Others had kissed her; they had made her feel loved, wanted and needed, and sexually excited, but not like this need and want. It was a demand that both of them exchanged at the same moment. She felt the urgency of his need and hers. She wanted to blame it on the week, the outbreak, the time, but she knew deep down inside it was the sheer need of both of them.

Paul drew back, releasing her and slowly pressed his forehead against hers and closed his eyes and though trying to block something or everything out. "Dear God, Denise! Give me a minute, give me a lifetime, but I think we need to stop and check on dinner."

"Yes," she agreed and stood up, surprised at the calmness in her voice and body, despite the pounding of her heart. "Sit here and finish your beer while I get it on the table. If you want to change the CD, please do." She walked into the kitchen and picked up the Italian bread and began to slice it with trembling hands, hoping she didn't slice off a finger. She glanced through the open section of the kitchen bar through to the dining room and saw him with his head laid back on the sofa, eyes closed.

She removed the lasagna from the oven and placed it on the hot pad on the table, next to the salad and hot bread. She walked to the doorway and said, "Are you hungry? Dinner is ready."

"Yes, thanks, it does smell delicious." He rose and walked toward her. She reached back to untie the bow on her silly yellow apron, but he reached and said, "Let me." She turned around and he lightly undid the bow and knot. She could feel his fingers lightly brush against her waist through the soft cotton sundress she had on. His heat was even greater than hers was. The two of them combined could create a volcano.

At dinner, Denise listened with interest to his stories of his life as a boy growing up around the world as the son of a diplomat. How he had attended so many schools that in the end his parents had decided tutors would be better than schools. So he was well versed in various cultures, and he spoke four languages fluently. His early university years he had spent at Harvard, and then at the University of Washington. After graduating from the microbiology department, he decided to enter the military as his favorite uncle had done. He had risen through the ranks so easily and effortlessly that it had even frightened him. He said, with honesty rather than conceit that it took very little in the few years to get to rank of Lt. Colonel. He was still years younger than his ranking peers.

"I did a lot of growing up in the military. I did a lot of evaluating the human being and the human mind and the cruelty of humans to one another. It was a mind-boggling experience during Desert Storm and one I hope never to have to go through again." His eyes were in a faraway place with pain and terror that was reflected in his eyes.

Then he turned to her. "That was a delicious dinner! I am afraid I am a bad guest. I could have brought dessert."

"No need. I have fresh strawberries and cream if you are interested, and I will put on a pot of hazelnut coffee," she replied.

"God, you are so good. Such a perfect hostess. Yes, that sounds delicious. Can I help you clear away the dishes?"

"No, I'd rather do it myself. Why don't you take your wine to the sofa, and put on some more music. I like your choices so far, and I'll do a quick clean up while the coffee is brewing."

She rose and started picking up the plates and watched him walk across to the entertainment center and look through her CD collection. He was tired, very tired, she could tell by the way he moved, the way he stood. This week had taken a lot out of him.

In a matter of minutes, Denise had the table cleared and the strawberries scooped into the Waterford sherbet glasses and covered with thick whipped cream. The coffee was almost ready. She placed the desserts on the wooden tray with two cups of coffee and a sugar and creamer with fresh cream in the dish. She walked into the living room and placed the tray of goodies on the table, finding him staring into the bookcase of her favorite collection with a faraway look.

"You are thinking about the outbreak in Connecticut, aren't you?" she asked.

"No," he said thoughtfully, "I was thinking about how to scoop you up in my arms, carry you off to your bed, and make passionate, abandoned love to you before I die."

In that moment when he turned to her with his clenched jaw and raw need for her reflected in his eyes, the need spread all through her body.

"Paul," she said softly, as she walked toward him, "Paul."

She felt his arms go around her waist, lifting her, with his other arm under her knees, he lifted her, as though she were a baby. She cradled her head against his chest, running her fingers through his hair. She released the band holding his hair and ran her finger through it and raised her lips to his. His lips came down on hers with that demanding, moving, needing desire, and she responded with all of her being. He carried her through the doorway and gently lowered her onto the bed and kissed her more forcefully and fully as they tore at each other's clothes as though to loose themselves from all the binders of life. The binders of their clothes, their needs, their desires, their demands, and the world.

They dissolved into one body on the bed and with one sweeping movement he was inside her. All she could do was feed on his mouth and his tongue and match each one of his movements with her own movement, until she reached ecstasy time and again, and he soared with her until they both exploded into oblivion at the same moment. He collapsed gently on top of her, not wanting to crush her with his weight, their bodies totally spent.

Chapter 14

Three Years Earlier

That dinner, that night marked the beginning of a six-week affair. Six weeks of sharing her condo, morning coffee and kisses, sharing showers and swims, sharing lunches and phone calls while he was away, sharing cooking skills and treats, stolen weekends at the lake, giving and receiving secrets, reading poetry and telling jokes. Denise was discovering many facets of herself through his eyes. And she liked the person she saw. This was a stronger, deeper woman, capable of giving as well as taking. Six weeks of bliss for them and then the trip to the Microbiology Conference in DC.

The flight to DC was longer than usual, with delayed takeoffs, busy people and a loaded jet. It seemed to take forever. Barrett and Denise, as usual, had seats together. Osgood and Harold were in the seats behind them. Paul was already in DC and had taken a suite at The Willard so they could enjoy the time they would have with each other. By now all of her group at Incline knew they were involved and had accepted it completely. Even Beth, who had bowed out gracefully, had never mentioned it again.

Barrett had done his usual "be careful" reminders, especially as the investigation had continued and the trail for the culprit was getting colder. The agency had already developed Michael's antitoxin and sprayed the contaminated area and so far no new cases had developed, even though the three of them knew that the antitoxin did not work. They were still holding onto their suspicions, and as the three musketeers, they had not included anyone else in their circle. Denise was having a problem keeping that secret from Paul. She was lucky that the time they spent together was spent on themselves, and they rarely discussed the outbreak, or their work, except for basic information. She could tell both Barrett and Paul were getting frustrated with the fact that they felt they were making no headway.

"How you doing?" Barrett reached over and covered her hand with his. He squeezed her hand as the plane lifted off, and he started talking very low and slowly to her about his trip to the Canadian Rockies when he was a child. He was distracting her with anything he could think of until the plane would level off and she could breathe again.

"Dad was not a happy camper," he continued the story, "with the fact that I had used his expensive fishing knife for a machete. But he didn't lose his cool; he just explained the difference to a ten-year-old boy between a machete and a fish-cleaning knife. Years later we joked about it when I gave him a new and very expensive one for his birthday. Okay?" he asked, as he felt her relaxing again, and he released her hand.

"Yes, thanks," she replied. "I'm grateful for your corny old stories. I wonder if they are true or just your imagination, though." She smiled.

"How can you say that? You've met my dad. You know what he's like and besides I'm surprised he has not told you most of these stories himself."

That was true. Of all her friends at Incline, Barrett was the only one whose family she had met on several occasions and they had shared dinner and picnics. His parents were a happy couple; married for forty-odd years and still enjoying each other's company so much. His family was a picture of a perfect family with a perfectly happily married couple. The type of marriage she knew Barrett hoped he would have one day.

They were lucky in that the crowd was small at the airport so they had a short time to wait to gather their baggage and the cab ride to the hotel was nice as Denise always enjoyed watching the monuments of her favorite city go by as she glanced out the window of the cab. This was a beautiful city with so much history. She never tired of it.

The desk clerk at The Willard gave her the key and summoned a bellhop to carry her bags. Denise felt a chill of excitement run through her body, as she knew she would be with Paul in a few moments in a different city, in a different hotel, in a different bed. Her heels clicked on the tile in the elevator as she walked in and pressed the tenth-floor button.

Using the card-key to unlock the door, the bellhop moved aside for her to enter first. She glanced over the suite Paul had taken and approved of it. The sofa was large and faced a huge entertainment center. She noted that their favorite CDs were scattered on top of the unit. She walked into the bedroom and noticed his clothes hanging in the closet. She was adjusting to having his clothes in her condo. She had given up the closet in the guestroom to him as well as several drawers in her dresser. It made her feel safe and secure in their love.

She tipped the bellhop and started to unpack. Paul had left one side of the closet for her and had taken the bottom drawers in the dresser, just like at home. She hung the suit bag up and unzipped it to remove her gown before it wrinkled too much. She hung the gown on the rack next to his tux. Glancing down at the bottom of the closet, she saw his dress black cowboy boots. She smiled. If it had have been anyone else she would have wanted soft, black wing-tips, but it was perfect for him.

He had called her earlier that morning, before she left for the airport, to tell her he would be tied up most of the day. He would get back to the hotel as soon as he could so they could have some time together before they went out to a quiet dinner, just the two of them. She had all the next day to get ready for the formal dinner that night.

Walking into the bathroom, she laughed out loud. Paul had left her a small bouquet of flowers, a bottle of champagne in the ice bucket, and candles around the garden tub, waiting for her to light. He had placed some scented bath crystals on the side of the tub and the rich, fluffy hotel robe draped across the gold make-up chair sitting at the dressing table.

She ran a tub of hot water, lavishly using the crystals, and stepped into the tub, sinking down slowly to adjust to the heat of the water. She had run it hot enough to turn her skin a deep pink. As soon as she had rested her head on the side and was breathing easy, the phone rang. She reached across the towels and lifted the receiver.

"Hello?" she said.

"Hi, there, did you find everything you needed?" came that delicious voice over the line.

"Yes, I did. You do realize you are spoiling me, don't you?" she replied softly as she let the heated water soothe her body and her soul.

"You deserve to be spoiled. You deserve this and much more, and I am going to give it to you in the future. I just wanted to call and say I love you and I should be back at the hotel by 7:30. I have made reservations at a quiet little bistro so we can talk. How does that sound?"

"It sounds too good to be true. I will be here waiting for you. I love you."

"See you soon. 'Bye."

"'Bye."

Denise had almost fallen asleep from the combination of the warm water, the relaxing music, and the candlelight, when the phone rang again.

"Yes?" She said.

"Well, hello. You sure sound comfortable." It was Barrett.

"I am. I am about to doze off in this marvelous bathtub. What do you want?" she asked.

"I hope you are not alone, so you don't drown." He laughed.

"As a matter of fact, I am alone. Paul will be here later. Now, why are you pestering me?" she teased him.

"Too bad you are alone, but on to other things. Have you seen or heard from Harold since we got here?" He seemed disturbed.

"No, he was behind me when we checked into the hotel. But I haven't seen him since. Why, have you lost him?"

"I haven't lost him. I just want to talk to him. He was a little frazzled this morning at breakfast before we left. He was a lot more irritated than usual, and I didn't get a chance to talk to him the way I wanted to about keeping his cool."

"He's probably visiting some museum or reading a book. Don't worry, he'll show up. He is so excited about tomorrow night. He'll be okay. Now leave me to my bath, okay?" she said softly, feeling the sleepy mood close over her.

"Okay, don't drown, but enjoy. 'Bye."

She didn't bother to answer, just replaced the receiver and slid further down in the tub to enjoy every minute of the bath.

She was awake, dressed, and ready when Paul arrived. After a few minutes of heavy petting and kissing, he whisked her out of the room and off to a waiting cab.

That evening at the bistro had proven to be more than she had ever hoped for. Paul was his charming, wonderful, caring self. The food was marvelous, the wine delicious and she indulged in a few glasses more than she should have, but that was made up for by the incredible lovemaking later in the night and early the next morning.

He woke her with a passionate, delicious kiss and she lost herself once more in this man she adored.

After a brief breakfast, he left for his DC office, and she went downstairs to get her day of pampering. She had scheduled an appointment with the hairdresser, and with the manicurist for a manicure and a pedicure. She was going to get the full treatment before the dinner tonight.

"Hey, there!" She recognized Barrett's voice across the corridor as she turned to go into the salon. "I see you didn't drown. Thank goodness."

"No, I survived," She laughed. She could feel the blush rising up her neck again as though he could tell what an incredible evening she had spent with Paul.

"Good. I found Harold last night. He was at Paul's lab doing some more reading and research. Paul gave him a card key. I don't think Paul even knew he was there. Harold got back to his hotel room around midnight, and after I had left so many messages, he called to assure me he was okay. He was very testy though. Still wanting to confront Michael about his antitoxin, but I talked him out of it. I told him we weren't ready to raise the issue yet, but I can tell you I am close, very close to finding the person. In fact, I would say it will be done within the next few days, if Harold doesn't blow it."

"Why didn't you tell me any of this yesterday on the plane?" Denise heard the irritation in her voice. "You were going to keep me informed about all things you learned."

"Listen, Denise," Barrett said as he reached for her arm and pulled her over into a corner away from the entrance to the salon and out of the busy corridor. "I *am* keeping you informed. But one, the plane was no place to discuss anything, and two, I don't have anything concrete to tell you yet. Trust me. I'll let you know as soon as I know, okay?"

"Okay, it's just that I feel lately you have left me out of the loop, and I miss that." She shrugged.

"No," he replied, "I haven't left you out of the loop. I have been so busy chasing leads and notes that I've felt like a dog chasing his tail. But I'm almost there, and you will know as soon as it all comes clear to me, okay? Now go enjoy your pampered day, and I'll see you tonight at the dinner." He reached over and squeezed her arm and brushed his lips against her cheek. He smiled and walked off.

Back in the room later, Denise slipped on her satin heels and smiled. The pampered day had paid off. She faced the full-length mirror on the front of the closet door and turned sideways to get a good, sidelong look. The black silk dress was perfect. It hugged her lines and showcased her ample breasts. The front dipped just enough to hint at a generous cleavage. She was pleased. Those few minutes or hours she could steal for working out each day had paid off.

"Jesus, Denise," Paul whispered, as he walked back into the bedroom from the sitting room. He had already gotten dressed and had left her the bath and the bedroom.

"You approve?" she asked coyly, knowing she looked great.

"Approve? It is marvelous! Great dress! Great body! Great woman! Maybe we should just stay in tonight?" he laughed as he pulled her into his chest.

"No way, not after all the work I had done to me today and the money I spent for this dress. We are going to go out and shine," she said as she reached up and kissed him on the lips. The delicious smell of his Stetson cologne made her press her body into his and feel the desire rising in him as it was in her. She reached up and pulled his mouth down to hers and filled his mouth with her tongue and her desire. He responded as well and let his hands glide slowly over the backless dress. As his hand moved around to the front to cup her breasts, his breathing came in deeper sounds, and she pulled away.

"Wait. Wait. Later. We have to be downstairs for the car in just a few minutes, and we both need to make this appearance. Believe me, if Martin and others were not expecting us, I would stay with you. Besides, look at you! You are gorgeous!" She walked around him and ran her hands over his broad shoulders, admiring his small waist and slender hips. The black tux fitted him perfectly, and the shining black boots made her smile. The short red ponytail was done up in a black tie. The contrast of red and black was fantastic. The man was beautiful, and she adored him.

The gilded, ornate ballroom was abuzz with conversation that she could catch only snatches of. Incline's reserved table had to be one of the most handsome tables there. Paul and Barrett looked dashing in their tuxes with the contrasting red hair and Barrett's dark brown hair and sparkling green eyes. Beth was outstanding in her peach-colored slinky thigh-high cut gown with the rhinestone straps. She had kept a tight hold on Martin all night. Denise had to admit Martin cut a dashing figure in his tailor-made tux splashed against his dark, Italian olive skin, the silver hair, and those green eyes that were almost iridescent. The silver mustache across his generous mouth helped to set off his delightful expressions of surprise when he recognized old friends or laughed at the jokes the dinner speakers delivered.

White-coated waiters circulated among the guests after the dinner as they mingled in the other spacious ballroom with a big band at the far end of the room. The shimmering crystal candelabra were at half-light to create a dreamlike atmosphere. Between the glasses of champagne and the lighting of the room, Denise felt she was in Wonderland with her Prince Charming.

The guests in the room were the intellectual elite of the medical establishment. The politically savvy types

126

were there because it was DC, of course, and a few celebrities were in attendance. It was a who's who sort of gathering. As she moved to a slow dance in Paul's arms, her eyes swept the room in all the glitter and glamour.

She spotted Barrett and Harold across the room in a heated argument, and it looked as though Barrett was losing the battle. With the soft light highlighting his brown hair and strong green eyes and his straight jaw line, he looked every inch an action movie hero. She had forgotten what a handsome man Barrett was, but tonight she had been reminded. She squeezed Paul's arm and look up at him "Excuse me, darling. I think I need to check on those two." She motioned toward the arguing pair.

"I think so," he replied. "Do you need help or would you rather I get us another glass of champagne?"

"No, I can handle it. Please get us another glass, and thanks." She walked toward the pair slowly. Coming up to Harold, she put her arm through his. "What is going on?" she whispered to both of them, hoping to quell their discussion.

"Denise, please tell this nutty neurotic spy that we have a serious problem that needs to be discussed with the company and with Martin," Harold said, as his angry glance caught her eye.

"Have you found out anything new or different that we can share with Martin or the company? Or are you just grasping at straws? We can't afford to approach these people without proof, because we still have no idea what and whom we are dealing with. I'm sure Barrett is doing the best he can, but I have to agree with him that right now we need to zip our lips. Don't you?" She squeezed his arm again, and he relaxed. She looked into his eyes.

"Harold, do you trust me?" she asked.

"Yes, you know I do, Denise. I just feel we are losing control of the situation and that there are no answers." He frowned.

"I know, but don't you see that if we have no answers we certainly can't ask the questions and alert the enemy, now can we?"

"No, I guess not. I am just not made for these games. It has been several weeks now, and we haven't made much headway. I can't quite put my finger on it, but I feel I *know* the answer. I have spent hours in that lab, going over more and better data and analyzing them and it just keeps getting more frustrating." He gave a dejected sigh.

"I know it does," Barrett replied. "We both know what you mean, but this is not the place or time to raise a red flag. Especially not tonight with this particular group of people."

"I have to agree with Barrett," said Denise. "In fact, I have an idea. Why don't we get out of here and walk back to the hotel, have a nightcap, discuss the older and better days we had during college and all the goofy things we did. I have had enough glitz and glamour, haven't you two?" She asked that as she spied Paul headed her way with the two glasses of champagne.

"Are you sure?" Asked Harold, noticing Paul walking in their direction. "Paul looks like he is ready to make an evening of it."

"No, he is as ready to go as I am. Besides we can all use some fresh air, right, Barrett?" she smiled.

"Right. Sounds good to me."

"Hello, all. Champagne for my lady," Paul said as he smiled and handed her the crystal glass.

"Paul, Barrett and I were just talking about leaving now, and taking a brisk walk back to the hotel and doing old memories over a nightcap. How does that sound to you?" she asked.

Paul slowly sipped his champagne and replied, "Sounds great to me. I've had all the wining and dining and dancing I need for one night. Let me get your wrap. I will meet the three of you at the lobby of the ballroom, okay?"

"Sounds good. Come on, Harold." She turned to get between Barrett and Harold and ran her arms through theirs.

"Should we say our good-byes?" asked Barrett. As both he and Denise caught Martin's eye; as he was dancing with Beth, doing a mean Twist.

"I think not," laughed Denise. "Those two are into the dance right now and don't need to be disturbed. Let's walk."

Denise felt the late evening air cooling against her skin as she stepped outside the hotel door. It felt good after that hot, noisy ballroom of people and loud music. Paul joined them and she took his arm as Barrett and Harold fell in behind them.

"Thank you for this," she whispered.

"You are welcome. I was ready to leave anyway. I can only take so much of that type of fun." He chuckled.

They walked along the sidewalk with Harold and Barrett already beginning the stories of college days and the lab disasters they had shared. Some of the events had been intentionally set up, some had happened accidentally. The night air and the soft whispered conversation added to the tranquil feeling of the evening.

In that moment, a hoarse voice cried out: "You idiots!"

A blazing hot light flashed out of the darkness and she heard the sharp report of a gun. A dark figure had stepped out of the doorway of a building and fired two shots rapidly into Harold's chest. Before Paul or Barrett could respond, the figure disappeared in the dark alleyway. As he passed the one lighted window, she caught a glimpse of *the dark hair and the heavy, black-rimmed glasses.* In an instant she was on the sidewalk, pushed down by Barrett. She was cradling Harold's head in her arms as Paul chased after the fugitive. Barrett grabbed Denise's hand

and placed the small Derringer from his ankle band into her hand, "Take this! I'm going after 'em! You'll be okay."

She vaguely heard the sound of running feet, and shouts as the first police officer showed up and took the gun from her hand. He screamed into his shoulder-held walkie-talkie for help and an ambulance. The buzzing in her ears was intense and all she could do was cradle Harold's head and watch the life drain out of his body. She was distantly aware of the dark red stains spreading across the pavement and covering the whiteness of her hands and arms. She rocked Harold in her arms, holding him close to her breast. She started humming a lullaby as though he was her child.

"Here! Over here!" She heard Paul's voice and Barrett's screaming at the police the direction the assailant had taken. There was a clatter of feet on the sidewalk, the shrieking of the sirens from the police cars, the ambulance, and the forcible removal of Harold from her arms. Someone picked her up and whispered over and over, "It's okay, baby, it's okay. It will be all right, I promise. It will be all right." She felt the gentle rocking of her bloodstained body against someone's strong chest.

She didn't remember the ride in the police cruiser back to her hotel. She vaguely remembered the whispered conversation with the house doctor, the questions and answers and the controlled voices talking about the fact that the assailant had gotten away. The last thing she remembered before she plunged into that deep, dark, drug-induced sleep was the face with the heavy, dark-framed glasses. Michael!!

Chapter 15

Three Years Earlier

Waking the following morning to a dull headache, Denise realized that it had not been a dream. It was real. She looked across the room at her crumpled black silk dress on the floor, her satin shoes lying nearby. She glanced down at the white tee shirt of Paul's that she was wearing. As she slowly turned her head to the other side, she was surprised to see Beth sleeping in the straight chair next to the bed. She was still wearing her peach gown and strands of hair were falling down in her face. She was in a deep sleep in what looked like a very cramped, uncomfortable position.

Rising up on her elbow to decrease the pain in her head, Denise reached over and shook Beth's leg and whispered, "Beth, Beth, wake up!" Beth woke with a start.

"Hello. Sorry I fell asleep. I thought I could stay awake, but it was a bit much, with the champagne, the action. How are you?" she asked in a concerned voice.

Denise considered. "Fine. Slightly out of it. It's true, isn't it? Harold really has been shot, hasn't he?"

"Oh, Denise! I am so sorry. Yes." She paused. "Not just shot, Denise." Another pause, Beth looked at her hands. "He's dead, Denise. He died last night. I know you guys were close. I am so sorry."

Silence. Then, "Where is Paul?" Denise asked as she rose up even farther to look into the living room.

"Gone out. He and Barrett are with the police. They are giving all the information they can to the police and helping with the composite picture of our friend, Michael." Her voice was tinged with pure hatred. "I never did like or trust that guy."

"I know," Denise said as she lay back against the soft pillows. "I always felt so uncomfortable when I was with him. Harold, dear Harold!" She turned her head as the tears flowed and the scenes from last night, holding him, flooded through her mind.

"Go ahead and cry. Get it out. You have been through a real ordeal. What a lousy way to start our trip to DC. But at least no one else was hurt."

"Have they picked up Michael?" Denise asked.

"No, he got away. Probably just as well, because Paul and Barrett would have shot him right there on the spot."

"Barrett?" Denise felt suddenly alarmed. "Where is he? Is he okay?" Denise again tried to get up and felt a sharp pain go through her head as well as her left elbow. She winced.

"Barrett is fine. He's with Paul at the station, as I said. They'll be back soon. You must rest. You have a sprained elbow from being forced down onto the pavement last night. Your headache is probably stress in spite of the medication the house doctor gave you. You sort of faded out on us. Of course, I can't blame you."

"How did I get here? I don't remember much after Harold was shot. I remember the shot, the falling down, the blood, the noise, and the sirens." She lay back again, trying to keep the memories at bay.

"After the accident. The guys brought you to the room. Called the house doctor and he gave you a shot. By the time I got here, they had you settled in and resting. I promised to sit with you while they went back to the station to help the police. You need to sit back and rest and just take it easy. The doctor says you are going to have a sore arm for a few days. Can I get you some juice, coffee, or breakfast? I can call room service. I think that coffee in the sitting room is about done for."

"Yeah, some juice and coffee, nothing else. If you are hungry, go ahead and order yourself something,"

Denise said as she again tried to relax and to banish the memories.

"I think I could do with a bagel and cream cheese. I don't think I could eat anything more than that." Beth walked across the room and Denise watched as she placed the order with room service. Beth came back in and sat down on the side of the bed.

"You're looking better. We were very worried about you last night." She smiled. "It's good to have you back."

"Thanks, Beth. It is good to be... alive. You don't look so great. And you have destroyed that gorgeous dress. I'll be fine if you want to go to your room and change."

"No, I promised him I wouldn't leave you. He made me swear on my life, and I did. But if you don't mind, I would like to slip on a pair of your jogging sweats, just to get out of this, if you don't mind?" she asked as she padded over to the dresser in her bare feet and crinkled evening gown.

"No, go ahead. Second drawer. Help yourself. Why don't you go ahead and take a shower. You will be out before room service gets here, and I'll be fine."

"You sure?" Beth asked. "If you want to talk, we can. Although I would love a hot shower; I feel so grungy right now."

"No, I don't want to talk, just yet. Go ahead and take a shower. I'll be fine. Honest."

Beth walked into the adjoining bathroom and turned the hot water on and gauged it until it was comfortable and closed the door to undress. Denise sat up and swung her feet off the bed. The pain in her arm was almost unbearable. She had never felt such a sharp, searing pain before. She glanced down and saw that her elbow was wrapped in an Ace bandage. She stood up and balanced herself trying to stand upright. As she moved slowly across the room, the pain let up some. She opened the closet door and pulled her jeans and a sweater off a hanger. She had no idea where she was going, but she had the feeling she had to go somewhere or do something. She slipped her feet into her loafers without socks and started through the living room to the front door.

She reached for the doorknob, turned it, and there stood Barrett. "What the hell? What are you doing out of bed? Where do you think you are going?" As he reached for her she fell against him with a sharp pain in her arm and once again she heard a soft voice, whispering, "Baby, baby, please don't do this. I will take care of everything." She could feel herself being lowered back into her bed and the shoes being removed and the jeans pulled off and the light top sheet spread over her. As she floated away she thought she heard more angry words of "Don't leave her alone for any reason, do you understand?" And another protesting voice, she thought she recognized as Paul's, "Don't ever tell me what I can or can't do or ask me where am I going or doing, do you understand? I can take care of Denise. I am very capable of that." She then felt a soft hand stroking her face, and she slept again.

At three o'clock that afternoon when Denise awoke with a lot more vigor than before, she heard Barrett, Paul, and Beth in the sitting room. She wasn't sure whether she could trust her stance yet so she called, "Hello, is anyone there?"

Paul was at the door immediately, crossing the room and raising her gently off the bed, cradling her in his arms and pressing her a little too harshly against his chest. "Welcome back, darling. I've been worried to death about you. You've been asleep for a long time. The doc said you needed it, but I wanted you awake with me. How do you feel?" he asked as he gently pressed his lips against the top of head. It felt so good to be in his arms again. So safe.

"I feel better. Lots better. I think I fainted. I was going to, I don't know. I just couldn't move very well, and I needed to do something."

"No, you don't need to go anywhere or do anything. We are taking care of everything. All you need to do is get some rest and get over this so we can go home and get back to our lives. That's all you need to do." He gingerly laid her back on the pillows that had been fluffed up by Beth as Paul had held her.

As she lay back on the pillows, she smiled at Barrett standing at the foot of the bed. "Hi!" he said. "How are you doing? I bet you have a hell of a sore arm, don't you?" He smiled.

"Yes," she smiled back. Those green eyes and that reassuring voice made everything okay. It seemed almost funny to be holding Paul's' hand and gazing into Barrett's concerned eyes.

"Yeah, it's pretty tender. What happened to it?" she asked.

"You were pushed down, out of the way. Maybe a little bit too hard, but at least to safety. It's a sprain, and it'll take some time, but it'll heal soon. I think everything else is in good shape," Paul answered her.

"Can you eat or drink anything now?" Beth asked, sitting down in the chair next to the bed.

"Just some orange juice, please. Nothing else right now. I need to talk. I need to talk to all of you," she said. "You have got to tell me what happened, and I have to tell you what I saw. I saw him. I saw the man who killed Harold." Her voice cracked as she said his name. Her dear friend Harold. She turned to Paul and grasped his other hand. "It was Michael. It was Michael!"

"I know," said Paul. "We saw him. We chased him, but he had a car waiting for him in the alley and he got away." He reached for her and hugged her close. "I am so sorry you had to go through this. I am so sorry about Harold."

She pulled back. "I know. I appreciate it. But something doesn't make sense. How did Michael know we would be there? We decided at the last minute to walk. No one knew we were leaving until we left. Any other time we would have taken the car. If Barrett and Harold hadn't been arguing and I needed to cool them down, then we wouldn't have even been on the street." She glanced over at Barrett, and as he started to speak, she saw it in his eyes. She read it, yes, someone did know they were leaving the ballroom. She remembered she had grabbed each man by the arm, encasing herself between them while Paul had gone to get her coat. She held Barrett's glance for what seemed minutes. She didn't want to leave the comfort and safety of those eyes. She also knew she would not say anything else right now.

She turned to Paul and looked into his loving brown eyes. "He must have been waiting for poor Harold to leave the dance." She shrugged and leaned against Paul's shoulder so he wouldn't see her questioning eyes on him. She looked past the side of his arm at Barrett and got the slightest nod of 'Yes, this is how to play it now. I am here. You are safe.'

"That is what we guessed happened. He was waiting for Harold. Apparently Harold had confronted Michael earlier in the day about his findings on the antitoxin. Michael couldn't take care of the situation then, while they were in my lab. So he decided to take care of it later. I am so sorry. I know how you felt about Harold. I want you to know that I had Michael checked out thoroughly. Also I had known him since college. I can't believe he did this. I think he is one of those geniuses who just snapped." He leaned her back and looked into her eyes. "I am so sorry I brought him into your life."

She smiled and stroked his cheek. "It's okay," she said. "You didn't know. How could you have known? I'll be okay. Don't think about it anymore. I'll be fine. By the way, where is Martin and how is he?"

"Out in the sitting room, on the phone. Trying to handle the press. Which reminds me that I need to get out there and help him," said Beth as she walked closer to the side of the bed.

"I'll return these," she pointed to the jogging suit.

"You're in good hands now. Get some rest. Call me if you need anything. We'll leave you two alone now. Come, Barrett. Duty calls," she teased, as she walked past Barrett to the door.

"Yes, I'm coming. I've a lot of things to take care of. You stay in bed and get better. Don't be wandering around anymore. We'll tell you what's going on. You just rest as Paul said so we can all go back home soon." He winked at her and she had never appreciated his friendship as much as she did now.

She smiled back. "Thanks guys. Now go on and get back to work. I'll be fine. I feel better already, but do remember you promised to keep me posted, remember the three . . . " she almost said the three musketeers, but stopped. She saw the recognition of the term in Barrett's eyes and didn't go any further. The term she had used for Harold, Barrett, and herself.

"Okay, I'm out of here! Take it easy! Paul, call me when you get ready to make some runs or check on anything, okay?" Barrett said.

"Right. Although I won't be able to stay in touch all the time or take you with me. You understand? I will let you know all I know and all I find out about the son-of-a-bitch," Paul said, as he rose to shake Barrett's hand and send him on his way. During the handshake Denise caught Barrett's eye again and recognized the concern but smiled back to let him know she was aware of the danger and that she could handle it.

"Whatever you can do for us or tell us, we'll be grateful," Barrett said releasing Paul's hand and walking out the door, closing it behind him.

Paul smiled down at her and reached over for the phone. "Are you sure you don't want something to eat?"

She shook her head. "Room service?" he questioned into the receiver. "This is Dr. Wagner, Room 719. Please send up orange juice and coffee for two, a western omelet, some fresh strawberries and some toast, please. Thanks." He replaced the receiver.

He turned and said, "I hope you don't mind. I haven't eaten since last night, and I'm starving. I want to run a hot bath for you and I want you in it for a good soak. I know the cuts and scratches are going to sting, but you need the bath to help you relax and rest, okay? You will do what the doctor orders, right?"

"Yes," she answered softly, "I could do with a nice, long bath."

She watched him move across into the bathroom and start the water. She couldn't be wrong about this man! She loved him too much. She knew him too well. This man who could write poetry, draw a tub of hot water, make brownies, laugh at anything, and coax her into anything. No. She was sure he knew nothing about Michael or Harold's death. He was not involved in any way. No matter what she could read in Barrett's eyes. He was wrong. She knew this man, and he would never be involved in a threat to her life. He came to the bed with that boyish grin and she knew she was right.

He helped her undress and gently slipped her into the tub. The warm water stinging the cuts and scrapes was a bit more that she had anticipated.

"I would get in with you, but I don't think either of us needs that right now, right?" For the first time, she did note his concerned look and how very tired he looked. He had been up for twenty-four straight hours, and it was beginning to show in his eyes, and in his day-old red stubble.

"No, you go eat your breakfast. I can handle this. You can bring my juice and just let me relax. I'll be fine." She smiled. "We'll talk later, I promise."

"You got it. I'll just hang out and wait for room service. I have to leave in a little while, and I'll get Martin or Beth to stay with you."

"I'll be all right by myself," she protested.

"Don't argue on this point. Because you won't win. Not with me. Not with Martin. Not with Beth, and certainly not with Barrett. Take your bath. I will bring your juice when it arrives." He leaned down, kissed her on the forehead, walked across the room, and closed the bathroom door.

No, she wasn't wrong about this man. He was not involved in this murder. He was not involved in this cover up. He was not involved in any way. It was obvious that he was as shocked and concerned about Michael as she was. Michael had been his friend and associate, so naturally he was devastated to find that he had betrayed him.

After the bath and juice, Denise found she still had very little strength as Paul helped her back to bed. He showered and changed into his jeans and baby-blue dress shirt. As he slipped the gun holster over his shoulder, she noticed how casual, how second nature that was to him. She knew he wore a gun, she had always known it, but today it really stood out in her mind.

"I've got to go now. I'm going to call Beth to come and sit with you. I'll be back later. It may be much later so I'll explain that to Beth so she can move some of her things in here. You will be up and about in another day or two, and we'll head home, okay?"

"Sounds fine. I promise not to get up again, unless I really need to. I think I'll just sleep. That bath was wonderful, but it made me sleepy again."

"Good. Get some rest." He sat down on the bed and cradled her in his arms. "I love you, Denise, I love you. I'll be back soon." He kissed her lightly on the lips and left.

She heard him calling Beth from the sitting room as she lay back and dozed. A few minutes later, she heard a soft knock on her bedroom door.

"Come in, I'm awake."

"Good," came Barrett's voice. He, too, had showered and changed into a blue, loose-fitting jogging suit. He walked immediately to the closet and pulled out her suitcase and started taking things from the closet and drawers and haphazardly packing her bag.

"Here, put this on," he said as he tossed her jeans and sweater onto the bed. "My back is turned, so get dressed and let's get out of here."

"What do you think you are doing?" she asked, incredulous.

"What do you think? I'm taking you home now. I'm getting you out of danger and out of here while the coast is clear. Now, I know you feel bad, but please, get up and get dressed. The car is waiting, and the tickets are ready. We are going home! Now!" His tone was demanding and short.

"I can't leave now. Paul needs me here with him."

Barrett turned to her and she couldn't believe what she read in his eyes. It was amazement. Her statement had surprised even herself. Barrett walked around the bed and sat down next to her.

"Denise, listen to me. I think Paul is in this up to his eyeballs, and you are crazy as hell if you think I'm going to leave you here with him. I don't know when he'll be back, so we are leaving *now*." He raised her face up to his and smiled, "Please, baby, you *must* trust me on this one." Denise had a fleeting thought that she recognized that word, that tone, but she couldn't be sure from where or when.

She edged herself out of bed and slipped on her jeans, sweater, and loafers. She felt as though she should leave a note, a message or something and then she saw her crumpled black silk dress on the floor with Harold's' blood on it, and she knew she had to leave.

Chapter 16

Bayside, Maine

Denise forgot her daydreaming of what had happened three years ago as she and Barrett walked into KC's, a dimly-lit seafood restaurant. Adjusting her eyes to the dark, Denise spotted Henry and Terry at a table in the back of the room.

"In the corner, in the dark?" teased Barrett.

"So what do you guys have for us tonight besides fried sea food? Which, by the way, smells delicious."

Henry pulled some papers out of his briefcase that he always carried with him, placing them onto the table. He reached for a red pen and started circling numbers.

"See these numbers? Identical with an outbreak we worked three years ago. Remember Connecticut? I didn't get out into the field on that one."

He turned to Terry, "Do you remember that outbreak? They ended up with ten deaths from seventeen cases. No confirmed involvement except some nut that worked for NCTR. A Dr. Michael Fitzgerald. He was never caught. Our lab technician, Dr. Harold Rushman, he was shot and killed. He was working on the project at that time." He turned to Denise for confirmation and saw the horror in her eyes.

"Gee, I'm sorry, Denise, I hate to bring that back up, but I wanted to give Terry some background and I will close this story of what happened three years ago by saying it is the same bacteria. The same pathogen with the same proportions. Identical. Look at this." He handed the papers to Barrett.

"Are you sure?" Barrett's voice cracked at the end.

142

"Yes, we've been running the same tests, and even new data, prints out the same exact results." He turned to Denise, who was also checking the numbers. "May I finish the story, now? For Terry. He is unaware of what happened to all of you with Michael, NCTR, Dr. Wagner and Harold three years ago."

"Yes, Henry. I am fine. It was just startling to hear all of that again after all these years. To be reminded of Harold." She turned to Barrett and smiled the 'I'm okay smile.'

"Anyway," Henry continued. "A lab technician who had worked for NCTR was identified as the assailant. He had been working with Harold at Incline for a few months on that outbreak. He was never captured, but he did go overseas later. At first there was talk that Dr. Paul Wagner was involved, since they were good friends and he had brought Dr. Fitzgerald into the study. But later he was cleared of all charges and has, I believe, spent the last three years trying to track down this killer. The way the two met was that Dr. Fitzgerald, after graduating from some college, then attending Amherst, was experimenting with growing these bio-germs in his lab at Amherst, in unauthorized sessions, and unbeknownst to the staff. When they found out, they fired him, locked up his lab, and destroyed or confiscated his papers, or at least Uncle Sam did. Then USARMRIID hired him to work for the Feds in their labs on the same project. Apparently, Dr. Fitzgerald and Paul had met at some seminars and become fast friends and got to know each other very well. Paul helped Michael enroll in the University Of Washington School Of Microbiology, and after graduate school Michael joined the military. Paul had given the military what they wanted, a crazed genius to work on their germ warfare, his thinking being that everyone won in that situation."

"Yeah, everyone except Harold," came Barrett's quiet reply.

143

"Now, Barrett, I know you were a close friend of Harold, but all of the investigations cleared Paul," replied Henry.

"Close to Harold? Henry, he was my best friend! We did things together away from the office, and then on top of that I was walking next to the man when he was gunned down..." He glanced over at Denise, and continued. "Anyway, we don't want to get into that. I always felt that Paul was involved with the whole thing, the outbreak, the cover up, all of it, and I have never really trusted him since. Of course, thank goodness after that fiasco he never worked with our agency again on anything. Michael was killed somewhere overseas and Paul went back to NCTR."

"But isn't it interesting that now, we have another outbreak, with the same numbers and make up, and Paul is on the scene again? That is a bit too coincidental for me. Have you told anyone else about this yet?" he asked Henry.

"No, not anyone. I thought I would run it past you, and then you could do whatever you wanted to with it. Besides, the site is full of folks, not only NCTR, but also CDC, and Health Department folks. I didn't want to involve anyone until we had to."

"Good thinking. And don't you tell anyone else for now. Terry, I know you belong to the state, but trust me, we need your help in keeping this quiet for the time being, because this can be as deadly as Henry says." Barrett turned to Denise and they both realized it was "deja`vu all over again."

"This time, it will be okay, and we'll capture this nut and close down his operation and take him out once and for all. *And* anyone associated with him," he added as an afterthought for Denise.

"I met with the sheriff this morning, and he has assured me all the contaminated asthma inhalers, nasal sprays, and cleaning solutions are off the shelves. We are assuming that the contamination was set in the local stores and not at the factory. We have a team at the factory investigating that, and so far everything is coming up clean."

Denise interrupted, "So here we go again. It's okay. I'm fine with all of this, and I don't think he'll get away with it twice. I might as well say it since we're all sitting here thinking it. You think it's Michael again, don't you? And there's a possibility that since Paul is here, he's involved also, correct? You think he was not killed after all, only reported dead."

Barrett sighed, "Denise, I think it's Michael because of the lab results and the tests. These numbers do not duplicate themselves that easily. Trust me. You know enough about micros. It's like DNA. It has its own fingerprints. There's only one host and it can't be copied. As far as Paul is concerned, I have no idea. I think we should give the man the benefit of the doubt, myself." Barrett continued, "Yes Denise. I think Michael is back to his old tricks. I think he has a reason for this and I am going to find out his reason and find him and destroy him."

"Well, here is the food," Terry interrupted. "It looks delicious. Let's enjoy our meal. Drop the subject now. We have given you two the information you need. You handle it from here and Henry and I will keep running our tests. My, this shrimp looks marvelous."

Denise tasted her shrimp and she knew it was delicious. She just couldn't savor it. Any other time she would have enjoyed it immensely, but today the subject, the ideas, the day's event had taken the taste out of everything for her. She ate slowly and pretended to enjoy it. She didn't want Barrett to know how upset she was with him, herself and the situation. She knew that Barrett's anger was coming from the fact that after the shooting in DC, Barrett had taken her back to Atlanta. He had stayed with her. He had handled the last two angry phone calls from Paul. Then Paul stopped calling. He had left Atlanta and gone back to Maryland. Barrett had sat with her through many lonely, crying nights of pain and realized he could not help except to be there as a friend and comfort her.

Paul had made only two attempts to see Denise and Barrett and some of his men had stopped him. Paul gave up. He did call every once in a while. She had changed her number a couple of times but in his position he could always get it. She felt she did owe him an explanation, and now three years later she could do it. Even though Paul had been completely exonerated in the case, she could never get past the fact that he was involved somehow, if only because it was his friend who took her friend's life.

Sometimes she knew that the reasoning was not fair to Paul, but then she would justify it by the fact that he lived a dangerous life, much more so than she did. So she would always be in a certain state of anxiety when she was with him. She would also always fear for his safety when he was away from her. She had decided that she did not want to live that way. She wanted a quiet, easy life now.

Denise also knew that tonight's conversation reminded Barrett of the fact that he had saved her life and that he had never forgiven Paul for placing her in harm's way. Months after the murder, when they were back in their settled life at work as friends, her memories had been coming back, and she had remembered the soft, loving, caring voice that had taken care of her in her shocked state. She had always assumed it was Paul, but it hadn't been. It had been Barrett. It had been Barrett who had cradled her in his arms, Barrett who had whispered to her and placed her in the police car and carried her to her room, while Paul handled the police and the manhunt. It was Barrett she had overheard arguing with Paul the following day, to stay away from her for her own protection.

It was months later when Beth confirmed all of Denise's memories. Beth, who had been there through the event and had played referee between the two men who cared so much for Denise. Beth, who now was married to Martin. That one event in Washington that night had changed so many lives. Harold had lost his life. Martin had realized he was living a boring, stale life with Eunice, his wife, and he had awakened to the fact that he adored Beth and wanted to be with her. So after an amicable divorce, he had married Beth and they were very happy. Barrett had lost more than anyone had. He had almost lost the woman he loved, and by the time Denise knew the facts and the caring and the pain he had shared with her, it was too late.

The pain, the heartache had lasted so long, and it had taken so much out of her that even now she just didn't trust her feelings for anyone. Even though she had been attracted to others and daydreamed about them. She didn't trust her feelings toward Barrett because he was her dearest friend. He knew her and knew everything about her, but she couldn't get past that incident. So they both had lost. They remained close friends and working associates, and sometimes she would catch herself staring at Barrett and his gorgeous eyes and wishing she could make the first move, but she couldn't. That night had cost a lot of people dearly.

Glancing up, Barrett noticed the local sheriff, Joe Thomas, walking into the restaurant and over to the bar. Barrett liked Joe. He had a lot to deal with now in this small community with the terror that was going on even though Incline and the other local and federal agencies were trying to keep a handle on it. Joe motioned to Barrett, and Barrett walked over to the bar to talk to him.

After a fifteen-minute discussion, Barrett walked back to the table. "Joe has confirmed it. The carrier was the asthma inhaler for Dr. Bishop and the saline solutions for the other cases. They have no fingerprints. No leads."

"Jeez," replied Henry.

Glancing up he smiled and said, "Look, its Sierra Connor. Hi, Sierra," he called and waved. Sierra waved and walked toward them.

Henry asked her to join them and she sat down between Henry and Terry.

"Maybe this will give us some time to compare stories on David, your wayward brother." He said the words as he motioned for the waiter to bring her a cup of coffee.

"I think we will leave you two to talk," said Barrett, as he rose and pulled Denise's chair out for her.

"Yes, we have a full day tomorrow, and I'm ready for a shower and some sleep," added Denise.

"Can I bum a ride with you guys back to the lab? My car is over there in the parking lot," said Terry.

"Sure, come on. Besides, we probably need a good navigator to get us back to town at night. We have got to get used to this area," laughed Barrett.

"See you tomorrow," Denise said, but Henry and Sierra were already in conversation about his friend and her brother, David.

After Barrett dropped Terry off at his car, he turned to Denise and said, "This is getting really serious with no leads. Joe just informed me that they have admitted fourteen new victims of exposure and that it looks like only two are going to make it. They have traced the agent to the inhaler in Dr. Bishop's office and the other cases have been traced to a drug store. They have taken care of that part by emptying all the shelves. Now the cops and we have to figure out why, who, and when. I feel for the sheriff. He's got his work cut out for him."

"Are you telling me someone just broke into an office and some drug stores and spread a deadly agent and left? No rhyme or reason to this madness?" Denise asked in utter amazement.

"That's about it. They got to Dr. Bishop first, and so far it looks like only one drug store. But I am afraid we are after the guy who left the disk behind. At least we have the diskette with Dr. Bishop's name and the others so maybe we can put a stop to this. That is the only lead we have.

Now we have our work cut out for us, too. We have to identify this strain and find the person and figure out where he got it and what his next move is likely to be."

-------- ------------------

-

The lone traveler sat in the airport reading the papers, and yes, there it was, the announcement of the death of Dr. Norman Bishop. Soon he would be reading about the death of Dr. Richard Bean, Dean of Sciences at Boston University. It had been so easy getting into the locked cars in the parking garage. Using several cars as decoys for the one Mercedes. Dr. Bean did love his Mercedes so much. A perfect opportunity for murder. Using the remote control that he'd help design during his military career, he had unlocked the cars that had electric locking systems. Then spread the powdery white mix inside the air-conditioning vents. When the engines were started and the air turned on, the drivers would naturally inhale the deadly bacteria. Such a beautiful car for such an ugly death. He smiled slowly, a smug, satisfied smile.

Chapter 17

Bayside, Maine

Denise noticed the flashing red message button on her phone in the hotel room as soon as she entered. She dialed the operator, who informed her she could check her messages by dialing the room number code. Denise dialed the number. She had three messages. Martin wanted to make sure all was well with her, Barrett and Osgood, and to let her know he was thinking about sending Clifford out for some field experience and for Denise to keep an eye on him.

The second message was from Teale. Things were jumping at the office but she would keep it all under control. She needed some phone numbers from Denise to track down some more information, and would Denise call her back tomorrow.

The third message was from Paul. It said simply, *"I will pick you up on Friday at 8:00."* Deja'vu!

Denise did not rest well that night. She didn't have nightmares, but she did have dreams of Barrett calling her name and of blood on her white blouse and of the flowers in her office drying up and dying. So she tossed and turned a lot.

The following morning in the coffee shop of the hotel, Barrett said, "I see you didn't get much rest either?"

"No, it was a tossing and turning night and not the type the song refers to," she laughed to keep it light.

"Are you okay? Do you want to go back to Atlanta and not deal with this project? You know you can. You know that neither Martin, nor I, would object to that. You can handle another project elsewhere, and we can replace you here. Do you want that?" he asked quietly.

"No, really I'm all right with this. And please stop asking me if I am okay. I think you have asked that twenty times since we got here. I appreciate it, but I am really okay. I am over all of that and past it. Three years is a long time, and I have dealt with it." She hoped he would buy her lie.

He did somewhat, with the reply, "I know you are over him, but everything that happened in that chain of events took a great deal out of you. Hell! It took a great deal out of me! I know you think I hover too much, but I just want you safe and happy. You know that, don't you? You know that I care for you and no matter how I feel about Paul, I just want you to be all right."

"Yes, I know where you're coming from." She sipped the hot coffee and looked at the doughnut. "I am telling you once and for all, everything is fine. In fact, I had a call from Paul, and I am having dinner with him Friday night," she said, reaching for the doughnut.

"You are kidding me, aren't you? You can't be serious! It is one thing to have to work with this man on an assignment, but dinner? Have you lost your mind? I don't care if God himself says he was free and clear of being involving with Michael, I don't care if all the courts in the land found nothing to charge him with! He still ran after Michael and left you there in the street with your dead best friend." By this time Barrett's voice had risen almost to a shout, and when he saw the shocked look on Denise's face, he stopped. "Jeez, Denise, I'm sorry. I am sorry. I didn't mean to bring that up again." He reached for her hand. She pulled away. She wanted to touch him, to hold him, but instead she pulled back and hated herself for it. She recognized the anguish in his face, the anguish in her heart, and she still couldn't deal with it.

"Its okay, Barrett. I need some air." She rose to walk out the shop.

He rose, "Do you want . . . "

"No, thank you," she cut him off, politely, but firmly. No company. After three years they had never really talked about the events of that night. They had been questioned separately by the police. She had spoken to Paul only sparingly on the phone. She had not wanted to see him again. It was not Barrett protecting her; it was her protecting herself. It took her weeks to convince Paul of that. He blamed Barrett. She blamed herself. She had believed that a love that strong could last through anything, but it couldn't, it hadn't.

151

She walked down the lane to the sidewalk and into the little town, checking out the store windows. None were open at this early morning hour, but she was not shopping, she was thinking, or maybe even trying not to think.

She could still hear Paul's voice on the phone. "For God's sake let me explain! Talk to me! See me! Don't throw this away! Listen to me!" She didn't. She couldn't, she was too numb and nothing he could say or do would bring her back. A small part of her kept hoping that in time the pain would pass and she would call him and they would talk. He would be able to explain it all away, but the day never came when she could make that call. Here it was three years later, and she had just found out that the loving, caring voice that night was her best friend's and not her lover is. One more bit of confusion to deal with. She had assumed that Paul had done so much to protect her, and he had for a short while, until Barrett carried her away to safety.

Even then, in safety and protection with Barrett, she couldn't get past the pain to reach out to him. She could see the love in his eyes. She could feel the caring in his voice, as he would tell her over and over again that everything would be all right. Her heart and mind wanted to reach out to him and touch him, but she couldn't let them.

Why was it Barrett who took care of her that night on that bloody street, instead of Paul? That was Barrett's best friend lying there in the pool of blood also. Why hadn't he chased the killer as Paul had? Why did he put that small pistol into her hand? Why had he come back? Why hadn't Paul caught Michael? He'd been right there within five feet of them. How could he have gotten away? All these questions now. She thought she had asked these questions and answered them years ago, but now she realized she hadn't. She wanted to go to the man in the coffee shop and comfort him, but she couldn't. Instead she was going to have dinner with the one man who had hurt

152

her so deeply three years ago that even now she couldn't move forward in life.

She parked the rental car in the parking lot of the state Health Department. It had been one week since the last discussion of Paul with Barrett. He had not brought the subject up again and neither had she. Paul had not showed up that Friday night as promised, and she had really been a bit relieved. She had told Barrett about the broken date, but he didn't comment, and she didn't pursue it with Paul or Barrett. She had seen Paul at the lab almost daily, but she had not mentioned the broken date and neither had he. She was sure that he had changed his mind about the date and decided it was over and that there was no going back.

She walked into her makeshift office and glanced up as Sierra walked in and sat down.

"Good morning, Sierra. How are you?" she asked.

"Not great. I'm concerned about Henry. Can we talk?" she asked. Denise noticed the tension in her voice and the concerned look on her soft, pretty face.

"Sure, what's going on?" Denise questioned.

"He's been getting lots of phone calls from his wife. Here at the office, at the hotel. All the time. Almost hourly. He can't stop them, and some of the staff have tried to cover for him by telling her he is out in the field, but that doesn't help. She gets very belligerent and raises hell. I hope she can handle his absences better then she has so for."

"Hmmm. Sounds nasty. Have you talked to Henry about this?"

"Yes," said Sierra. "He told me she was emotionally ill and that he had sought help for her on numerous occasions and that she really goes berserk when he is out of town. This time, even he seems amazed at the amount of trouble she is creating. She's threatening suicide and crying and everything. You know, Denise, I have known all of you for only a few weeks, but he seems a really nice man. He has gotten back in touch with my brother David and we have been sharing phone conversations and stories. In fact, Henry has asked David's opinion on this outbreak and the lab results, and David has consulted with him. David keeps trying to work his schedule in so he can fly back here and work with us if only for a weekend, but he is so swamped in California that he just can't get away."

"That's too bad. From what Henry has told me of David's background, he would be a valuable asset. We certainly could use all the help we can get right now. Terry and Henry feel like they're going in circles and Barrett goes ballistic each time a new case is reported. It's not an easy situation, but, getting back to Henry, what do you want to know?"

"I guess, what I am asking," replied Sierra, "is just how serious is Ingrid with these suicide attempts, and how involved with her is he?"

Denise thought for a moment because she was treading on thin ice here, discussing her friend's private life with someone she hardly knew. But she believed Sierra only had Henry's best interest at heart.

"I think he loved her very much at one time, but her illness destroyed a lot of that, and now he feels a sense of obligation to her. Is she serious about the suicide threats? I think so. I think Henry believes so also. In fact, I have heard that she has actually tried on two occasions. I wonder, though, whether anyone ever knows how serious a threat like that is. I certainly don't. I'm sorry you are going through this with him, but I think he appreciates your being there. I think he likes you a lot, and he needs a good friend now," Denise said, recognizing with that statement she was releasing Henry from her heart and her thoughts. She also was thinking that Sierra would make Henry a wonderful mate.

"Thanks, Denise, I hope you don't think I was just being nosey. I really do care about Henry, and I worry about him and what he's going through right now."

"That's nice, Sierra. I'm sure he appreciates it. All I can say is just be there for him, okay?"

"I can do that," said Sierra, as she got up and walked to the door. "I'm glad you're here Denise. Thanks."

Denise smiled. "Things will be fine, Sierra, don't worry."

Two days later, Henry seated in Barrett's office, confided to Barrett and Denise that he would have to fly home for a few days to take care of Ingrid, because she was getting worse with her threatening phone calls at the office and the hotel. They assured Henry that they understood and that things would be fine until he got back. Terry was working hard on the new samples they were receiving from the latest outbreak.

Sierra walked into Barrett's office, glanced at Henry and smiled, and he smiled back. "Barrett, this is the list of names of the victims and the list of those with active cases. Paul had mentioned you wanted this to check to see if there might be a link between these cases and location."

"Thanks, Sierra. Henry was telling us he is heading back to Atlanta for a few days to take care of a few things and that he will be back," Barrett said, aware of the growing relationship between the two.

"Yes," she smiled at Henry. "He told me. I am sorry he is being pulled away right now, because Terry feels he is getting close to isolating a new strain, and David's last call was very interesting in that he agreed with Henry and Terry."

"David?" Barrett questioned.

"Yes, my brother David in California. He went to school with Henry years ago. And now that Henry is working on this particular stain and David is familiar with this strain, they are sharing notes."

"I hope that's okay," said Henry, looking at Barrett, "I know I didn't clear it completely with you. But I did mention it to you a couple of weeks ago. I got the feeling it

155

was okay with you. Especially since I had known David for years and because he has seen this type of behavior in the bacteria with his work."

"No, that's fine. Where does he work?" Barrett queried. Denise was amazed by the coolness of his voice when she could see his green eyes flashing concern and questions.

"He's at the Chemco Labs, in Irvine, California. Do you need the phone number and address?" Sierra asked.

"No, Sierra, just curious. In this job we always run into people we know. I thought he might be working for one of my buddies out there. You know what a small world it is. Look at us. We show up and our lead researcher is an old buddy of your brother's. As I said, small world." Standing up, Barrett extended his hand to Henry. "Take care of things at home, Henry. Hope you find everything okay. Get back to us as soon as possible. I do need you to follow through on this project for us, and I would hate to see it get settled without your involvement."

"Thanks, Barrett. I feel the same way. I'll be back in a couple of days, and we'll press on. Thanks for your concern," Henry said.

Henry rose to leave the room. "I will walk you out," said Sierra with concern.

"Thanks, Sierra."

After they had left, Barrett walked across the room and closed the door. He turned to Denise, who was sitting in the corner chair lost in thought about Henry's problems and loss.

"Do you know any more about Sierra's brother David? Also check these names and see if they match the ones on the disk," he said.

"Yes, they match. What in the hell is going on?" Denise's high-pitched voice gave rise to her concern. She handed the list of names back to Barrett.

"And no, in answer to your question about David. I just know that he is a very bright microbiologist; been

156

doing the same type of work as we are. Lives in California. He's single. Gets back east to visit his family whenever he can. Sierra thinks the world of him, and so does Henry. Even though Henry hasn't been with him in years, they certainly have enjoyed getting reacquainted on the phone. Wouldn't it be a nice twist in fate if Henry could work something out with Ingrid and wind up with Sierra. They do make a cute couple? Do you see something?"

"What?" Barrett mused as though interrupted in thought. "No, I'm always interested in new people. It would be nice if Henry could get some peace and quiet in his life. He's a very nice guy and deserves it, but don't count on it. Emotionally ill people -- Ingrid, for example-- create chaos in other people's lives, and that is not easy to deal with. It would be great if everyone lived happily ever after, but that rarely happens. Speaking of that, do you have plans for dinner tonight? I was thinking of going to a new restaurant I spotted outside of town."

"Sorry. I have plans. Maybe another night." She rose to go back to her office.

"Okay, another time. See you later." Barrett reached for the phone as she walked out. Thank goodness he had been distracted so he wouldn't question her more about tonight. She didn't want to have to explain about dinner with Paul.

Paul had called two days after the "stood up date." He had just wanted to talk, but when Denise mentioned he had stood her up, he explained to her that he thought she would have called back and said either yes or no. Denise did not want to tell him that she had assumed he would just show up like he had done years ago. That was her mistake for falling back into the routine of the old days.

The exposed anthrax victims who were able to do so had filled out the questionnaire or their families had, so that afternoon she had visited the hospital and picked up the questionnaires. Later that afternoon she had driven to Dr.

157

Bishop's home and as she sat across from Carol Bishop watching the teary-eyed expression of a woman who had just lost her husband, Denise glanced across the room to the top of the piano and noticed the framed photo of Carol and the two boys, with the glass covering missing.

"I hate to bother you at a time like this, but I just have a few questions? I know you have been through this with the police, but it won't take but a minute, and it may help us a great deal," Denise said.

"I understand," Carol sighed. "I'll do anything to help find out what is going on. But as I told the officers I have no idea if this is a bio-terrorist who would want to hurt Norm. He had no enemies that I knew of and I thought everyone liked him. It is so hard to believe this has even happened. I have had a hard time explaining it to the children."

"I know. I'm sorry," Denise said as she walked over and picked up the picture. "Nice family picture." She smiled warmly.

"Yes, it was in Norm's office. That's the reason for the missing glass. The glass had been broken in his office. It was his favorite picture."

"Had Dr. Bishop had any threats lately, or unhappy, complaining patients or anything unusual in his daily routine?" Denise asked.

"No, all of his patients appeared to be very happy with him. I wasn't aware of any calls or threats. You can check with his receptionist at the office. Or the hospital staff. He had been his usual, happy self. You know, we had been playing tennis two days before he died. The policeman told me that they think the inhaler he used that night when he started wheezing was what carried the bacteria. Isn't that amazing?"

"Yes, amazing and frightening," Denise said. "That's the reason I'm trying to find out all the information on his days before the incident. We think someone broke

158

into his office and either contaminated his inhaler or replaced his with another one."

"It is just so hard to believe," Carol sobbed.

Denise had left the young wife and mother feeling helpless. She couldn't answer the woman's questions because she had no idea what she was looking for except some kind of monster.

Denise parked the car at the side of the restaurant in the lighted area. She was getting to know the small towns around the area they were working, but this was the first time she had been to this restaurant. She had worn her baby blue shirtdress and beige heels. She was aware that she hadn't gone to a lot of trouble to make herself up. She was glad of that. It meant another milestone she had passed. She would not knock herself out to impress him again. Denise felt the knot in the pit of her stomach, and she was having second thoughts. Maybe she should drive away and call him later and apologize for canceling. From the tone of the last conversation she was sure he would understand.

As she sat there trying to decide, she was stunned by the knock on her car window, and she looked up. She looked up into those loving brown eyes that had given so much to her and had taken so much away from her at the same time.

She rolled the window down. "Hi."

"Hi, yourself! You seemed lost in thought. I thought you might be considering changing your mind as you sat there. That's why I walked over," he said.

Denise smiled. He was still reading her mind. She would have to be on guard tonight.

"No, just thinking about several things that are popping at the office. You know what it is like, busy, busy, busy," she lied.

He opened the door for her and reached in to take her arm and help her out. Still helping her as though she was in pain--and the funny thing was she *was* still in pain, emotional pain. She didn't want to look at him again until she could control her breathing and her life.

"Busy day?" he asked. "So was mine. I also heard Henry was leaving to go back to the Atlanta. Is that true?"

News travels fast, thought Denise. It had been only three hours ago that she and Barrett had said goodbye to Henry.

"Yes, his wife is not doing very well. He will be gone for a few days and then come back and finish this project. I hope we can all finish it soon. I'm getting antsy also and ready to go home." She smiled.

"I know. This one is dragging on. My report today says we have six more cases and three more deaths. This has got to stop soon or we are going to have a local panic on our hands. I hate to think about that," he said, as they had reached the entrance to the restaurant, and he held the door open for her.

"Good evening, sir," said the host.

"Good evening. Reservations for Wagner, please."

"Oh, yes, Dr. Wagner, special reservations even though they were not needed tonight, but we do appreciate them. Please follow me."

Oh, God! Thought Denise, special reservations. What was he up to now? She knew that he had already figured out he could get to her. Just a brief push and she would be gone again. She was fighting as hard as she could with her emotions, but she knew it was a losing battle.

"How is this?" the host asked.

"Perfect. And thanks for the consideration," said Paul as he pulled out the chair for Denise. On top of her plate was a single yellow rose, and in the ice bucket was, she was sure without looking, her favorite champagne.

"I hope it's not too much. I just wanted you to enjoy tonight. I thought giving you a few of your favorite things might do that. Was I wrong?" His concerned look was melting her heart.

Finding it impossible to respond directly to that, she murmured, "I think just a quiet evening with talk would have been sufficient, but thanks. The rose is lovely."

"Let me pour the champagne," the host offered.

"No, that's okay. I can do it. Give us some time. I will prompt you when I need the menus. The lady and I have a lot of catching up to do, and we don't need any distractions. Is that all right?"

"Oh, certainly, sir. I'll keep an eye out for you. Just wave when you're ready to order. I'll leave the menus. Take your time. No rush." The host handed Paul the menus and walked away. Paul seated himself across from Denise. She was looking at the rose, but she could feel his eyes covering her face from the top of her hairline to the bottom of her chin.

"May I pour you a glass of champagne? It's a very good year," he teased. It reminded of her of all the other glasses of champagne with him, and she felt the knot in her stomach again.

"Yes, thank you. I am sure it is an excellent year, as you put it. All of this was very thoughtful of you, Paul. It wasn't necessary, but thoughtful. I had promised you an evening to talk and answer questions. I understand what happened about your last invitation, but we're here now, so let's talk. As a thought, why not call the host over and order an appetizer to hold us over for a bit because we have a lot to talk about."

He smiled at her, "Thanks Denise." He moved his arm slightly, and the host was there in a moment. "May I serve you?"

"Yes, please bring us your appetizer plate with a serving of each treat you offer. We don't care what it is, two of each, please."

"Of course, sir." The host left.

"Now for some conversation, be it good or bad. At least we are together and I have your undivided attention. Let me get a few pleasantries out of the way and you can fire away." He smiled. "How are you? What have you really been up to and have you missed me?"

Chapter 18

Bayside, Maine

Waking the next morning Denise felt such an ache in her head. She sat up in the bed and thought she might be sick. But she forced the vomit back down. What was wrong? She glanced over at the clock and noticed she had been asleep for several hours. The scenes of lovemaking with Paul were coming back to her. She remembers meeting Barrett in the hotel lobby when she arrived at the hotel and her statement to him, "Don't ask." Barrett had just nodded okay and walked away. She thought she knew what she was doing but she wasn't sure.

Now she had to get some balance in her life and get to work on this outbreak. Her private life was going to have to take a back seat to this problem. She showered quickly and buzzed Barrett's room.

His sleepy voice came on the line "What?"

"Well, aren't we a grump this morning?" she teases, hoping their friendship would carry them over the brief encounter of last night.

"Sorry, I was planning on sleeping in a bit this morning. How are you?" he questioned.

"I'm ready to go. I slept forever. I need to get back to the office or the site. Have I missed anything?"

"No, the results are still being tested against other agents, and Terry is still hitting blank walls. The police have no leads at all. No one was seen in the area. We have no leads and no ideas. No labs have reported any stolen agents from Plum Island, CDC, or any other research lab across the country. Of course a small vial of one deadly bacterium would be rather hard to trace. I thought both of

163

us could use some down time. Also there is a bit of sad news, but I don't want to tell you over the phone. Meet me in the coffee shop in, say, fifteen minutes."

"See you there," she replied.

Denise showered quickly and slipped into her blue jeans, red cotton pull-over sweater, and hiking boots. No matter what Barrett had to tell her, she still planned to get some work done today. She wanted to spend some time in the lab with Terry, and she wanted to run the questionnaire by a couple of doctors at the hospital who had handled the first few cases.

Walking into the coffee shop, Barrett, dressed in blue jeans, a beige polo shirt with the Incline logo over the heart, and a baseball cap, stopped to buy a newspaper at the counter. He waved to Denise.

"Good morning, 'Nise," he said, sitting down and motioning for the waitress.

"Yes, sir?" said the waitress, walking up to the table.

"Coffee for now and lots of it, please," Barrett requested.

"Bad night? Bad day? Bad news? What is going on?" Denise asked.

"Yes, bad everything. Martin called, and it appears that this is really sad." He stopped.

"Well, just tell me, and get it over with," she snapped.

"Ingrid, has killed herself," he replied.

Denise felt as though a brick wall had hit her. It took a minute to gather her composure.

"What happened?"

"By the time Henry got home, she had already taken a bottle of sleeping pills. He rushed her to the hospital; they pumped her stomach, but it was too late. He is not in good shape. He blames himself for being away and all that. Somehow he has to realize that she was just a sick woman and there was nothing he could do for her except get professional help," Barrett sighed.

"Poor Henry," Denise replied. "He is such a nice man. I can't imagine. Should we go back for the funeral, or what can we do?"

"No, I asked Martin. He is attending and a few other close friends and relatives. I think Henry wants to keep it quiet. Martin says Henry is holding up okay, considering."

The waitress set the coffee cups and an insulated pot of hot coffee in front of them. "Call me when you get ready to order."

"We will, but it may be a few minutes. Thanks," Barrett replied. She left.

They agreed to meet first thing Monday, but both of them knew they needed the weekend to digest all that had happened in just a few short days.

Walking into Barrett's makeshift office the following Monday, Henry could feel the looks of concern and compassion from his fellow workers. He had never been good at showing affection or expressing emotions. This time he had to accept their kind words and thoughts. Martin had called and asked if he wanted Barrett and Denise to come back to Atlanta for the funeral, but he had assured them that was not necessary. Now he had to face them and talk about what had happened.

"I am so sorry to hear about Ingrid's death," came Denise's soft words as she embraced him. Tears glistened in the corner of her eyes.

"Thanks, Denise. It was unexpected, but she had been sick for sometime."

Barrett reached for Henry's hand "I am also sorry, Henry. If there is anything we can do please, let us know. Are you sure you should come back so soon? Aren't there a lot of other things you can be taking care of at home?"

"No, the estate will be probated in a few weeks. Her family has gone back home, and I think the best thing for me is to get back to work. I need to keep busy now," Henry said, as he slowly sat down in the well-worn chair.

"Do you want to talk about it?" Denise asked as she walked over and sat down in the straight-back chair. "Can I get you coffee or anything?"

"No, truly, I am fine," replied Henry, picking up the latest lab printout from the desk.

Barrett and Denise explained the latest findings from Terry's lab and also from what Paul's group had told them. All the time Denise's mind was wandering to the suicide of Ingrid Osgood. How could this have happened? Everyone knew she was mentally ill, but no one suspected she was that sick. To take her own life with an overdose of sleeping pills! Besides, if her doctor, and Henry, and all her friends knew how sick she was, where did she get the sleeping pills? Surely no reliable physician would have given her a prescription for sleeping pills. Henry also knew better, but Denise was not going to ask too many questions, because she could tell by his expression that Henry was not ready to deal with a lot of questions. He could barely get through each day; he didn't need anymore pressure.

The intercom buzzed and Barrett reached for it.

"This is Barrett," he said.

Barrett listened for a moment and exclaimed, "Damn! You have to be kidding!"

Listening to the response, he replied again, "Yeah, thanks, we'll get right on it."

"Guess what, gang?" he asked.

"What?" Denise responded, concerned by Barrett's outburst.

"We have another outbreak. In New Hampshire. There are five cases of exposure so far. We are due up there within the next seven hours. Well, Henry, it looks like you will be kept even busier."

"Okay, let me speak to Sierra about travel arrangements," Henry said. "I think she'll ask her staff to take care of the arrangements for us. I'll meet you back at the hotel in one hour. That okay? I wanted to see Sierra and go by the lab and talk to Terry for a few minutes. At least I haven't unpacked yet," he smiled tentatively. Henry walked out of the office and down the hall to the one friend he felt he could talk to and confide in at that time, Sierra.

"This is getting out of hand, isn't it?" Denise asked.

Barrett wasn't sure whether she was asking about the outbreak or Henry's condition. He assumed it was the outbreak. "Yes, I'm concerned because it looks like the same strain from the preliminary data. The problem is we haven't gotten a handle on this outbreak even after days of work and now we have another one. Denise, do me a favor, as soon as we get to the New Hampshire site I want you to get me a list of all victims exposed, their names and addresses, places of work and places of exposure. Get it to me as soon as you can. Be sure and bring the case list from here with you also. I want to check a few things. Apparently this one has been traced to air conditioning vents in cars."

"You are kidding! Someone is putting lethal bacteria in car vents? This is unbelievable," she replied in shock.

"We are going to work our asses off until we find this maniac. We can't let this happen again. We have go to get on this right now and handle it. The police were on top of this one fairly quickly. I will meet with the detective heading up the investigation as soon as I get there. Please take care of getting those lists together for me. I have a feeling our only hope is linking the cases in some way. I need not remind you, this has to be kept very quiet."

"Sure, I can do that, but what are you looking for?" Denise asked.

"I will share this with you, but it goes no further than this room, for the time being. Not Henry, not Paul, not anyone else, do you understand?" He frowned as he asked her.

"Of course, but tell me."

167

"I have a feeling, an unhealthy, ungodly feeling that someone is using this lethal agent to kill certain people. They are not using a large deadly agent to wipe out a large area or a town. I think they are using it to murder someone, knowing it will be investigated as a lethal outbreak of a deadly disease. None of the authorities will think anymore about it than as an outbreak. I think it is the same person who left the disk. I think it is a person who has a connection with doctors."

"You can't be serious!" Denise exclaimed. "How could anyone do such a thing? What about the innocent people? Even kids? The person had to know that other people would be hurt by this."

"Yes, that is what scares me. We may be dealing with someone who knows the consequences of his actions and doesn't care. He doesn't care if it is kids, old folks, mothers, and fathers, whoever gets sick and dies. He's probably out to get only one or two people. Now, if my theory is correct, we have to find the common link between these people. That is why I need the list of cases from all outbreaks, especially as the outbreaks occur, so we can compare names. I know there is a connection. I just have to find it."

"I will get the list from here and the list in Maine now. And I will call ahead and ask for the list to be ready when we get there. Who is our contact in New Hampshire?"

"Dr. Stevens; Marie Stevens is the State Epidemiologist," Barrett replied turning and dialing the phone to call for more information.

Sierra stood and wrapped her arms around Henry. She was glad that he was back with them. She wanted to take care of him now and help him get past this terrible ordeal.

"I'm so glad you're back," she said as she released him.

"I'm glad to be here. Thanks for the flowers and the card, but mostly thanks for the phone calls. The calls got me through a lot of bad nights. It was good having you to talk to each night and knowing you were back here. You are a dear friend and I am so thankful you are here."

"I will always be your friend." She smiled into his eyes. The ringing of the phone broke off the chance for another quick hug.

"This is Sierra Connor," she answered into the receiver. "Hi, there. Good to here from you! Guess who's standing here next to me?" She asked. She could see Henry waving his hand to warn her that he did not want to talk to anyone. She smiled and said, "It's David."

Henry reached for the phone "Hi, David. It's good to hear from you. "Yes, thank you." He replied in the phone to the condolence offered by his best friend. "I know. I appreciate that. I'm just lucky to have your sister as a good friend to be here with my other friends and me. Thanks, but I don't want to talk about it now," he said in an uncomfortable voice. "Besides, we have another outbreak. Somewhere in New Hampshire, so the team is headed out right now. I have to make some travel plans with Sierra and then hit the road. When are we going to see you?" he asked in a hurried voice. "That'd be great. Seeing you in a couple of weeks would be fine. I know Sierra would like to see you, and so would I. What? No, all I know is that the strain looks the same. There are only a few cases right now. We just got the call and very little information except it may be the same agent. I'll call you when I get there, and we can compare notes. I'll give you back to Sierra." He handed the phone back and started to walk away.

"David, hold on a minute," Sierra said as she pressed the hold button. "Henry, wait." She walked to him and squeezed his arm. "I am sorry you have to leave since you just got here. I will see you when you get back. Do call me. I'll call Margaret now and get the locations and time needed for your flights. Take care, and get some rest."

She rose up on her toes to reach his cheek and kissed it softly.

"Thanks, Sierra. I'll probably call every night. Also talk your brother into coming soon. I could use his company personally and professionally. I'd like to discuss this outbreak more with him." He smiled and turned and walked away.

Barrett had rounded the corner to overhear the last statement of Henry's. "Who were you going to talk to about the outbreak, Henry?"

"David. Remember Sierra's brother, David Connor? He has some experience in this field and I thought I would compare notes with him. He might have some input that we are missing."

"Oh, that's right. David Connor. I had forgotten. Yes, if you get to talk to him, let me know what he has to say, but let's not deal with anyone else. This needs to stay in-house until we know what we are dealing with. I have to pick up some things from the front office. See you back at the hotel. By the way, if you're going to Terry's lab, ask him for the file on the latest antitoxin test he has for me, and bring it along. Henry, where is David working now?"

"Somewhere in Irvine, California. I forgot the name of the agency. Sierra knows," Henry replied as he started walking off again.

"Henry, how long has it been since you have seen David?" Barrett asked.

"About seven or eight years, that's one of the reason it was a nice treat to run into his sister here at the Health Department. Why?" Henry turned and asked.

"Just curious. I'd like to meet him one day, when he comes to visit. You're right. He might have a new insight into this problem. See you later, Henry," Barrett replied, walking into the direction of Margaret's office.

Barrett's mind was racing now as he headed to the front office to pick up the information on the latest outbreak and to make a few phone calls. How long had

Henry known David? Why hadn't David shown up at the Maine site when they were working on it? What did he look like? What am I? Am I so desperate that I'm getting suspicious of everyone? When things did calm down a bit, Barrett thought, he would have to look into David Connor's background, just to satisfy his own curiosity.

Rushing for the gate to catch the flight to New Hampshire; Denise saw Barrett and Henry just ahead of her in the walk-through tunnel to the plane. It had not been easy, but all of them had packed and made the flight on time.

She sat down next to Barrett and buckled her seat belt. Reaching over, she pulled out of her briefcase the lists of names from the Maine outbreak as well as the list that had been faxed from the Health Department in New Hampshire.

"The lists you asked for," she said. "Hope you find what you are looking for."

"Yeah, me, too. Not quite sure what I am looking for, but thanks," he replied.

Chapter 19

Madison, New Hampshire

The plane had already taxied to a stop at the terminal when Denise remembered that she hadn't had a chance to call Paul or anyone else about this trip to New Hampshire. She felt okay about that because she was trying to forget her personal life for a while so she could focus on this outbreak. The staff morale was low now. They had not come up with anything in Bayside, and now there was another outbreak here in Madison, New Hampshire, with possibly the same substance.

Denise and Barrett retrieved their carry-ons from the overhead bins. Both had learned a long time ago to travel light, and to keep it with you at all times. The laptop and the overnight bags were all they needed.

The Madison airport was the size of a large city's bus station. The different-colored plastic seats were bolted to the floor. The five gates could accommodate sixty or seventy people at the most. It was very easy to pick out Dr. Stevens standing at the gate as they deplaned.

"Dr. Stevens?" Denise asked.

"Yes, I'm Marie Stevens. Please call me Marie." She was a pleasant-looking woman with shoulder-length blonde hair and clear blue eyes. There had to be a bit of Scandinavian blood in her family line.

"Hi, I am Denise Gibson. This is Dr. Barrett Hayden, and this is Dr. Henry Osgood. We are all from Incline. I think you were expecting us?"

"Yes, the folks in Maine had called and told us you were on your way. Thanks for coming so promptly. The preliminary data look the same as those in Maine, but we will do some more tests. Our labs are in touch with your labs. I'll brief you as we walk. The car is right outside. I have you checked in at the Holiday Inn. I thought we'd go to the lab and let you meet our technician, then to the hospital, and then if you like, to the site. The site is only a few miles away. How does that sound?"

"Sounds fine," said Barrett. "We can stash our bags anywhere until we make it to the hotel. I think right now we would rather go to the hospital first and then to the lab, if that's okay. I need to make sure the symptoms are the same as those in other exposed victims."

"Fine. We'll head for Madison General. I think the staff will be very cooperative. Needless to say, they're scared stiff. We have a very good man in charge, and he has taken all the necessary precautions."

Carrying her briefcase as well as her laptop, Denise stepped out of the car and into a mad house of TV and newspaper reporters. Their TV trucks with antennae shone in the morning sun. Barrett and Marie had already gotten past the mob. Passing the security guards and entering the cool interior of the hospital, she pushed her way through the crowd of reporters and onlookers. The number of people who had already gathered at the hospital was amazing to her. Where were the security guards or the police? She caught a glimpse of Marie further down the hall and Denise forced her way through the crowd by showing her ID badge and cornering a guard. "Can you help me?" she asked.

"Sure, hold on," he said as he took her laptop and grabbed her elbow, "let me help you get through this or you will never make it."

"Thanks, I do appreciate it. I just need to get down the hall to the conference room. Have you ever seen it like this?"

"Nope," he replied, "and it is only going to get worse. We have already called in for more help. I don't think these people realize how much trouble they create with their pushing and shoving and in a hospital no less. But for now we have them contained to the first floor and that's where they'll stay until we can get all of them outside the building." He pressed her shoulder to guide her through the last throng of bodies and pass the red barrels with yellow *no trespassing* tape stretched between them that had been set up to cordon off the crowd.

"Thanks a million," she said, pointing to the end of the hall toward the room that was her destination.

"Any time, Miss. You be careful and when you start to leave, try the back elevator, just to be safe," he said, walking back to the disorder down the hall.

Denise noticed the familiar odor of disinfectant as she entered the quieter halls heading for the conference room. It was an older building that had been remodeled in a more modern style. The freshly painted walls were the traditional beige color but the floors were covered in a deep maroon carpet and there were some very nice paintings on the walls. The quarantine had already gone into place. She wondered if the patients and visitors to the hospital were aware of that rule. This end of the hall was a lot quieter and emptier.

She spotted Marie at the entrance to the conference room. Walking up, Marie introduced the men standing in the hall, "Dr. Robert Baker, medical director of this hospital, and Dr. Forrest Blair, the state health commissioner, and this is agent Tom Lacey, with the FBI, who is heading up the investigation. This is Denise Gibson. She is with Dr. Henry Osgood, and Dr. Barrett Hayden from Incline.

"Dr. Osgood, Dr. Hayden, Ms. Gibson, we're glad you are here and so quickly. We have just received the teams from CDC and NCTR. They are up on the third floor with the last of the seven cases we have isolated. We have already had three deaths, and it doesn't look promising for the others. Also, Ms. Gibson, this is the latest updated list we have compiled of the cases that have been reported so far." Dr. Baker handed Denise the updated list and she turned to give it to Barrett.

"Thank you, Dr. Baker," she said.

"I appreciate the list. I can't say we are thrilled about being here. What have you observed so far?" Barrett asked as he reached for the list from Denise and quickly scanned it.

"It has all happened so fast. Dr. Marjorie Greenspan, a young resident, admitted the first case and thanks to her quick thinking, after noticing the purplish hue to the skin of two patients and the respiratory problems, she had the patients isolated immediately. That cut down on the contact with the other patients and staff. Even though we know it is not contract by person to person contact we do not want to take any chances. Unfortunately, it was a doctor who was our first case and our first death."

"A doctor? One of your staff?" Barrett asked quickly.

"No, a vacationing physician. Dr. Richard Bean. He has a summer home in this area. He was divorced, and we knew him socially. He played golf with some of our staff and always offered his services if needed. He spent about two months every summer here. He had sent us patients with minor injuries when he had encountered them on the beach. Cuts from driftwood, insect bites, injuries of that nature."

"Dr. Richard Bean from Boston University?" Henry asked, as he reached for the list from Barrett.

"Do you know him?" Barrett asked.

"If he is the same Dr. Bean at Boston. He was on the staff of the Microbiology School. He taught most of my classes. Is that the same one?" Henry looked over at Dr. Baker.

"Yes, it is the same one. Dick is . . . was still teaching at Boston University. He would get away during summer break and come here. It's a small world. Dr. Osgood, you were one of his students?"

175

"Yes, it is a small world. What about the other cases here in the hospital? What can you tell us about them?" Henry asked, crossing the lobby to the elevators.

"Are the other cases locals or vacationers?" Barrett asked, as they were riding up in the elevator.

"I think he is the only visitor," replied Dr. Baker. "The second case was a young girl who lived in the area. By the way, the area where we think it was contracted has been isolated and cordoned off. It is a site by the ocean, north of Hampton Beach and, as you can guess, close to Dr. Bean's summer cottage. We will have to pull the charts on the other cases. This is just a list of names you requested earlier before you left Bayside."

Agent Lacey turned to Barrett and said, "Can I speak to you two for just a minute?"

"Certainly," replied Barrett.

"Let's step into this exam room for a few minutes." Lacey led Barrett and Denise into a deserted examining room containing only a bed, a chair, an exam table, and a floor lamp. Closing the door behind him, he sighed. "I don't have to tell you folks that this new outbreak in our area is getting to everyone around here. We have seven cases and the first four of them have been traced to the air vents in their cars. These doctors are admitting cases that may not be related and are after effects causing the police and doctors to think they are contracting the illness at other locations. This doesn't give us much room to breathe."

"What precautions have you taken there?" asked Barrett.

"We had the parking garage closed off. We impounded all the cars that had used that garage. Our investigators, as well as some of your team, investigated each one of the cars. They found some traces of a powdery substance, which proved to be anthrax. Can you believe that?" asked Lacey.

"How did he get it into the cars?" Denise asked.

"That is what is so amazing. There was no sign of breaking and entering. So he either had a key to each car, which is doubtful, or a remote control, something like a garage door opener that could program the locked systems and unlock the doors. Our investigation showed that all victims had electrically locking cars. Also we have been lucky. So far we have found only ten contaminated cars out of all the cars parked in that garage."

"That's what I was afraid of," said Barrett. "What we are dealing with, I think, is someone setting off pathogens of a lethal disease to kill just a few people. Not an entire town. Remember the Tylenol scares back in the 'eighties?' I think this is a copy-cat killing just with a more powerful element."

Lacey whistled. "Jesus, if that's true, what now? We have no idea where this nut is heading or what his next move is. Do you have any ideas?"

"Not yet, but we are following up on a few leads. I will drop by your office later and tell you about them. Right now I need to check on a few things here and I'll get back to you. Thanks for your input, Lacey. I know you have your hands full but the best you can do is try to keep the media out of this and settle down the hospital staff and others who know, because I would be willing to bet your epidemic is over for now."

Agent Lacey walked down the hall heading back to his makeshift office. Barrett turned to Denise. "Listen to me I wanted to tell him more information, but not all of it, not now, because I think he could do more damage than good. So I'll give him some info on the cases in Maine, but not all of it. Not the disk, not any connection we have made or will make. Do you understand? This has to be our secret for now."

"Yes," whispered Denise, too scared to think, much less reply to any questions. She couldn't believe that what they were talking about had taken place in this little town, in this small hospital.

Walking down the corridor, Denise noticed that the hospital had a more subdued quietness than hospitals usually have. It was almost the quiet sound of death. Not even fright, just death.

Arriving at the nurses' station, Henry took the chart on Dr. Bean from the top of the counter. Denise picked up the chart on the young girl, Becky Riley, and Barrett took the other charts from the counter.

"It *is* my Dr. Bean," Henry said. He handed the chart to Barrett. The record page showed the vital signs that were so familiar with the other cases; high fever, malaise, cough that developed into severe pneumonia, a coma and then death.

After Barrett finished with the chart he turned to Dr. Stevens. "Where are the other patients?"

"Down the hall in the isolation area," she replied.

"How are they doing?" Barrett asked Dr. Baker.

"I'll ask. Here is Dr. Greenspan, who recognized the problem with the first patient."

He called the young resident over and made the introduction.

"How are the patients?" Dr. Baker asked.

"I am afraid that all but two have died. It is the fastest moving bacterium I have ever seen. It has not responded to our antitoxins. I left Dr. Wagner and the doctor from CDC in the room. They are taking nasal swabs as well as blood and urine samples. If you want to join us, the protective gear is on the shelf next to the station," she said, pointing to a cabinet with the stacked yellow gowns, gloves, and protective eye wear.

"I think I'd like to join the team in there," said Henry, walking over to the cabinet. "How about you two?"

"No," said Barrett. "Henry, you go ahead and get the samples back to our lab and CDC's lab. Let's leave the state lab out of this one. Their folks can send their own cultures. Denise and I have some other things to deal with." Guiding Henry by the arm, Barrett led him off to a corner of the office; "Before you suit up, can you look at this list and tell me if you recognize any other names or anything that might be helpful?" He handed Henry the printed list that had been given to him earlier.

Henry looked at the list and said, "This is Maine's list. Why, Barrett, what am I supposed to see? It's the same names, Dr. Bishop and now Dr. Bean. Wait! What was Dr. Bishop doing in Maine?" Henry asked.

"Henry, he lived there. He had left teaching and had set up a private practice in Bayside. He had treated most of the victims of the first outbreak. We think he was contaminated by way of his asthma inhaler. If this is your Dr. Bishop, then both of these men taught at Boston University when you were there, correct?"

"Yes, but why? What does this mean?" Henry asked, as he sat down in the nearest chair. Barrett could tell that Henry was shocked by the death of his two professors.

Standing up again, Henry finished getting into the protective wear and started into the isolated area. Barrett stopped him and said, "This has to be kept quiet. I mean no one, no one, including CDC, NCTR or the FBI must know about this yet. I'll explain it to you later. Do you still want to do the blood cultures?"

"Yes, more than ever. I'll be okay. I won't say anything to anyone. Just let me do my work so I can help find out what's going on with this bacterium and how we can stop it. I can't believe this is happening!" He started to walk away and then turned to Barrett and asked, "You don't think I'm involved do you, Barrett?"

"No, Henry, I don't suspect you. I do worry about your safety since you know two of the victims. So while we're here in New Hampshire, you stick close to Denise or me. Let me know where you are at all times. I'm going to leave you now for a short time to take care of a few things. When you finish your lab work, come back here, and Bob, one of my men, will be here at the door. He will take you back to the hotel and help you get checked in and settled. Okay, Henry, will you do that for me?"

"Yes, Barrett, I'll do that, but please do stay in touch with me, and let me know what you come up with. I have to know. Don't leave me out of this, okay?"

"I promise, Henry. You will be the first one I call. And, Henry, I really am sorry about the death of your friends."

Barrett walked back to Denise. They said their good-byes to the doctors, explaining that they would be back within the hour with some other security people, and stepped into the elevator. Each time Denise started to speak, Barrett would squeeze her arm to discourage any talk. He assured Marie that he'd use a cab and pick up a government car as soon as they got back to the Health Department office.

Outside on the street, Barrett called Bob, one of his agents, on the cell phone and told him to get to the hospital and stay with Henry until Barrett got back. He then waved to a cab that was parked out front. Once they were seated in the cab, he gave the address for their hotel, the Holiday Inn, to the driver.

Barrett turned to Denise and said softly, "Listen to me carefully, Denise. We've found our connection, but now we need to know why and when. When we get to the hotel I want you to get on your computer and check all your databases and others. Call in all your favors and find out all you can on these two doctors, at Henry's university for these several years." He was quickly scribbling down names, dates, and locations. "Be as discreet as possible. Also pull all the information you can on Henry." He saw her distressed look in her eye. "No, I don't think Henry has any idea what's going on, and I don't think he's in danger, but I can't be sure. Rerun that disk Bob found and see what other information you can find."

"This is turning into a three-ring circus. What do all of these people have in common with Henry, his professors at Boston University, and Amherst College? What exactly are we dealing with? Were you correct days ago when you thought it was a nut case, a person out to even the score with someone, and using deadly bacteria to do it? Who would do such a thing?" Denise asked.

Barrett shook his head, "I'm not sure. But I think we have a genius in germ warfare that's out to get rid of some people, and he's found an easy, safe, undetectable way of doing it by charging it off to a deadly disease outbreak. That's why I need as much information as you can get me on these people. What else do they have in common besides a college, a teaching staff, and the field of microbiology?"

Denise hesitated. Then she said, "I'll get right on it. I ought to have something for you soon. I just wish I knew what I was looking for. I need more than names, dates, and places. I need a common thread," she sighed.

"Right now this is all we have, and I think once you get started you'll find the common thread. Just hang in there and work on it. You are our best hope now. I don't want to alert or call in anyone else to start probing this information. Not yet, anyway?"

"It's Michael, isn't it?"

"I don't know. It certainly looks that way, but we won't know for sure until we check a few things. I know you have already thought of this, but do run our friend, Dr. Michael Fitzgerald, through your database also, and see what you come up with on him. It may be nothing or it may be everything."

The cab pulled up to the hotel and Barrett reached over and opened the door. "I have to do a few things. Check in and try to get adjoining rooms for all three us, Henry, yourself, and me. In fact, demand it!"

Barrett waved a bell-cap over to help Denise with the bags and pushed his carry-on bag across the seat.

"Take this, please, and help the lady with all these bags."
He tossed the bell-cap a twenty-dollar bill for his trouble.
Denise didn't hear the address he gave the driver as they
drove away.

Denise set up her laptop with the phone in her hotel
room and went online into her secured databases. She
started checking the names, dates, and places that Barrett
had given to her. There it was! The dates and times that
Henry Osgood had attended college at Boston University.
Henry had done his graduate work at Boston also. His
entire academic career was listed in front of her. She
printed out the listing of his classes and professors. It was
the same as Barrett had mentioned. She was hoping for
something on Michael Fitzgerald, but he wasn't in any of
Henry's classes. In fact, for a six-year period he was never
mentioned as attending Boston University. She was
disappointed.

She re-ran the diskette and noted the names of the
two professors who had now died and the listing of their
classes and class schedules.

Denise's mouth felt dry with fear as she kept
checking the information, thinking that at any moment his
name would emerge or some other connection, but there
was no connection. He had never attended the same
school.

Glancing around the room at the usual green and
beige-decorating scheme of a Holiday Inn guestroom to
clear her head, Denise noticed that her everyday planner
book had fallen out of her briefcase and fallen open to the
page with Paul's old name and address. Organizing her
thoughts, she started keying in the information on his
military and university background.

She knew of his medical and military careers. When she
found it, she began reading. It was the same data she

already knew. Both Paul and Michael had attended graduate school at University of Washington. The university had the best school of microbiology in the country.

The interesting thing was that Michael's records had just disappeared. He had started graduate school but the records did not show his undergraduate work or schools. Where did he come from? Then she saw it. He had attended Amherst, Amherst College of Massachusetts. Amherst located in Boston. He had attended only for a few semesters before he transferred to the University of Washington. She keyed in a few more commands and found the listing of his classes and professors on the database of the University that she had linked on through the Net. He was in the Boston area but not at the school. At least she had the location, but there was no mention of the problem that Terry had mentioned that night back in Bayside about Michael's work being stopped, confiscated, and destroyed--or picked up by Uncle Sam, namely NCTR. She would have to dig deeper.

As Denise was trying to find any connection with the cases, Barrett was meeting with Lacey outside the parking garage and was being briefed on Dr. Richard Bean.

"He wasn't a well-liked man," Lacey said. "He was the type who loved money and loved to flaunt it. Turned a lot of folks off, if you get what I mean. He loved flashy dates, flashy cars, flashy jewelry, not the typical conservative doc."

"Any connections to underworld ties or anything that would have created this problem for him?" Barrett asked, as they watch the technicians in their PPE suits scour the area with detecting equipment. Once again it was as though a scene from an old science fiction movie had evolved on Madison's main street.

"None that we can fine yet, but we're looking. He did like to bet, but let's face it, our friends in the mob will deal with a lot of things, but not biological stuff, don't you think?

"God, I sure hope so. Nowadays, I don't know who is dealing with what. But at least I don't think they would want to knock off a lot of people in a town and lose all their customers, do you?"

"Who knows? Or on another note, my cop instincts are telling me that this is a local guy not a foreigner, because of the location of this particular death. We don't get a lot of different folks in this town. So it had to be someone who could mill around the garage and not be suspicious looking. Look at this." He flipped up an artist's canvas pad to show what the police artist had drawn for him, sketching the garage and the contaminated cars. "The cars are randomly selected, probably by his ability to open them with his remote control device. He had to wander around and slip into each one for a few minutes to disperse the agents into the vents. But the one thing we did get back from the lab is that the amount of spores on Dr. Bean was stronger than on any other case. More dosage of the agent. Any thoughts on that?" he asked.

Barrett nodded, as though a bell had just gone off, "our guy may have been after only Dr. Bean and the rest of the victims were unlucky enough to have electric car locks."

"Bingo," replied Lacey.

"Who was Bean seeing in the past few months, women, friends?"

Lacey pulled his pad from his white shirt pocket and flipped it open. "A Miss Stacey Hursh lives over on Fourteenth Street, Bel Air apartments, apartment 2B. I understand she is another story in herself. Be careful." He smiled.

"You want to go with me," teased Barrett.

"Nope, I will leave this one to you, as I have some more leads to run down. I will be in touch soon."

"Thanks, Lacey, thanks for the info and the help. Say hello to the family." Barrett headed for the rental car.

Finally, from the ringing of the apartment doorbell several times, Stacey Hursh appeared, dressed in loose-gauzy material with tear stained makeup and uncombed hair. It was apparent she was upset.

"Miss Hursh?" Barrett asked in a calming voice.

"Yes," she whispered through the half-opened door.

"I'm Dr. Barrett Hayden from Incline and I need to talk to you about Dr. Bean. I know this is hard for you, but I need all the information I can get right now."

"You don't look like the police," she said opening the door and motioning Barrett into the lavishly decorated room.

"I'm not a policeman. I am a special investigator with Incline Investigations. We are looking into the death of Dr. Bean on another level."

"Please sit," she tried to smile and sat down across from him. "Can I get you a drink, soda, coffee, anything stronger?"

"Yes, a soda would be fine, if its not too much trouble."

"No, no trouble," she said.

"Anything stronger or in your soda? I'm having one more shot of Scotch myself."

"No, soda is fine." He replied.

She returned with her makeup a bit tidier and her hair combed, handing him a glass brimming with red wine. Smiling a little, she leaned over. "Now, what can I do for you?"

"This isn't exactly soda," he said, as he took a small sip and set it down on the table, "I need a bit more information about Dr. Bean, if you don't mind. We are trying to figure out who would want to hurt him, much less murder him."

"Murder him? I thought this was a case of anthrax which I though he had contracted at the hospital from one of his patients or doctor friends," she cried.

"No, Miss Hursh, we are dealing with something a little more serious." He realized he was taking a chance confiding in this woman. "My agency believes it is a madman who might have been after Dr. Bean only and the other people just got in the way."

"Why am I not surprised? Please call me Stacey," she smiled. "Richard had a way of pissing people off. In fact most of the time he was a son-of-a-bitch, but hey, I loved him in my own way." She took a large gulp of Scotch.

"How did he piss people off?" Barrett asked, watching a little trickle of Scotch drip down and onto her luscious white top.

"He was a rich pig and he flaunted it. Instead of enjoying it and sharing it or even being nice about it, he was a pig. Insulting busboys, waiters, valet parkers, everyone. He was the type who was rude and obnoxious."

"To you also? I can't believe anyone would be rude to you, Stacey," he whispered.

She smiled. "Thanks, I try to be nice at all times to everyone myself, but yes, he was mean and rude to me. He came and went as he pleased and he showed me no respect, no respect at all. I hate to say it, but I don't think I will miss anything, but his money." She laughed.

"I am sorry to hear that. Anyone should know how to be nice to a lady like you, " Barrett replied with a wink.

"Barrett, how long you going to be in town?" she purred.

"Only tonight. Tomorrow I have to leave for DC. Another problem, but thanks for the information and when I come back I hope you will let me call you." He knew he would never talk to her again, but it always helped to keep channels open in case he needed to get more information.

"I'd like that," she said.

"Good," he replied. "By the way, do you know anyone who might want to hurt Richard?"

"Just pull a name out of a hat and you will have everyone. No limits, no thoughts." She smiled.

Walking him to the door, Barrett detected a heavy sigh from her, but that was about all of her emotional state she shared with him. She touched his sleeve. "Come back Barrett and we can talk some more."

"I will. I will be back soon," he whispered as he pulled the door closed behind him.

Apparently this Dr. Bean was not a real crowd pleaser with anyone, Barrett thought, as he headed for the rental car and thoughts of a soft bed, the hotel, some peace and quiet and rest.

Chapter 20

Nags Head, N.C.

It has been so easy locating **him** and following **him** through his daily walks. He was so predictable. Going for his late afternoon walks and then leaving his old, gray, tattered sweater on the bench. It was so easy to lift the nasal spray from his sweater pocket and replace it with the contaminated one. Getting the agent into the other nasal sprays had been a cinch. Now, it remained only to fly up to Boston for the last act to finish the job. It's all too brilliant; too good for this world.

Bayside, Maine

It was nearly a week later after the New Hampshire outbreak. Denise, Barrett, and Henry had returned to the setup in Maine, the makeshift offices in the Health Department, the hotel rooms. In the time she had spent in Madison Denise had talked to Paul only a couple of times about the cultures and the investigation. He had accepted the fact that no personal decisions were going to be made or discussed in the middle of this outbreak. He also appeared distressed about not being able to control the situation at both outbreaks. The outbreak in Madison had wound down. No more cases had been reported. They had lost the seven cases that had been admitted on the same day but thanks to the swift action of the young resident at the hospital, the hospital and staff were spared an epidemic.

Sitting at the same table at KC's restaurant, eating fried seafood with Barrett and Dane from CDC, and with Henry and Sierra, who had become a couple, Denise felt eager to get started on the reports that Terry had generated from his labs.

They had become regulars at KC's and were recognized and accepted by the town locals. Barrett had been disappointed and yet not surprised by the findings of Denise's report about Michael's history. It had certainly cleared Henry, but Henry was still confused and wanted to know more about the common connection between his professors and their deaths. Barrett had made several discreet visits away from the sites but he never disclosed them to Denise or Henry. She knew Barrett was following up some ideas and leads but she also didn't really want to know what was involved.

Paul was making frequent visits back to Bayside, but he had very little to do with Denise, Barrett, or Henry. Everyone was so demoralized that they had come so far with the investigation and still had no clear-cut answer.

"I think we need to examine the area again. Maybe we missed something," Dane, the tech from CDC, who had been adopted by the Incline group, wondered aloud.

"I don't know, Dane. We have been over the area, the data, and the cases. It is so baffling. This nut is really good. First the use of asthma inhalers and then randomly selected cars in a parking garage. This maniac has to be stopped and soon. We usually find our fugitives and take care of them. How about you?" Barrett asked.

Dane smiled and said, "Man, we go all over the place, investigating everything from A to Z. Sometimes we get lucky: sometimes we don't. But we are out there looking for bugs created by other bugs, bad food, animals and so on and not two-legged maniacs. We get the headlines for the good investigative work and we don't release the facts on the outbreaks that just go undiagnosed or never answered. It is a game of science and chance. We catch hell for not being fast enough or smart enough, not talking enough, but we have always been there working our asses off and protecting this country from things they haven't even heard of. We will continue to do that because that is why we are here and that is why we went into the public health service. To serve. Well, enough of that, I have to admit this one is a little out of my league and my territory and I suppose that is why you guys are here. That's why we love it, right?" He took a deep swallow of his beer.

"Yeah, but we need to get lucky soon," Henry said, as he chewed the greasy fried shrimp. "This is going on forever. I'd like some answers. I need to know what's going on. All I can do is keep helping Terry run the specimens. Besides, you know Martin is going to call us all back home soon."

"Home? Home? Is there such a place?" said Barrett. "I don't remember a home, a bed, anything except this place and this delicious food. This, by the way, has helped add a few inches to my waist."

"You look fine," said Denise. "Besides, I know you are still up every morning at the crack of dawn, getting in your three-to five-mile jog."

"Well, it is getting harder and harder . . . "Barrett was interrupted by his beeper. He glanced down at the number on the panel. "Shit! It's the office." He jumped up and walked over to the counter, pulling his phone from his pocket. He punched in the numbers and listened carefully. The expression on his face went from concern to shock.

"Let's go, guys!" he said, as he tossed three twenties onto the table. He didn't want to talk to anyone; he just wanted his people out of there.

"See you, Dane. We will be in touch." He waved Dane off as he put Denise and Henry into the rental car.

"What now?" Henry asked, knowing it was not going to be good news.

"We have an outbreak in North Carolina near Nags Head. So far, it looks like the same strain, and the people in charge have taken the necessary precautions. They have quarantined the area, isolated the patients, and called in the groups. They have reported six cases, with one death so far. Needless to say, we are headed to the hotel to pack a few things, make a few calls and get going." He reached down for his phone in his briefcase. Punching in the numbers, he heard the ring, "Hello, Susan? I just got off the phone with the big guy. Tell me the status of travel arrangements." He listened to Martin's secretary, Susan, go through the necessary explanations.

"Thanks, Susan. Just to let you know: It will be Denise, Henry, and me. All three of us are going on down to North Carolina. I think Henry can use the new samples to compare with Maine and New Hampshire. Book us as close to the site as you can. You have? Great! What's the name of it?" he asked. "Thanks, Susan. You're a lifesaver. We'll be in touch." He replaced the phone. "Well, we're on our way to Nags Head. Tickets are at the airport. We're in a quaint little motel called the Sea Spray. I can just imagine the decor, but that's life. The mobile unit is on its way. So grab your swim suit, your sandals, and your money, although we will never get to use them, and lets be off again."

Rushing through the airport to catch the departing flight, Denise realized she would never get used to this rushed traveling. Whatever she had left at the room in Maine, she would have to pick up at the next location. They barely made the gate and were seated when Barrett leaned over and said, "Our friend is in the back of the plane and is making the trip with us. Just wanted you to know."

"Our friend?" she asked. She couldn't play guessing games now, she was too rushed, too tired, and too frustrated with coming up with nothing on her analyses.

"Yes, Paul. Apparently they got the call also. So he will be along for the ride."

"Oh," she replied. Even though the past week had been hectic, she hadn't had a chance to think too much about Paul or anyone. Barrett had not mentioned that last night she had spent with Paul and neither had she. They had once again settled into their comfortable friendship routine of working, eating, talking and traveling.

Nags Head, N.C.

Taking the elevator up to the balcony suites that Teale had gotten the three of them felt good to Denise. Maybe Martin or Teale had recognized the burnout in her voice, in her e-mails, and in her faxes. Maybe because they had been away for what seemed months, Martin had decided to treat them.

Opening the door to her suite, Denise was pleasantly surprised by the soft yellows and greens of the room. The bell-cap opened the French doors onto the balcony. The view from her room was unbelievable. She stepped out onto the balcony and breathed deeply the salty, warm air of the Carolina coast. Looking to her left she saw Barrett on his balcony two rooms down from her. They waved and laughed.

Turning around and facing the bedroom, Denise moved into the muted room. Realizing that the bell-cap had not closed the door, she started for it when Paul walked in.

"Hi, helluva a place, isn't it?" He smiled.

"Yes, are you here? Are you staying here?"

"Of course, next door. I thought you knew. I saw you board the plane, in your usual rush. I guess it's just the fates, yes?" He reached for her. And as he did she let him take her and hold her and kiss her hair. She needed it. It had been so long since anyone had just held her. She melted for a moment. Just for a moment.

Stepping back and placing her hand on his chest, she said, "Wait, what is this?"

"This is a man kissing and touching a woman he has missed so much. It's very natural, very honest, isn't it?"

She stepped toward him again. "Yes," she said simply.

They stood in their embrace for several minutes, not moving, not kissing, and just swaying in each other's arms. She didn't want to think. She didn't want to decide. She just wanted to feel something, anything.

"Dinner tonight at eight?"

"Yes." He reached down and kissed her on the forehead and was out of the door before she could open her eyes.

A sudden knock at the door jarred her out of her reverie. Was it a dream, or was he just here in her room with her in his arms?

"I see you have made contact," came Barrett's remark, as she opened the door.

"Yes, I have made contact. I think." She shook her head as though to come out of a daze.

"Let's go. I called downstairs and got us a car. We are headed out to the site. Henry is taking a cab to the Health Department to do some looking around there. We'll join him later. You ready? Do you have your things?" She knew he was asking because of her befuddled movement and gaze.

"Yes, I have it all, let's go." She didn't want to talk about it.

Driving to the hospital in the gray sedan, Denise could feel the soft, warm breeze on her face and arms through the window she had rolled down. The change in scenery, temperature and atmosphere was magical. She liked this place, even if she was here to investigate another deadly outbreak. She liked this place.

Barrett turned off the main road and followed the paved side street to the back of the hospital. Arriving at the hospital, they both recognized the Health Department cars, the NCTR vans, the FBI agents in their familiar dark blue suits, the CDC epidemiologists and the Incline biohazard transport truck,already there.

Opening her door and stepping out, Denise realized that this entire scene was becoming very casual to her. Too casual! One should never get this complacent with a deadly bacterium or with death. As she looked over at Barrett, she saw a grin cross his face, and she looked to see whom he had recognized.

Clifford was walking down the back steps toward them.

"Hi, there, welcome aboard." He smiled.

"Hi, Clifford. When did you get here?" Denise asked.

"Last night. Martin sent me out to help you guys save the world. Besides you sounded a bit tired on the last conference call. And another good thing--I helped Teale make the arrangements for the accommodations."

"So you are responsible for that. Thank you. Very nice. Especially after the Holiday Inn in Maine. It's very nice."

Clifford turned to Barrett, handing him a printout. "You're welcome. Barrett here's your list of cases. So far ten cases and three deaths. The local team did a good job of isolating it and testing for the strain. I guess everyone on the East Coast is a bit concerned since the other outbreaks haven't been identified yet."

Barrett glanced at it and said, "Did you make sure Henry got one?"

"Yes, I gave it to Dr. Nick Hampton, the State Epidemiologist, to give to him. I wrote the cell phone number on the list, in case Henry needed to reach you."

"Thanks, Clifford. Good man. I appreciate your taking care of this. Once again, we are right on the situation early, so maybe this time we can get a break and finally come up with an answer."

"With luck and good investigating, you can," Clifford's voice responded, tinged with eternal optimism.

Quickly getting her things together, Denise walked over to the Incline van to speak to the crew. Paul walked around the corner of the van, passing her. He didn't speak. He walked over to Barrett, reaching out and shaking his hand. "It looks like it's the same. My people have done the test, run the numbers, and it's the same. I'd be willing to bet on it. There are a couple of other things you need to know, Barrett."

Barrett looked at Paul expectantly, "Hell, I'm afraid to ask."

"It seems the carrier this time is nasal sprays"

"You have got to be kidding! Aren't those things supposed to be sealed and shrink wrapped?"

"No, unfortunately nowadays, some of the boxes are not sealed and most of the bottles are made of plastic and can be easily punctured with a syringe or easily dusted. We're wasting our time at this hospital, except for talking to the cops."

"Jesus, Paul! Do you know what this means?" Barrett asked. Both of these scientists were man enough to forget any personal differences when they were dealing with as deadly a situation as this one.

"Yes, it means we have yet another outbreak, set by a nut. I can't decide if he is doing this for money, for politics, for show, or what?" He said, "No one has received any calls claiming responsibility. No ransom demands. Nothing! What is this idiot after anyway?" He turned to Barrett.

"I don't know. Maybe he is not after anything. Maybe he just likes to kill and destroy."

"Are you kidding?" Clifford moaned after overhearing the last comment and moving closer to Barrett. "Are you saying all of these outbreaks have been set by a nut, just for the fun of it? I can't believe that." He whistled.

Barrett glanced across at Paul and recognized that they were thinking the same thought. Yes, we have another outbreak, set by the same person. A nut who has found a clever and easy way to get rid of anybody he wanted to. Who demands or wants nothing. But Barrett still wasn't ready to trust Paul or share anything with him. Paul wasn't going to share anything with Incline, either. Incline was the small bio-terrorist unit out of the White House and was lucky to be invited to investigate these outbreaks. It was a small outfit compared to NCTR and CDC. Incline was there only at the agreement of the other two agencies.

"Come on, Denise, let's talk to some of the crew," Barrett said, as he quickly walked away from Paul and Clifford. Denise could feel the resentment, the confusion, and the frustration in everyone. She smiled at Paul and motioned for Clifford to follow.

"Clifford, this is not for discussion. Learn this real fast and right now. No more outbursts like that. If you think, feel, or see anything you don't understand, you see me first. Keep everything to yourself until you get to Denise or me. Do you understand?" Barrett said flatly.

"I know, Barrett. I am sorry. I will be more careful. It just floored me to think that all of this for the past several weeks has just been the handiwork of a nut case," Clifford said simply.

"I know. It was a shock to me also, but all the data, all the tests keep coming up the same. So bear with us."

They spent the afternoon on site, examining samples and talking to the other technicians. Most of the techies agreed it looked the same as the other outbreaks. The three agencies at the hospital had almost the same people at all three outbreak sites, and by now everyone knew each other. No spores had been discovered anywhere in the area where the body of the last victim had been found. Things were getting stranger and stranger.

Denise talked to Dane about what he was looking at these days and how he was dealing with it.

"All I want to do lately is just get home, get into my single-engine plane, and just fly away and lose myself," Dane admitted wistfully. "How about you?" he asked.

"Well, flying is not my gig, as you know. I think I want to get back to my house and sit on my patio and read a good book. No phones, no people, no travel, but I think that's a long way away for now. See you back at the hotel," she called as she walked away.

Driving back to the Sea Spray, Barrett answered his cell phone. "Yes, I've got it. Well! Well! What do you know?" He smiled, replacing the phone.

"What was that about?" Clifford asked from the back seat. He sat up to hear the answer.

"Some very good information that might just check out before the day is over. I have to make a few more calls, but we are getting there, slowly but surely. We are getting there."

When they arrived back at the Sea Spray Hotel, Denise made her excuses to Barrett and Clifford and went to her room. Barrett left to talk to the police.

As she was stepping out of the shower, Denise looked around the bathroom. How many hotel bathrooms had she been in now? They all looked the same. Maybe this one was a little nicer. She had almost forgotten about her nice, cheery condo. She stayed in touch with her neighbor, Nancy, who took care of the plants and just generally kept an eye on her place. Maybe she would get home soon.

The phone rang. It was Paul. "I'll pick you up in fifteen minutes," was all it took.

Paul's rented Sebring convertible sped across the blacktop with the wind blowing and the music blaring.

Denise felt as though she was a teenager again. He reached over and squeezed her hand. She smiled. There was no need for words; he couldn't hear them anyway. Besides, they both knew she was back where she belonged. With him.

Pulling up to the secluded restaurant on the Outer Banks, Paul parked away from the lighted area. He turned to Denise, "Are you okay with this, dinner, me, you?"

She smiled, "It doesn't matter whether I am or not. I think fate has decided that this is the way it should be." She leaned her head back against the seat and closed her eyes, inhaling the soft, salty night air and smiling.

In an instant she felt his lips on hers. With what seemed no movement at all he was there, without touching any part of her body except her lips. She returned his kiss, opening her mouth to receive his tongue and his kiss. With the second probe of his tongue his arms had encapsulated her, and she had taken him into her opened arms. It was all so natural, so real. She reached up and stroked his face and then reached behind him releasing his ponytail and accepting the fact that this was the way it was and that she was too tired to fight it. The movement of his tongue with hers, his gentle caressing of her breast, his hand gliding over her knee and thigh was so natural. He pulled back and looked at her with those aroused, glowing brown eyes. "How hungry are you?"

She pulled his face closer to his and replied, "I am just hungry for you, that's all." He pulled her over to himself, and starting the car, he drove. Damn the seat belts, damn the world, and damn the nut with the killer disease. Tonight was theirs, and they recognized that with their sixth sense.

Stroking his face and kissing his neck as Paul sped along the black top, she realized he had no idea where he was going. After a while he pulled onto a dirt road and followed it back to a deserted cove. No house, no people, just a dock with a small, broken down fishing boat.

Opening the door, he pulled her to himself and lifted her out of the car. He carried her toward the boat and set her down on the dock. He removed his coat, tossed his holster off to the side, removed his shirt and spread it down on the dock to create a makeshift bed. She wanted to laugh. How thoughtful he was! She didn't need a bed, a mattress, a song, a dance, anything. All she needed was him . . . his mouth, his eyes, his tongue, his touch. And that is what he gave her as he devoured her and she devoured him. No words were spoken, no commitments made. Just sheer love and joy for the pleasure of each other. She lost herself in him again and gave herself completely until she was totally spent and then she turned to him smiling and fell asleep in his arms.

The singing of the beeper aroused her out of a deep, satisfied sleep. Paul raised her up half way off his arm to reach his beeper. "Damn. Sorry, darling," he said as he reached over for his pants. Clicking off the beeper and glancing at the neon-lit panel, he murmured, "Here we go again." He laid her back down on his rumpled coat and shirt and walked to the car to retrieve the phone. He placed the call and talked quietly for a moment and then walked back. He dropped to his knees beside her and stroked her face, her neck, her breasts, and her belly.

"Each time I am with you I think it couldn't get any better, but it does. The last time we made love and you left me, I thought I would die and then tonight it was even better; perfect. I do enjoy you; I love being with you, and I love you." He reached down to kiss her shoulder.

Denise cradled his head against her shoulder and felt his hair on her breast, "I love you, too," she whispered in his ear.

He squeezed her other shoulder and looked at her. "Thank you for this, thank you for coming with me, thank you for being you, but now yet again it is back to the real world."

She laid her head down on the wooden dock. "Bad news?"

"No, same old news. Report in. The usual."

She sat up and smiled. "Yes, I know. Thank you, Paul. Thank you for this."

Chapter 21

Nags Head, North Carolina

Arriving back at the hotel, Denise decided to treat herself to a nice, hot bath. They had said their good-byes in the lobby. She didn't care or want to know where he was going. She was too happy and too satisfied to care. Paul had taken her away for a few hours. Away from this scary, frightening place where nothing was known anymore. Her formal education, the best medical education of her peers could not help them put their finger on the culprit right now. She took the elevator up to her room, let herself in, and crossed to the bath, discarding her clothes one piece at a time. She started the water, making it hot so she could relax, sprinkling the hotel bath salts in the water as it bubbled up. She walked back into the bedroom to retrieve her nightgown out of the bureau. She noticed the red message light blinking.

She retrieved her hotel voice mail; she heard Barrett's voice, *"I'm sure I don't have to ask you where you were tonight. I hope you get back in time to get this message. Meet me in the lobby at six o'clock in the morning. No bags needed. We will be doing a one-day trip. Dress for comfort. If you don't get this message in time, take the first flight back to Bayside and meet me at the Health Department. I'll wait for you there at the office until eleven o'clock. Then I have to take care of something. I'd like you with me, but if that's not feasible, if you get there late, just wait at the office. Do not try to call me or track me down. Just wait. I am very serious about this. Just wait for me."*

She glanced at the nightstand clock. It was four o'clock. She had time. She could take a much-needed bath, take an hour's nap, wake, dress, and meet him downstairs. Should she call him and tell him she would be there? No, he was probably asleep. Let him sleep. She set the alarm on the clock for 5:30.

Listening to the bath water still running, filling the tub, she slipped on a cotton tee shirt, opened the balcony doors and stepped outside. The night air was stark, still, and beautiful. She looked in the direction of Barrett's balcony. Lights were off. Of course he was asleep. As she moved back toward the door she thought she caught a gleam of a red-burning cigarette on his balcony, but no. She was tired. She needed rest.

Waking to the blaring alarm, Denise realized that she felt as though she had the one-hour sleep that she had just experienced. The warm, soothing bath had helped her relax for a brief nap, but the alarm had roused her out of that sleep. She didn't want to get up, she didn't want to go, but she had to. She knew that Barrett was counting on her and she needed to follow this through to the end.

Slipping on her jeans, her pink polo shirt, and her tennis shoes, she felt better. She took the elevator to the lobby and met Barrett in the coffee shop. She gulped her first, much-needed cup of coffee. Barrett sat across from her, dressed in his baby blue polo shirt, jeans, and running shoes.

"Rough night? Sleep well?" he smiled.

"No, a very good night. Slept like a log. Where are we headed?" She wanted the answers now.

"We are going to do a quick day-trip back to Maine to pick up some information or someone, whichever comes first. You didn't mention this to anyone, did you?" he asked.

"No, of course not. Why are we going back to Bayside? It's Sunday. Very few people will be at the office. The labs will be running at full speed, but no one else," she protested.

"We have another dead professor of Henry's, and it was done by a nasal spray. I talked to the local FBI agent and detective last night after we left the hospital. He gave me all the needed information. Hopefully this one makes only the sixth case. They've cleared all the store shelves in town of the nasal sprays and inhalers since this news. So far the local health departments and officials are keeping the media away from some of this, but the media are going to be on top of it before too much longer. You can't go around clearing off shelves of certain medications without someone taking note of it. I know hardly anyone will be at the offices today. That's the reason we need to go back today. It's a little investigation I need to do, and I thought you might like to come along. Of course, if you had rather sleep in, you can."

"No, I'm here. I'm ready to go. I have to tell you, Barrett, that I am scared. I have handled a lot of cases before, but nothing like this and this bothers me. We have no idea what or who we are looking for or where they are going to strike next. It is like playing blind man's bluff!" she said.

Barrett reached over and squeezed her hand. "I know. I've only been in this situation once or twice before, and it is frightening, but we can handle this, and I think by the end of the day I will have some answers for all of us."

Driving to the airport, they barely talked. They were in their own little worlds. Barrett in his investigative world of do and don'ts, seek and find, think and do. Denise in her confused world of Paul and this deadly outbreak.

"I visited the wife of one of the victims last night. She sat there in a daze, barely able to concentrate on her answers. She was fairly young and attractive, but this had taken its toll on her. She was the wife of Dr. Stanley Grant. She was sitting there in this old, tattered gray sweater, probably his, hugging herself as though to keep warm. It was pitiful," Barrett whispered.

"Dr. Grant. Henry's friend? What is this all about? Was Mrs. Grant any help?"

"No, she's still in shock. She couldn't think of any reason anyone would want to hurt her husband, and also we hadn't told her the entire truth. I thought I would let the cops tell her that it might be a deliberate plant and not an outbreak."

Denise didn't even try to think of where they were headed and why. She didn't want to talk about it until Barrett was ready to tell her. He parked the car at the lot on the private plane terminal side of the airport. She glanced over at him. "What? No Delta?" she asked.

"Not today, sweetheart. It's just you and me. Come on. I've reserved it. You know I'm a good pilot. Let's go."

She knew he was a good pilot, yes. She had been up with him several times on sightseeing tours of Atlanta, San Diego, and other areas, when he was trying to help her get over her flying phobia, but rarely had he flown a plane for investigative purposes. She stood in the lobby of the plane rental office, shaking the sleep from her eyes and thinking that only Barrett would go to all of this trouble. He filed his flight plan, paid with his credit card, and scooped up the log with the flight plan. "Has it been checked out, Fred?" he asked the young man at the front desk.

"Yes, sir. We did it first thing this morning. She is gassed-up and ready to go. The weather looks good. You should be in good shape."

"Thanks, Fred. I should be back later tonight, but if not, then tomorrow. If longer than two days, I'll call you. You have my card, my number, and all the info you need, okay?"

"Sure. Have a good trip. See you later."

Barrett wrapped his arm around Denise's shoulder as he walked her to the door and pulled it open for her. "You are okay with this aren't you, 'Nise? I just need to get back to the site, and I thought you might find it interesting."

"I feel fine. I wish you would tell me what's going on though. I hate being in the dark. You know that," she replied.

"I know, but I'm not sure of this, I'm still looking for the key, but I think I've just found it. I don't want to tell you until I am sure. That way, neither one of us will be disappointed." He opened the door of the Cessna on the passenger side and climbed over into the pilot seat. Denise climbed in, slamming the door securely. That was one thing she hated about flying in small planes; they were just too damn small.

Buckling up his belt, Barrett reached over and pulled her strap tighter and kissed her on the cheek. "Hold on, baby. We'll be up in a minute and off to never-never land." Denise watched how expertly Barrett handled the controls as he backed out of the parked position and headed up the runway. She leaned back and closed her eyes. She felt only a tiny lurch as the plane lifted up and she finally opened her eyes when she felt him squeeze her hand. "We're up," he said.

Glancing out the window, she could see the incipient sunrise, a wondrous sight with the hues of pink, red, yellow, and purple. She thought of the old song: The blue of the dawn meets the gold of the day. It was beautiful. She smiled at Barrett, and he smiled back.

Bayside, Maine

The flight took about three hours, and Denise was thankful there was with no turbulence. It was a quiet, easy, trip and she had napped most of the way. Arriving back at the small airport in Bayside, Barrett rented a car, and they headed for the hotel.

"I need to pick up a few clean shirts," he joked. "If you need anything from your room, go ahead and get it now, because we may be in North Carolina for a while."

Denise's hotel room looked the same, except cleaner from the work of the maid service. They hadn't given up their rooms because they didn't know when they might be returning. They had left so quickly for the other site that she had grabbed just a few things. Even now she didn't see anything she needed.

She met Barrett in the lobby. He had a new stuffed duffel bag, and she noticed that he had slipped his wind breaker on over his polo shirt even though it wasn't that cool. Then she realized why he had the jacket. As they started out the hotel door, she motioned for him to go first since he had the bag. She glanced at his back and saw the imprint of the holster against the jacket.

"Where to now?" she asked reluctantly.

"Now we go to the lab and pull a few folders, and then we may go sight-seeing, if you are up for it?" He smiled.

"Whatever," she said. She didn't know if she was scared, or being silly. She hadn't felt great since she had awakened from her sky-nap, and now to know he was armed and not talking was a bit disturbing, but she trusted him completely.

Walking through the Health Department halls on a non-work day was eerie. Even though the guard at the front desk had recognized them with their badges, it was still weird to be on the floor, which was usually abuzz with people, talk, and laughter. Now it was filled with deep silence. Denise's tennis shoes made little noises as she followed Barrett to Sierra's office and flipped on her desk lamp.

"Sierra's office?" she asked.

"Yeah, she has some information on Henry and she had the latest reports from Terry in the lab. He was comparing the Maine samples with the North Carolina samples and the New Hampshire samples just to be sure. Here it is." He picked up the computer print-out apparently left for him, because the folder in a sealed, official envelope had his name printed across the top. Barrett then reached over and thumbed through the Rolodex until he found the address he was looking for. He read it twice as though to memorize it and then he switched off the lamp and pulled Denise's hand. "Let's go."

Driving out the scenic road, Denise turned to Barrett. "Is there anything you want to tell me? Now?" she asked.

"Not yet. I hate to be so secretive, but think of it this way. You are with me. If I am right about what I think, you will know right away. If not, I'll tell you one day when I have recovered from my embarrassment of being wrong." He winked at her.

"Barrett, this is not funny now. I know you are carrying. I know you have taken and made several discreet phone calls. Now tell me what is going on. Also, were you on your balcony this morning at four o'clock, smoking?"

"Yes, I have my gun. I wear it most of the time; you just never notice it or think about it. Yes, I made phone calls. I always do. Yes, I was up at four o'clock this morning. Question is what were you doing up at that time?"

She glared at him and said, "I couldn't sleep, so I stepped out onto the balcony to get some fresh air. Are you going to tell me?"

"Not yet. I'll tell you we're headed to see Sierra. I need some more information from her on a few people, and I'll tell you this: whatever you see or hear at Sierra's, do not say a thing. Just keep your cool and remain quiet, and we just might walk out of there with the answer. I promise you that."

They pulled into the drive of a small gray bungalow with red shutters, and a carefully landscaped yard. Denise approvingly thought this would be the type of home that Sierra would live in.

Barrett knocked on the door. They could hear music from the stereo inside. Sierra opened the door, wearing shorts and a tee shirt. "Barrett, Denise, what a nice surprise! What in the world are you doing here? Excuse my appearance; I was taking it easy."

"No, excuse *us,* Sierra," Barrett said. "May we come in? I have just a couple of questions about this file you put together for me." He opened the folder and started to pull out some papers.

"Come on in," Sierra said stepping back inside to let them pass. "Can I get you some coffee?"

"I would love coffee", said Barrett with a smile.

"Yes, coffee would be fine, if you have some." Denise automatically replied. She was following his lead and had no idea where he was headed.

"I have coffee. Please come in and have a seat." She motioned them to a cream-colored sofa covered with multi-colored throw pillows. The bungalow was tastefully decorated with bright colors and very good prints on the wall. The drapes were a soft sea-foam mist, but insulated for the cold Maine winters. It was a very cozy place. Denise sat down, but she noticed that Barrett started moving around the room as though checking it out.

"What do you like in your coffee?" asked Sierra's from the kitchen.

"Black is fine for both of us." said Denise. She caught Barrett's glance and he crooked his finger to motion her over to the bookshelf. She walked over, looking at him, and then he slowly took her hand and squeezed it and with the other hand he pointed to the silver framed photograph on the bookshelf. Denise turned in the indicated direction and came face to face with a photo of Michael!

She could feel the scream start at the back of her throat, but she raised her hand to her mouth and cupped it herself. Barrett squeezed her hand again and walked her back to the sofa and sat her down. She couldn't breathe. Her heart was pounding, her mental processes frozen. This couldn't be! Not here, not now! The man who had killed her best friend, the man who had taken so many lives. The man who Barrett was chasing. Paul's best friend, and hopefully now worst enemy was here in Sierra's house!

"This is a nice surprise. Of course you will have to forgive this mess," Sierra said, as she pointed to the Sunday paper strewed across the coffee table and floor.

Denise was slowly returning to herself. She took the cup of coffee from Sierra, surprised that her hand was not shaking like her insides. She was breathing normally now, but she couldn't bring herself to look at Sierra or the photo.

"Please don't worry about it. It should be us apologizing to you for just dropping in. We had gone by the office to pick this up, and I had misplaced your number, but realized I had your address, and since it was a nice day for a drive we thought we would take our chances. I hope you don't mind?" said Barrett.

"Oh, no, not at all. Are you back from North Carolina? Is Henry with you?"

"No, just a day trip, I'm afraid. They're keeping Henry really busy right now. Denise was also admiring your garden out front. Those are beautiful flowers. Aren't they, Denise?" He touched her hand.

"Yes, Sierra." Denise couldn't believe how calm her voice sounded. "Do you have a garden in back? Could I impose on you to show it to me?"

"Certainly. I love to show my garden off. Bring your coffee and I'll give you the grand tour. Barrett coming?"

"Yes, but could I impose on you to let me make one phone call and then I will join you girls."

"Of course. The phone is there on the desk," Sierra said, pointing to the desk in the corner that held the phone, a few books and another picture of Michael.

209

Barrett walked over to the desk as Denise followed Sierra through the dining room papered in dark crimson wallpaper, into the kitchen decorated in a country motif. Denise couldn't believe her mind was admiring Sierra's decor at a moment like this. At least her mind was working despite her shock. She was listening to Sierra describe the flowers in her garden, and what each one was, and how much trouble it was to maintain them, how she loved gardening and she could only enjoy the fruits of her work for a few brief months in the summer.

Denise tried not to stare at Sierra as though she was looking at a lunatic. She wanted to grab Sierra and ask her, 'What the hell are you doing with that picture in your living room? Don't you know who that is?' But Sierra didn't know who he was even now, while she knew people where out looking for a maniac. Sierra kept talking about the weather.

Barrett opened the back door and descended the steps slowly. He walked close to Denise and put his arm around her waist and she relaxed in his embrace. He was here. She felt safe, but there were so many questions to be answered.

"This is beautiful, Sierra. You should be proud of it." Barrett was responding to Sierra's lectured tour. "I am afraid we have to be leaving soon, but I need to ask you a couple of questions about the file in the house. Can we go back in?"

"Of course, I'm sorry. If you get me on the topic of my gardening, I do get carried away," Sierra laughed.

"No problem, you should be proud of it, and thanks again for sharing it with us. It really is beautiful. I know Henry enjoys it when he is here with you," Barrett answered.

Sierra blushed. "He does. He is a very good gardener himself. He's given me several hints about growing certain plants in this area of the country. He has had dinner with me several times here, and we have sat out in the garden. I think it has helped him recover from his loss." She led them back into the house and through the kitchen, the dining room and the living room.

"Why don't you finish your coffee?" Barrett said to Denise as he seated her on the sofa. "I want to go over these numbers with Sierra." He smiled.

"Thanks," was all Denise could respond.

Barrett walked over to the desk and picked up the folder lying next to the photo.

"Are these the final numbers on the lab test that Terry ran yesterday against the samples we sent him from North Carolina? Is this the latest test?" He turned to Sierra so she could see the numbers. She stood next to him and looked at the printout. "Yes, those are the latest ones. See the date and time on the printout. Those were the tests he ran yesterday. Why? Is there a problem?"

"No, we just keep coming up with very similar numbers, and it is beginning to bother me," Barrett said. He looked from Sierra's face to the photo taking in the same dark features, eyes, and hair.

Picking up the photo, he asked, "Sierra, who is this, if I may, ask? I see a few pictures of this fellow around your den. Is this your favorite person? Don't tell me Henry has competition?" He teased her.

Sierra reached over and took the picture from Barrett. "Of course not! This is my brother, David. He is handsome, isn't he? I can't wait until he comes back for a visit. I do miss him. He stays so busy that I fly out to California to visit him. In fact, Henry and I were talking the last time we were together about the two of us making a trip out to California to visit David since he can't get here."

"Oh, yes, he is a microbiologist also. That's right," Barrett pretended his memory was coming back with the information on David. "He and Henry attended school together at Boston University. I remember now. David has been helping Henry with consultations on these latest outbreaks," Barrett continued.

211

Denise dared not look at him. She knew she would scream or panic or do something foolish if she even glanced at him now. Besides, from the tone of the conversation it was as though Sierra was very proud of her brother and had no idea what a monster he really was. "Of course," thought Denise, "Sierra doesn't know. She doesn't know him as Michael and neither does Henry. Both of them know him as David. Henry knew this man at college." Henry had never met Michael or seen a picture of him. He had not been on that outbreak three years ago in Connecticut with Harold. Denise couldn't take anymore. She stood up and cleared her throat.

"I am so sorry, Barrett, but we need to get going. We still need to make several more stops before we head back. Thanks, Sierra, for the coffee and the tour. It was very kind of you to let two wandering drifters drop in on you at home," Denise said, touching Sierra's' arm for comfort. Of course Sierra didn't know she needed comforting because she didn't even know anything was wrong or that Barrett had just stumbled onto the key to the whole case. A key that everyone had been out searching for and it had always been right here under everyone's nose.

Sierra smiled. "It was my pleasure. Are you heading back to North Carolina tonight?"

"Yes, we needed some more clothes, a few books, and these figures, so we decided to take care of everything at one time," replied Barrett. "Thanks so much for the hospitality. Speaking of David, I hope we do get to meet him soon. I know Henry says David has been a great deal of help to him throughout this investigation. By the way, I know David and Henry attended Boston U. together, but where did David do his graduate work?" Barrett asked casually.

"He spent a brief time at Amherst, and then he went to the University of Washington. He graduated from there with honors and then did some work with the military, and now he is in Irvine, California with Chemco, working with them," Sierra donated all the helpful innocent information.

"That's right. Henry had told me David was in California. Well, thanks, Sierra, for everything. Maybe when we get back here the four of us can get together for dinner."

"That would be nice," said Sierra. "Barrett, would you say hello to Henry for me? We talk every night, but still say hello for me."

"I sure will, Sierra." Barrett walked toward Denise, taking her arm and guiding her out the front door.

"Bye, Sierra, and thanks for the coffee. We will see you in a couple of weeks. I love your place," came Denise's words as she tried to sound as casual as possible.

"You're welcome. Come back to see me. Have a safe trip back!" Called Sierra from the door, as Barrett and Denise got into the car.

Barrett started the car and backed out of the drive and drove away before he spoke. "I was afraid of that. It was too easy. There were too many coincidences. In New Hampshire, when Henry recognized the names of two of his old professors, and then today, he confirmed Dr. Grant. The latest victim, as another professor who had taught both him *and* David. They were both in the same classes."

Denise laid her head against the seat and turned to Barrett. "Tell me all of it. Every bit of it. Even if Paul is or isn't involved. You have just scared me to death by making me look at that monster's picture. Now tell me the whole story, and don't leave anything out! If I am going to relive this hell and go through this again you are going to tell me all of it, do you understand?" Her insistent voiced pierced her ears.

"Yes, baby, I know. I will. Sit back and listen and I'll tell you all I know; all I have found out and all I have pieced together. Just bear with me."

On the way to the airport, he told her again how Henry had recognized the names of the professors he and

213

David had shared at Boston University. But the one thing Henry didn't realize was that after David's senior year he had left and gone to Amherst College under the assumed name of Michael Fitzgerald. His work at Amherst earlier had been condemned and he couldn't get any support, and he wanted to continue in that field. After Amherst had told him no, he couldn't work in that area, he still continued. He was doing some lab research on bio-germ warfare that he wasn't supposed to be doing. He wrote the papers and presented them to the board again, hoping for a grant to continue his research. Instead he got the shock of his life, because the board did not want anything to do with his research, no matter how far advanced it was or how significant or important. So they refused to accept the papers, much less publish them from their university. They confiscated his work, his lab, and all of his findings. Enter our good friend Dr. Wagner, who had met David as Michael Fitzgerald at some seminars earlier. He took one look at the work our Michael was doing and immediately prepped him to be the new golden hair boy for NCTR. Paul had already left the University of Washington and was working his way up the ladder in the military. He got Michael enrolled at the University of Washington to do research in that field. He left out a few minor details about Amherst because he knew how brilliant Michael was but also how controversial his studies in bio-warfare were becoming.

"I do believe Paul knew him only as Michael and is probably not aware of the David Connor person. How much he was or wasn't involved in the Connecticut outbreak I don't know. I don't think he knows what Michael is after here in Maine, New Hampshire, or North Carolina, because unless Henry has told him then he isn't aware that David and Michael are one and the same. I think Paul thinks we just have a nut case on our hands, which we do, but Paul doesn't know the reason or motivation behind Michael.

"After graduating with honors from Washington, Michael joined the military to do his own research unrestricted, because, let's face it, they would rather have a genius of his caliber on our side rather than against us. That unit lets its researchers have their way as long as they produce. Besides, how many colonels do you know on active duty who can get away with a ponytail and cowboy boots?" Barrett's question flowed through Denise's mind. Yes, how many?

"And Sierra. Is she involved?" asked Denise, trying to absorb all of this.

Barrett continued his story. "I don't think so. Sierra has never seen or heard of Michael either. Just like Henry. But that does explain why David has not been here to visit Sierra with all of us around. He keeps finding reasons not to. He could meet with Sierra and Henry in California, and they would know him as David. If you, Paul, or I were to see him, we would know him as Michael. My only concern now is, what is Michael's next plan?

"Dear God," Denise said as she sat up straight in the seat. "Is Henry in danger?"

"No, I don't think so. Besides, Bob is with him. I told Bob to stick close. That is the reason I wouldn't bring Henry today. In case my suspicious played out and David did turn out to be Michael. I didn't want Henry alerting Sierra, who would alert David. The only problem now is will she mention to David that we looked at his picture or will she just tell him we stopped by, or will she not tell him anything? I called Martin from the airport and asked him to put Sierra's phone under surveillance. And her house. So if she does call David or visit him, we'll know about it. I'm going to check in with them now. I may be gone for a few days. You just hang tough and stay on the cases, and I'll be in touch with you as soon as I can. Do not talk to Paul about this, at least not yet."

Returning to her hotel room after the three-hour return flight, Denise collapsed on the bed. The flight, the story, the truth, all of it, was a bit too much. Barrett had dropped her off at the front door and left on another trip for more information. She had promised not to mention the day's events to Paul, until they knew what he knew and where he stood on the story. The phone must have been ringing for some time before she rolled over to pick up the receiver. It was Paul. She had not bothered to check her messages when she had gotten back late last night. Now she had to deal with him and keep her mouth shut.

Chapter 22

Nags Head, North Carolina

It was just beginning to get dark as Denise stepped out of the shower. She had to get ready to meet Paul for dinner and then call Barrett at the office. Denise knew she had to talk to Paul, and she wanted to see him, but she found herself in the same situation as years ago; she could not trust him.

Passing through the lobby, she met him in the drive-through section in front of the hotel. He got out of the car and walked around it, opening his arms to her, and she walked into them. She held him for a few moments but this time she didn't feel so safe.

"Denise, where have you been? Why didn't you call me and let me know where you were and what was going on? I have been out of my mind with worry," he said.

"Barrett and I had to check out some ideas, and I had no idea where you were so I just left. I'm back now and all is well. It is a beautiful night, isn't it? Now its back to the world of intrigue and show, isn't it?" She turned to him and looked into those gorgeous brown eyes, hoping they would not deceive her again.

"I don't know about intrigue. Maybe drudgery would be more like it," he said, as he released her and opened the car door for her.

"So, what did you two find out? Anything interesting or anything that I need to know?" he asked.

Denise felt the cold chill run up her back and responded, "No, it was a dead end. Barrett thought he had found something on a lunatic microbiologist, but it wasn't there."

"I thought as much. Have you ever heard of Dr. Samuel Drefter?" he asked.

"No. Also Barrett and I have decided that this is not Michael, if that is what you are thinking. What have you been up to, anyway? Do you have anything for us? Who is this Dr. Drefter?"

"Just a name that keeps coming up. No, I keep hitting dead ends also and spinning my wheels. After a while it gets very frustrating. Also I wanted to let you know that I will be leaving tomorrow for a short trip to New York, and I am not sure how long I will be gone. That's the reason I wanted to see you before I left. I may be gone for a while," he said, slowing down, reaching over, cupping her face, and kissing her cheek.

She loved the touch of his hand on her face, and she responded, but then she drew back and smiled. "Where are we going?"

"I thought we'd try a new place that's just opened. It is supposed to have good food, great atmosphere and all of the amenities we need."

"What type of amenities do we need?" she asked, smiling

"You'll see," he replied.

The drive to the restaurant was filled with conversation of office gossip, and the latest news coverage by CNN and all of the other networks about the outbreaks as both of them tried hard to veer away from the daily happenings at the office. After weeks of the investigation, both of them were tired of the subject and all the discussions that went with it. They wanted time to have a normal, happy, conversation without the real world invading it, at least for a few hours.

The dinner was a delightful fare of seafood, with a superb wine list. Denise was feeling much happier and freer as they drove back to The Sea Spray, although she was also experiencing a feeling of nostalgia as she listened to the soft jazz on the radio.

"Thanks for seeing me again. The last time with you was unbelievable," Paul said. "I know these past weeks have not been easy for you. My coming back into your life, your questions about Barrett, the unsolved outbreaks. I know these things have taken a toll on you, so I am grateful that you agreed to spend some time with me."

"I have tried to put all of this into perspective. It has been difficult. Sometimes I feel I have no idea whether I am coming or going, but I have to get a grip on it. I am an adult woman and have to be in control of my life."

Paul pulled the car into the parking lot of her hotel and reached over and took her hand in his. "Can I come up for a few minutes?"

"Sure. Do you want me to order up a nightcap from room service?" she asked, as she got out of the car.

"No, I think just some talking and listening is all I need for right now. Besides, as I said, I wanted to let you know that I will be leaving in the morning and I may not be back for a few days. We have another problem. I have to look into, unrelated to this one," he reiterated.

Switching on the light as she entered the room, Denise flet the dismal aura of her hotel room. She was tired of it. She missed her pleasant, homey condo. She wanted to get home, and soon. Maybe the evening, the dinner, the wine, and being with Paul had made her moodier than usual.

"Have a seat." She pointed to the sofa. "I'll be right back," she said, excusing herself and going to the adjoining room to change into some sweats. She remembered times gone by when she would have put on a silky gown, but not now, not tonight.

Walking back into the room, she noticed Paul's look of disappointment, or was that just her imagination?

No, he probably had thought she was changing into a sexy gown.

Sitting down across from him, she said, "so where are you headed, and what is going on?"

"Just more grunt-work," he said. "Nothing for you to be concerned about. It's not related to the case in any way. Just off to another city, another problem." He leaned his head back against the sofa. "What about you?" he asked. "What will you do when this is over? Go back home? Back to your life in Atlanta?"

"Of course. What else would I do? That is home, that is where I want to be. Besides, my whole life is there, my house, my job, and my friends. Where else would I go?"

"I don't know. Maybe I was just thinking out loud. I have been doing a lot of that lately," he said, as he brushed his hand through his hair and leaned forward.

"Would you like some coffee?" she asked.

"No, thanks. That's probably the last thing I need."

Turning to him, Denise could see the indecision in his eyes and she reached for him. In a moment powerful arms were around her. She could feel the need building up in each of them. Once again she didn't care. She returned his kisses from the depths of her soul. She wanted him; she wanted to be with him. She needed him. Without any explanation, she started to cry. "Denise, what's wrong? What did I do? What is it? Please tell me?" He begged as he cradled her in his arms.

"I am so tired. I am tired of the death, the uncertainty, everything that has been going on, and now Barrett is off on his wild goose chase for Michael . . . "

"Michael?" Paul asked. "I thought you said Michael wasn't involved." He gripped her shoulders and turned her toward him, "You told me Michael wasn't involved. Do you know something about him? You have to tell me! This is very important. It is important to this outbreak, but more important, it is essential to our relationship. If you know where Barrett has gone, you have got to tell me! Please, Denise!"

She sat up and wiped the tears from her cheek. She couldn't take anymore. She might lose both of them now but she was willing to risk it for her own peace of mind. "Barrett has found out that Michael is David Connor and David Connor is Michael."

"What the hell? How is that? I have investigated both of them!" He seemed puzzled.

"I don't know exactly. Except that when Henry knew him in undergraduate school, it was as David. Yes, he is Sierra Connor's brother. When you met him and knew him at Amherst, he had already assumed an alias because of the trouble he had run into with the research he was doing at Amherst."

Telling the rest of the story that Barrett had told her took only a few minutes. It felt as if a great weight had been lifted from her shoulders. She knew Barrett would be furious, but she had never been good at playing this spy game with these guys. She might regret this later, but for the moment she had to let it go.

Paul, pulling her up from the sofa, encircling her in his arms, said, "Denise, this is the best thing you could do. I know you are still not very trusting of me, but now I can prove to you that I was not involved with Michael three years ago or today. This has been an issue with me since D.C. Now I can show you I was never involved. Besides, Michael is a real threat, and I need to find him for everyone's sake. Now, please tell me where Barrett has gone?"

"I have no idea. He put a tap on Sierra's phone and someone to watch her house. He thought if David tried to contact her, then he would know where and when. He is determined to catch this guy."

Paul pulled her into his chest, and, kissing her hair, he muttered, "Denise, I have to go. I have to go find both of them and take care of this, and I have to do it now."

"Now? You are leaving now?" she jerked back and shouted.

"Yes, time is very important now. I will be back, and I will tell you everything that went down. I promise."

"I don't want to know," she cried. "All I want is for you to promise you will not hurt Barrett and that you will be careful. That's all I want. Do you understand?"

"Yes, I understand completely. I will call you later."

Watching Paul leave, Denise felt extreme uneasiness over what had just occurred. She had to reach Barrett now and warn him. She grabbed the phone and started punching in the numbers for his pager. All of the training she had taken with the security agency had not been worth it until now when she didn't want any more. Now, more than ever she understood why Barrett had left his position at the FBI and gone into private security service.

Keying in her phone number for Barrett's pager, Denise realized she might have just made a deadly mistake. Telling Paul about Barrett's findings might cost all of them dearly. Especially Barrett. She was not made for this type of work. She didn't like dealing with lying, spying, cheating and terrorists. She then called Dane and asked him for the biggest favor of her life.

Chapter 23

Boston, Massachusetts

Barrett turned off the beeping on his pager and checked the number on the LED panel. It was the Sea Spray's number, probably Denise. He would call her when he landed in Boston. Now he had to get to the hotel David's phone calls had been traced to. Landing at the small airport, Barrett recognized Dick Hanson, one of his best agents, standing inside the terminal gate.

Shaking hands and walking, Barrett asked, "What have you got for me?" He pulled his backpack over one shoulder and pointed toward the closest exit door.

"Your suspect is staying at the Amherst Arms Hotel. It is a sleazy dive downtown. We have had it under surveillance since your call. We haven't seen the suspect enter or leave, but he is still registered there. He hasn't checked out yet."

"Good work! Thanks, Dick. Anything else I need to know?"

"Yeah, you may not like this, but we followed your hunch on your friend Denise," looking at his notepad and reading. "She had dinner with Col. Wagner three hours ago. He took her back to her hotel, stayed about fifteen minutes and then left in a rush. He headed for the Nags Head airport and picked up a company plane with a few of his associates, and filed a flight plan for Boston. On top of that, it seems that your phone lines at the hotel had a bug on them. It must have been placed recently, because we had just swept your room two days earlier. So someone is looking for something on you. I can't tell you how secure or unsecure your phone has been for the past few days. Sorry about that."

"That's okay. I was expecting as much. I just had a page from Denise, so she must be trying to reach me to tell me what's going on. I'll call her now." Reaching into his briefcase, Barrett pulled out his phone and punched in the Sea Spray's number, asking for Denise's room.

No one answered.

Barrett clicked the phone off, cutting Denise off. He knew she would be angry that he had not called her right away but he didn't have time to deal with her feelings right now.

"What is the address of the university?" He turned to Dick, who was driving the car.

"Just a few miles up the main street. Do you want more backup or just the two of us?"

Barrett pulled his gun out of his shoulder harness and slipped the clip into the Beretta. "I think we can handle this one ourselves. Be alert though. Others may join us at the last minute. So watch your back."

Paul had left Denise and while driving to the Nags Head airport, he had called ahead and reserved one of the agency's planes. He then called Henry Osgood and asked him to meet him at the airport, if Henry was interested in closing this case. Besides, Paul felt he could use Henry's services in taking care of any open vials of this bacterium, if confiscated. He rarely involved civilians in his work, but this time he could accomplish several things with the help of Henry. He would have an expert microbiologist with him to handle any spillage from the vial. Having Henry there would help convince Denise later that he, Paul, had no involvement in this outbreak. He was making a lot of bad moves and he knew that, but they had to be made. He had broken standard procedure by involving a civilian, by not calling his contact and alerting the staff, and by letting his personal feelings get involved with his work. But

Henry could be useful because he knew the layout of the campus, the buildings that Paul didn't have time to check out with his staff.

Henry was standing on the tarmac as Paul pulled the car into the restricted zone. Walking over to Henry, Paul extended his hand and said, "Thanks for coming, Henry. I think I have a handle on this man, and we need to take care of it right now. I usually don't involve civilians in an operation such as this one, but I decided you could be useful. It could be dangerous, so if you don't want to participate, tell me now, and you can get out and there will be no hard feelings." He looked at Henry as he signed off on the log for the plane and handed it back to the clerk.

"No, I want to go. I know it could be dangerous. I know the risks I am taking, but we have got to put a stop to this maniac before more people are killed. Where are we headed?"

"Amherst," replied Paul.

"Amherst? Do you mean this has something to do with the college? I know three of my old professors were victims, but I didn't think a university would be involved."

"No, Henry, it's not the school. It is a nut who attended the school. I need your help in identifying certain areas of the campus and the building locations, if you are game for this."

"Yes," Henry answered in a muted voice, still trying to figure out what the one link with him, his school, and the dead professors was.

"Good. Let's go."

Dane had agreed to pick Denise up and fly her to Boston. She signed onto the Net, punching in Boston and the address she had for Amherst College of Massachusetts. The laptop had printed out a map she and Dane could

225

follow to the campus. She was scared of the flight, and fervently hoped Dane was as good a pilot as Barrett.

As Paul and Henry arrived at Logan Airport, Paul figured he was probably fifteen or twenty minutes behind Barrett. He and Henry got into the car that was waiting for them at the airport and Paul called his contact.

"Are they here? How many? Where are they? How long ago did they get here? Where are they now?" Paul asked the pointed questions in rapid succession on the phone.

After hearing the answers, he snapped the cell phone closed. He turned sideways to Henry, keeping one eye on the road but talking to Henry. "Henry, do you know how to fire a gun?"

"Yes, I'm a good marksman. I try to do some hunting every once in a while. I am handy with a rifle, handgun, or shotgun. Why?"

"Good," Paul said, pulling out the .38 special. Handing it to Henry, he said, "Take this. Get comfortable with it. I don't want you to use it unless it is absolutely necessary. I don't want you injured. I want you to be able to protect yourself. I think we are going to run into only one person. My sources tell me he is a solo nut. He doesn't belong to an organization. We are fairly sure he is working alone, on his single vendetta against the staff and the school."

"Paul, can't you tell me who it is?"

"Not definitely yet. I want to be very sure myself. We have made one positive ID and we think it is my old friend Michael Fitzgerald," replied Paul in a husky voice.

"Michael? From years ago, I thought he was gone or dead. I thought your group had taken care of him some time back."

Paul glanced at Henry. "I thought we had, too. Apparently, he has gotten away again, but now we have him, and we can stop him this time."

"Why Amherst? What is he planning?"

"I think he plans to contaminate the entire school campus. The buildings, the classes, the faculty locations-- everything on campus. It's his sick way of getting back at the people and the school for what they did to him."

In the remaining time it took Paul to drive to the campus, he explained the findings he had made about Michael and his destroyed career before Paul had met him and given him a chance as a student at the University of Washington and in the military service.

"You mean to tell me, knowing he was a nut doing research in bio-warfare, you still took him and offered him a position to do research for your organization."

"Of course. Some of the best people in our group are intelligent nuts," Paul said with a short grin laugh.

"I don't find this amusing at all," said Henry, in a disbelieving voice.

"Think of it this way, Henry. Hadn't you rather they work for us than for others. Like our friends in Iran or Iraq? At least this way we can take advantage of their brilliant minds and keep some type of control on their allegiance."

"Allegiance? Are you kidding? These people don't have any allegiance to anything or anyone. Maybe to money or to some sick idea of the Utopian world they are looking for."

"I know, Henry. Believe me, I know more than you do about that. For the time being, that is the best we can come up with, so bear with us," he said, as he pulled up to the entrance gate that read AMHERST COLLEGE. Paul drove the car past the sign and parked a block away.

"Henry, now, this could prove dangerous. Are you sure you want to do this?" he asked one last time.

227

Henry took a deep breath and said, "Yes, I have to do this, because too much is at stake for me and others."

Opening the car door, Paul turned to Henry and said, "In case Michael sets off another canister of the agent, I need you here to tell my technicians how much antitoxin is needed to combat it."

Getting out of the car, closing his door softly, Paul turned to Henry and said, "Ready?"

"Ready."

Michael sat in the dark basement of the chemistry building. He was thinking about his phone call earlier today to Sierra. She had been very happy about his supposed trip to Europe, and she had agreed that she and Henry would fly to New York City to visit with him before he left. It would be a good reunion and a good send-off for Michael. He was glad Sierra had found someone for her future. It was even better that it was his old friend Henry. They'd make a good couple. Sierra needed someone in her life. Especially now, because once Michael left the country, he would not and could not ever come back.

The calculation he had made earlier in the day had assured him that if he spread the agent in the air vent compressor at the site, then the entire building would be contaminated within hours.

As soon as the students entered the buildings with the air conditioning fans blowing, they would breathe the bacteria into their lungs. He would empty other vials into each building's condenser. He would empty one also in the administration building and one on each main floor and at the entrance to each building. The agent would remain virulent as long as the moving air kept it floating. As soon as any person inhaled it, that person would contract the disease. Michael waited for the footsteps of the guard upstairs to ascend to the second floor before he would go upstairs and spread the hideous contents of the second vial. The inhalation mask he was wearing was uncomfortable and hot, but necessary.

Dane and Denise arrived at Logan in a rush. Incline had sent a car. Denise gave the address and the directions to the driver and they headed out for the campus. Denise prayed she would not be too late. Dane was elated about being involved in an intelligence search instead of a bug search.

Barrett motioned for Dick to go around to the back of the chemistry building and to let himself in through the back entrance. Barrett was going in through the basement window. He glanced at the miniature map he had created from Michael's lost diskette and memorized the location of the basement windows and the stairs leading up to the hallway. Rounding the building, he used his jack-knife to pry open the lock on the basement window. Laying his backpack on the ground and taking the inhalation mask out of the bag, he pulled it over his face. Maybe it wasn't necessary at this time but he couldn't afford that risk. He had packed two masks. One for him and one for Dick. He had reminded Dick to put it on just before entering the building. The plan on Michael's lost and found diskette indicated he would release it only inside the building and not outside. Barrett hoped the nut stuck to his plan.

Paul and Henry inched up to the chemistry lab and Paul grabbed Henry's arm. He motioned to the black bag he carried, and Henry took it and unzipped the bag. Paul reached in and pulled out the black outer-space-looking ventilation masks. Henry wanted to reject his, but decided that in his best interest he had better accept it and put it on.

Paul motioned to Henry to follow him as they headed for the side door of the first floor of the chemistry building. Henry's heart was pounding as he watched Paul easily unlock and open the door with a lock pick. No alarms, no bells. They walked in and closed the door. No lights were on, and Paul removed his mini-flash-light from his pocket. The light shone on the floor of the main storage room. The room was filled with office supplies, papers, books, computer disks, computer printer cartridges, lab boxes of test tubes, and other supplies. Slowly walking to the door that led to the offices, Paul put his finger up to his mask to ask Henry not to speak. Gently turning the doorknob, he opened the door to the administration office's secretary's room. Henry had been in here several times years ago; it had not changed at all. His presence tonight was completely different from years ago. He could still feel the atmosphere of knowledge, the books, the papers, and the works. He noticed freshly waxed floors and the slight hint of cleaning polish the maintenance man had used earlier on the desk.

Paul turned to Henry and winked as if to let him know that now they would be entering the main hallway. Henry took a deep breath and moved toward the glass-topped door that led out into the hall. Paul turned the doorknob and eased the door open slowly to avoid any creaking sounds. The door didn't creak. It opened slowly and quietly. They both tip-toed across the hall to the staircase. One staircase went up to the open second floor; the other one went down to the closed door leading to the basement. Paul froze, taking his Beretta out and clicking the magazine into place. He seized Henry's arm and motioned to the stairs. They heard the sounds of footsteps softly coming up the stairs from the basement. Turning his flashlight off, he reached over and pressed his arm across Henry's chest and pushed him fast against the wall. Whoever was coming up the stairs would pass right by them. The intruder would never notice them if he weren't using a flashlight.

Denise and Dane entered the first floor of the chemistry building through the side door, which had been left open. Denise could barely breathe. These were the scenes she had never developed a taste for.

"What's that?" Dane whispered when Denise pulled her .38 Special from her purse and laid her purse on the floor.

"A gun, Dane. That's the reason you are going to stay here in this storage room. You are unarmed, and this may get out of control. I can't afford to have anything happen to you, agreed?"

"Yes. No way, you won't get an argument from me," he replied, sitting down on the closest box.

Denise patted him on the shoulder and smiled. She started toward the door. She would have to feel her away along because all she knew was that the door opened into the hall.

Michael had an uneasy feeling as he was quietly ascending the staircase. He couldn't identify it, but he felt someone else was near. He knew the night watchman was making his rounds on the second or third floor by now. Reaching the top step of the staircase, Michael stopped. Turning right, he headed into the information offices. Starting across the corridor, he stopped without turning, and listened again.

In the dark corridor Paul reached his arm across Henry, pressing even harder against the wall and watched Michael crossing the hall diagonally across from them. As he started to move, he heard other footsteps coming up the stairs. Apparently the mask had kept Michael from hearing the same steps.

'Shit,' thought Paul. 'I thought he would be alone. I never thought he would have an accomplice.' But if he remained calm he could get both of them.

Reaching the top step, in the dark hallway Barrett caught a glimpse of a figure reaching to open the door to the Information Room. Gripping his gun and stepping out in the hall, Barrett flipped the overhead light on.

"Freeze, Michael," he yelled.

"Freeze, yourself!" screamed Paul from behind Barrett.

Michael turned to fire as Paul fired twice. Both bursts of gunfire hit Michael in the chest. Blood splattered onto the wall and spewed from his chest.

Paul turned and pointed his pistol at Barrett. Barrett raised his mask and gasped, "It's me, Paul."

"Damn, Barrett! I almost shot you. What the hell?"

Henry dropped his gun to the floor.

The sound of running steps heralded Dick coming around the corner. The shouts of the guard two floors up came, "What the hell?"

"Easy, Paul, it's Dick, my man," Barrett shouted. Denise entered the hallway and stared across the hall at Paul and then Barrett. "It's me," she shouted.

"Damn, Denise. What the hell are you doing here? Where the hell is your mask?" Paul shouted.

"Dane and I are here," she screamed, realizing that she was probably in a contaminated building.

Barrett screamed back, "Take this, damn it, put it on." Pulling his face mask off he tossed it to her.

"Where the hell is Dane?" He was still shouting as she pulled the mask on.

"He's downstairs," she cried.

"Well, get him, and get the hell out of here!" shouted Barrett.

Pulling the mask off, Denise ran back into the storage room. She grabbed her purse and Dane's hand. Dane was still seated on the box.

"Come on, Dane, the building has been contaminated. Let's get the hell out of here!" Climbing out the window and running out onto the campus, Denise started toward the front of the building, where police cars and other vehicles had started arriving, sirens were blaring. Dane followed at a fast pace.

Paul lowered his gun. Barrett holstered his gun and walked over to Michael. He raised the mask and pulled it off. Paul turned to Barrett, "I hated to spoil your show. But I had to end this one myself. Especially since he was my friend years ago. He had already cost me so much in my life. I couldn't believe he had gone so wrong. How did you figure out he would be coming back here?"

"David!" shouted Henry through the mask. "It's David Connor! You have shot the wrong man! You have killed an innocent man!" he cried, as he knelt down by David and cradled his head.

"No, Henry," said Barrett. "David is Michael and Michael is David."

"What are you talking about?" Henry's voice sounded disbelieving. "I've known this man for years. He is not your nut Michael!"

"Yes, he is." came Paul's quiet reply. "I knew him as Michael when he worked for me. Barrett knew him then also. You knew him as David. That's the reason he didn't come back to visit Sierra after the outbreaks started. He knew he could be identified by all of us as two different men."

The guard came running down the stairs, at the ready. "Stop. Be still!" he commanded.

"Easy officer," said Paul as he slowly reached for his ID and slowly showed it to the guard. "We need your help. We have a contaminated building. It has been sprayed with anthrax. Is anyone else in the building?"

"No, not that I know of," came the guard's astounded voice.

"Good, let's take this body outside and make the calls from outside. I think this is one time the police and other investigators won't mind our moving the body. Considering the circumstances, let's get the hell out of here."

Paul, Dick, Barrett, and Henry slowly lifted Michael's body from the blood-smeared floor and headed for the door.

At that moment the doors burst open with strange alien-dressed men shouting and shoving. A group of masked men took the body from Barrett and Paul and started for the outside. Barrett saw the flashing lights of the police cruisers and ambulances outside producing a weirdly melodramatic atmosphere and Paul took care of explaining to the local authorities the events of the night. The beating of the helicopter's prop as they hovered overhead shining an eerie spotlight on the building added to the drama. After several seconds of identifications and explanations, the NCTR van pulled up and the space-suited technicians started to close off the area with the *"hazardous material"* tape, as others in their biological containment suits began working in the basement and other contaminated rooms of the building. Another group headed for the upstairs to make sure there were no more dispersing devices set to go off.

After removing the mask and sitting breathlessly down on the grass, "So, how did you know he would show up here?" Paul asked Barrett.

"We found a disk he had dropped weeks ago. It had the names of the professors he planned to knock off. Three of them he had already gotten rid of. As a last after-thought he decided to take his revenge out on the

234

university. Sick man. How did you know where I was headed?" Barrett asked.

"Yeah, very sick. I had you followed. Sorry. You weren't sharing a hell of a lot of information, and I had to get this guy. And Denise . . ." Paul turned to Henry. "Henry, are you okay?" He asked.

Henry, staring at the blood-smeared face of his good friend, looked up at Paul, and said, "I don't understand. I've known this man for years. He was a good, kind man. He was a brilliant scientist. What happened?"

"Not now, Henry. We'll tell you later," said Barrett.

Standing up, Barrett angrily said to Paul, "What in the hell is Henry doing here, anyway? You shouldn't have involved him. He could have easily been killed."

"I know. I just wanted him to see what was going on, and I needed him to confirm that we could handle the bacteria that have been set in the basement. But I don't think he can even think now and . . ."

They were interrupted by one of the suited men in NCTR garb. "We only found one hot area downstairs and we can contain that one, but I suggest you folks move further away from the building and also find the wash-down vans right now!"

"Henry, there's nothing else we can do, but go home." He paused. "Are you ready for that?" He helped Henry up and headed toward the van.

Henry looked at Barrett. "What am I going to tell Sierra? What is she going to do?" He seemed dazed.

"I don't know, Henry, but I know you can handle it. Besides, she has you to help her through this. Remember that the one thing you two have is the memory of the good man known as David and neither of you was aware of the Michael. She will need you now, Henry, and I think you will need her."

"Speaking of a *her*," said Paul. "I guess one of us will have to explain the rest of this to Denise. What do you think?" He turned to Barrett.

Barrett smiled, "I think she needs you and wants you, Paul, so I'll leave that up to you. Make sure Henry gets home safe and sound also," he said, as he looked over at Denise walking toward them. He went over to Dick and took the backpack from him. "Thanks, Dick. I have to go down to the police station and finish up this paperwork and explanations but later can I buy you a beer?"

"Yeah, but I think I'd rather have a straight shot of whiskey right now, maybe a beer later," said Dick.

"Yeah, after the paperwork, let's get plastered. When we are through here. I am through for a while. I need a drink, my own house, my own bed, my own life, right?"

"Right," replied Dick.

"See you, Paul. Henry, you call me if you need anything. If you have any other questions that come up when you really start dealing with this, call me and I will be glad to answer them. I am going to be heading back home to Atlanta tomorrow. I'll let the staff clean up the things in Maine, New Hampshire, and North Carolina. I don't think there is much more we can do now that the culprit has been caught. But seriously, if you do need me for anything, you or Sierra, call me," came Barrett's concerned voice as he walked away.

Paul felt drained as he stood before Denise. There she stood in complete disarray. It was obvious she had not been thinking about what she was doing when she had railroaded Dane into the trip to Boston. He had left her only hours ago.

"Paul, oh, Paul," she cried, as she reached for him and fell into his arms.

"Shh . . . it's okay, darling, I'm here. I'm okay. It's all right. It's all over. Everyone is okay. It was a trying time for everyone, especially Henry."

"Henry? What in the hell is Henry doing here in Amherst? How did he get here? I didn't think he knew about Michael being David," she said pulling away from Paul.

"I brought him with me."

"You what?" she exclaimed.

"Here, sit down and let me explain this to you." Paul led her to the concrete columns along the walkway away from the steps. Sitting down next to her and taking her in his arms and placing her head on his chest, he squeezed her tightly.

"I called Henry as soon as I left you and asked him to come with me. I didn't press him. I thought he needed to know the truth and I also knew that he knew the layout of the buildings on the campus, and I needed someone to tell me how to deal with an accident or spill of the agent, if that happened. Don't worry, Michael only got some of it released in the basement and we've contained it. All of us were safe. We had our masks and he didn't get a chance to set any more off."

"Who killed Michael?" she asked quietly.

"I did," he whispered.

"God, Paul, I am so sorry. I can't believe you had to go through this. It hurts, doesn't it?" she said.

"Yes, but it's something I have gotten used to over the years. It will fade soon, and I won't think about it. All I care about now is spending some time with you and being with you. Mostly I want to reassure you that I had nothing to do with Michael's activities three years ago in Connecticut or with these outbreaks. I was as taken in by Michael as Henry was by David. Henry will have a hard time dealing with this, but as Barrett pointed out to him tonight, Henry can help Sierra, and they both can get through it together."

Paul lifted her face to his, her face with its sheen of tears, saying, "I love you, Denise, and I want to be with you." He kissed her full on the lips and she responded to his kiss, his touch. She let herself be pulled into the undercurrent she knew only as Paul.

Hours after the debriefing from the police and phone calls to Martin, Barrett sat in the bar, finishing his fifth beer with Dick. He knew he should get up and go back and talk to Denise, but why spoil Paul's scene. Paul could have the job of answering all of her unanswered questions. Besides, Paul was what Denise needed and wanted. Barrett didn't have time to deal with licking his own wounds now. All he wanted to do was to drink himself into oblivion for a couple of days. Go through the hand-over of the project, the debriefing, and then relax and get over it. Then start dealing with the real insane world again. He lifted his glass to Dick and made his fifth toast to good-looking women and insane killers.

Epilogue

Atlanta, Georgia

Barrett sat in his office, three days after his wild night in Amherst. He could still feel the after-affects of his celebrating. His head still had a tinge of a hangover. But he was feeling better about being back on the job. Henry had dropped by the office and told him that he and Sierra would be spending more time together. They had held a small private ceremony for David in his hometown of Bayside. Henry was going to take some personal time off and stay with Sierra. Henry had been through a bad year, what with Ingrid's death and now the death of David. Yet things were looking up with his relationship with Sierra. There was a future there.

There were two soft knocks on the door, He said, "Come in."

He glanced up with a startled look. Then a slow smile crossed his face. "Hi there," he said, as Denise entered his office.

"Hi, yourself. You look like hell." She sat down and crossed her legs.

"I still feel like hell. Dick and I tied one on for a couple of days okay, and I am still paying for it." He ran his hand through his hair as though it would smooth out the pounding pain in his head.

"I know. I heard. Why haven't you called?" She arched her eyebrow in challenge.

"Call you? I figured you would be tied up between moving back home and getting settled again. Not to mention taking on a new assignment as well as a new roommate."

"What new roommate?" she mocked, certain he was joking.

239

"The Colonel, of course," he replied.

"You are not a very good security man, are you? If you were, you would know by now that there is no new roommate, and certainly no Colonel in my life." She smiled.

He stared at her, incredulous, "Are you serious?"

"Yes. But maybe you are interested in a new roommate?"

"God, yes," he said, as he rose from the chair and walked around the desk. Taking her into his arms he looked down into her eyes and smiled. "You do know I love you, baby."

"Yes, I know that. It just took me a long time to accept it and get around to appreciating it, but I am here now if you want me." Denise felt, for the first time in years, the security in his arms she had been searching for all these years.

She had realized that night with Paul in Amherst when he had declared his love for her that his lifestyle, his life, his complete disregard for people and lives, such as Henry's, and his taking Henry to Amherst, that the fantastic love was just superficial. That type of love and life was not what she needed or wanted. She needed stability and a safe family life and the special excitement of Barrett's love.

She had hoped Barrett would call her, but he hadn't. So she had come to him-- a wiser, surer person with no more questions about her life and what she wanted to do with it.

The End